Ink's Whirlwind

Iron Punisher's MC Book #2

by Ciara St James

Blurb

As Ink watched his president fall for a woman, he's thrilled to realize that he's sure he's found his too. Even better news is the two women are best friends. Everything looks to be perfect. Or it does until Ink realizes Alisse isn't willing to give him the time of day.

He's spent months trying to get her to give him a chance. She keeps shooting him down with allegations of him being a man who can't commit to one woman. She accuses him of only wanting conquests, not a real, lasting relationship.

Ink has had enough when he finds his woman has gone out on a date with another man. This leads to a confrontation followed by someone trying to take her at gunpoint. The club still has enemies out there. Is it them? Or is it someone else?

Meanwhile, Ink discovers that Alisse and he have a past he doesn't recall. It answers a lot of questions and leads him to being able to convince her to give him a real chance.

Just as Alisse gives in to Ink's pleas, his past walks back in the door. Alisse is afraid of what this means for them. A secret is revealed, and this causes only more worry and strife. Is it the truth or a lie?

Meanwhile, her life isn't her own, as the club keeps her and her best friend under guard. As more dangerous things happen, the club is forced to consider that the enemy they were worried about might not be the enemy who is determined to take Alisse away from Ink.

Thankfully, the club isn't willing to stop until they get the culprit, remove the threats, and get an answer to a mystery. All Ink is praying for is to be able to fully claim and love his Whirlwind forever.

Copyright

ISBN: 978-1-955751-36-0

Printed in the United States of America

Editing by Mary Kerns @ Ms. K Edits

Book cover by Tracie Douglas @ Dark Waters Covers

Warning

This book is intended for adult readers, It contains foul language, adult situations, discusses events such as stalkers, assault, torture and murder that may trigger some readers. Sexual situations are graphic. There is no cheating, no cliffhangers and it has a HEA.

Dedication

This book is dedicated to those who are lucky enough to get a second chance, even if they didn't realize they missed out the first time. I truly believe things happen when the time is right, not necessarily when we think they should.

As always, a huge thank you to by editor, Mary, and several ladies on my beta team- Amanda, Kelly, Teresa, Karen, Stacy, Angie, Leslee, and Kim. The team read this and caught things that had gotten past me and Mary despite our best attempts to catch them all. It never fails that there are some. Alas, we're all human.

Iron Punishers Members

Holden Grier (Reaper) President w/Cheyenne

Creed Donovan (Maniac) VP w/ TBD

Jamison Tyrell (Mayhem) Enforcer w/ TBD

Killian Hardison (Ratchet) Road Captain w/ TBD

Damian Tatum (Crusher) SAA w/ TBD

Austin Kavanagh (Ink) w/ Alisse Jackson

Derrick Tatum (Lash) w/ TBD

Vance Halliwell (Tinker) Treasurer w/ TBD

Aidan Priestley (Spawn) Secretary w/ TBD

Carter McKnight (Sandman) w/TBD

Braxton Russo (Shadow) w/TBD

Dante Braun- Prospect

Dillion Braun- Prospect

Reading Order

For Dublin Falls Archangel's Warriors MC (DFAW), Hunters Creek Archangel's Warriors MC (HCAW), Iron Punishers MC (IPMC), Dark Patriots (DP), & Pagan Souls of Cherokee MC (PSCMC)

Terror's Temptress DFAW 1

Savage's Princess DFAW 2

Steel & Hammer's Hellcat DFAW 3

Menace's Siren DFAW 4

Ranger's Enchantress DFAW 5

Ghost's Beauty DFAW 6

Viking's Venus DFAW 6.5 (free novella)

Viper's Vixen DFAW 7

Devil Dog's Precious DFAW 8

Blaze's Spitfire DFAW 9

Smoke's Tigress DFAW 10

Hawk's Huntress DFAW 11

Bull's Duchess HCAW 1

Storm's Flame DFAW 12

Rebel's Firecracker HCAW 2

Ajax's Nymph HCAW 3

Razor's Wildcat DFAW 13

Capone's Wild Thing DFAW 14

Falcon's She Devil DFAW 15

Demon's Hellion HCAW 4

Torch's Tornado DFAW 16

Voodoo's Sorceress DFAW 17

Reaper's Banshee IPMC 1

Bear's Beloved HCAW 5

Outlaw's Jewel HVAW 6

Undertaker's Resurrection DP 1

Agony's Medicine Woman PSCMC 1

Ink's Whirlwind IP 2

Reading order for Ares Infidels MC

Sin's Enticement AIMC 1

Executioner's Enthrallment AIMC 2

Pitbull's Enslavement AIMC 3

Omen's Entrapment AIMC 4

Cuffs' Enchainment AIMC 5

Rampage's Enchantment AIMC 6

Wrecker's Ensnarement AIMC 7

Trident's Enjoyment AIMC 8

Fang's Enlightenment AIMC 9

Please follow Ciara on Facebook, For information on new releases & to catch up with Ciara, go to www.ciara-st-james.com or www.facebook.com/ciara.stjames.1 or www.facebook.com/groups/tenilloguardians

Ink: Chapter 1

I was slowly being driven insane, and I was almost at my wits' end. I thought of how Alisse looked when she laughed at something Cheyenne, my club president, Reaper's, old lady said. She'd thrown back her head, exposing her sexy neck, that I wanted to go over and bite. She'd been all I could think about for the past four months, ever since Reaper met Cheyenne and fell head over heels in love with her. One look at Alisse, and I felt like I'd fallen into a whirlwind.

I'd almost stumbled when I saw her come through the door of the ER where we were all waiting. She'd been called because Cheyenne had been hit by a car while at lunch. I saw the appreciative looks my brothers gave her when she came in. I was shocked to hear her say she was looking for Cheyenne and Reaper.

Days later, when she came to the compound with Cheyenne to attend one of our parties, she'd affected me as much, if not more. She was a decently tall woman; I'd guess around five foot six. Her figure was what I could only call lush. She had curves for days and that ass of hers that could make grown men weep. Her skin was a light mocha color, making it obvious she had some African American in her as well as Caucasian. Her hair was a dark brown with lighter streaks in it and it was wildly curly, hanging down past her shoulders. When she was close, you could see that her eyes were a light green, which stood out against her hair and skin.

After that memorable and harrowing visit, she'd moved into the compound temporarily, in order to protect her from the men seeking Cheyenne—men from an outlaw MC called the Soldiers of Corruption, although that wasn't the name we were told at first. Cheyenne freaking out and trying to run with Alisse had exposed their lie. I'd been thrilled that she'd be where I could see and talk to her every day. That thrill had soon turned to frustration because Alisse wouldn't give me the time of day.

She came to the clubhouse often, even when Cheyenne wasn't with her and she talked and laughed with the guys, but she would ignore me. Every time I attempted to talk to her or get close, she'd find a way to scurry away. The next few months had been a lesson in patience, and I wasn't a patient man. Despite me telling her that I wanted her, she refused to let me get close to her.

She had the notion that I was a man only looking to fuck her, then walk. I'll admit, that had been how I had handled women in the past. After my first really serious girlfriend years ago, I had wanted nothing to do with a serious relationship. Sex for the sake of sex was fine with me. I made sure that the women I slept with knew that was all it was and that we were not exclusive. If they started to get possessive or demanding, I'd cut them loose.

However, that was the last thing I wanted to do with Alisse. I wanted her to be with me and only me. I wanted her in my bed, my house, and not for a few nights or weeks. I'd gone and done the one thing I thought I'd never do. I fell for a woman and I fell hard. Her remarks about me being a manwhore and unable to commit to one woman pissed me off. Nothing I said could convince her otherwise.

I'd talked to Reaper about it more than once and he eventually told me that she had shared with Cheyenne, that she knew me from a long time ago. I didn't know how that could be. I would have remembered a woman like her. If we'd ever hooked up, I would have remembered her. She was unforgettable. Every time things seemed to get more relaxed between us, something would happen and we'd go back to square one. More than once, she'd run off upset, and I had gone after her. Kissing her had been a fight, but I'd gotten a few. They were the best kisses of my life.

After taking down Serpent and his cronies and then Reaper and Cheyenne's wedding right before Christmas a couple of weeks ago, I thought things were finally straightening out between us. Again, I was wrong. Well, no more holding back. I was done. After hearing what I had just heard, it was all I could do not to tear the clubhouse apart.

Apparently, Alisse wasn't at home tonight. She was still staying here with us, since we couldn't be sure the rest of the Soldiers of Corruption MC wouldn't come after her for being friends with Chey. We knew they were out there and suspicious about the four members of theirs who went missing—Serpent, Loon, Chubbs, and Tires, especially since Serpent had been their VP and Slither, their president's son. Unfamiliar riders had been spotted in town, riding bikes with stolen plates.

So, why was it with this threat still hanging over us, was she outside the compound? Because she was on a fucking date with another man. I was seething mad. When I'd asked one of my brothers where she was and he'd reluctantly told me she was in town on a date, I thought my head was going to blow off. I was headed for the clubhouse door when Reaper caught me.

"Ink, calm down before you go anywhere."

I swung around to glare at him. "Calm down! How the fuck am I supposed to calm down when my woman is on a goddamn date with another man? Why did you let her go? Why didn't you call me?" I practically yelled at him.

"She's a grown woman. I can't tell her she can't go. As for why I didn't call you, I didn't want you to go find them and kill the guy. I waited for you to get here."

"It's not safe for her to be out alone. You know that. Hell, she and Chey still haven't gone back to work for Dr. Simpson more than two days a week because of this," I reminded him, as if he was likely to have forgotten.

"I know, and I didn't let her go alone. Dante went along to keep an eye on her. She wasn't happy, but as long as he stays out of sight of her date, she accepted my stipulation. If he sees anything even remotely suspicious, he knows to call us immediately."

"Does this man having his hands on her or kissing her qualify as suspicious behavior he'll call about?" I asked, clenching my fist.

"No, it doesn't. For God's sake, you two need to figure this shit out."

"Don't you think I want to? She won't let me. She keeps going back to the same old shit about me not wanting her for more than sex and that I can't be with just one woman. That's utter bullshit. Who is she on a date with? Do we know him?"

Reaper sighed. "He's a guy she met when he brought his aunt into the clinic to see Dr. Simpson. From what I understand, he started talking to her and then a few days later, he came back and asked her to go to dinner."

"I want his name."

"His name is Alex Liberty. I have Spawn looking into him as we speak. If there's anything shady about him, he'll find it."

"He doesn't need to be shady for her not to be around him. She's mine and I'm not going to let some fucker think he can take her away from me. Where did they go for their date?"

He looked at me for a full minute before he answered. I knew it was because he was trying to gauge how volatile I was at the moment. I could've told him very and that it wasn't going to lessen until she was back here where she belonged... with me.

Sighing, he yelled, "Mayhem, Crusher, get your asses over here."

The two men hurried over to us.

"Yeah, Pres, what do you need?" Mayhem, our

enforcer, asked.

"I need you two to go to town with Ink and make sure he doesn't kill the guy Alisse is at dinner with at the Grove. I expect you to keep things under control."

Crusher, our sergeant-at-arms, snorted. "Yeah, why not give us the hard job? You know he's going to lose his shit. I want hazard pay for this."

"You get paid that already, asshole. If your brother lands in jail, your asses are mine," Reaper warned them, giving them his best scary look.

"Ah, man, this is going to be a hellacious night. Come on then. Let's get this over with," Crusher grumbled.

I didn't waste time. I followed them out to our bikes as soon as we grabbed our jackets and gloves. Since it was January and cold as hell, at the last minute, I decided to take my truck rather than my bike, like I normally would. It would be too cold for her to ride back on my bike.

"Hey, let me go get my truck, then we can go," I told them. They both nodded and waited as I got on my bike and rode the relatively short distance to my house. I parked it in the garage and got into the truck parked beside it. My brothers, not having to worry about a woman problem, had gotten on their bikes and were waiting for me at the gate. I waited impatiently as it opened to let us out.

I took the lead. The Grove that Reaper mentioned was the best fancy dining place we had in town. That's where people took someone they wanted to impress or romance. That's where another fucking man had my woman. I sped up.

Alisse:

I tried not to sigh and hoped I had an interested look plastered on my face. Tonight was a mistake. I knew it would be the moment I gave into desperation and said yes. I had told Alex I'd go out with him in the useless hope that he might grab my interest and make me forget about the man who really ruled my every waking moment and most of my sleeping ones, Ink.

Just thinking of him sent a shiver of need through me. God, why couldn't I get over this infatuation I had with the man? Just because he happened to be one of the sexiest men I had ever laid eyes on didn't mean anything. There were lots of sexy men. So what if he had deep olive skin, hair and eyes so black they looked like sin? His sculpted lips, strong jaw and nose, and chiseled cheekbones made me want to kiss him all over. His dark hair that hung to his shoulders made my hands itch to run through it when he had it down and itched to take it down when he had it pulled back.

Don't get me started on his body. He was tall, a few inches over six feet. He had broad shoulders, rippling muscles and all of it was covered in mouth-watering tattoos. Combine those things, and I knew I had to be crazy to think I could forget him.

Add to it the fact that I'd been secretly in love with

him since I was sixteen years old didn't help. Eleven years hadn't managed to erase my obsession. Every man I tried to be with had always fallen by the wayside because he wasn't Ink. Only Ink wasn't ever going to be the man for me, no matter how much I secretly dreamed he would be. He was a first rate manwhore, who couldn't stick to one woman, even if his life depended on it.

Had that stopped him from driving me insane these past four months, since I ran into him again? Hell no. He wouldn't leave me alone. Every time I turned around, he was there, talking to me, touching me, trying to kiss and convince me that he wanted me and only me. Did I have stupid written on my forehead?

I never imagined when I moved back to Bristol five years ago that he'd be here. I thought he'd left years ago. In five years, we somehow managed to avoid running into each other until that fateful day his club president, Reaper, saw my best friend, Cheyenne, and fell head over heels for her. That's when I had the pleasure of seeing him again. Walking into the ER that afternoon and seeing him standing there in his motorcycle clothes and cut had floored me and almost made me turn around and run the other way. If it hadn't been for Chey being hurt, I would have.

He hadn't let me forget he was near since. Hence, me accepting a date from a guy who did nothing for me, which sucked, because Alex was a very good-looking man. He was tall, fit, had dark blond hair and was around my age, or maybe a couple of years older. He was some kind of banking manager. He drove a nice car, was polite and smelled good. His clothes were nice and looked expensive, like the watch he wore. So why in the hell wouldn't my heart even speed up one beat when I looked at him?

He caught me on a really down day and I gave in to my self-pity. Hell, it wasn't like I had never been with a man who wasn't Ink. I'd tried more than once, but every time I did, it ended in disaster. The really fucked-up thing was, he didn't even remember me. See, I was just one of numerous, faceless women for him. I had too much self-respect to be another notch on his belt. Besides, it would make it super awkward when I'd see him after it was over. It wasn't like we could avoid each other. My bestie was married to his president now, and they were expecting their first child.

Alex cleared his throat, jerked me out of my head, and got me to focus back on him. I instantly apologized. "I'm sorry, Alex. My head seems to be somewhere else tonight. What did you say?" I would concentrate. I would enjoy this night out. I would allow this man to try and engage my attention.

"Are you alright, Alisse? You've been quiet all night. If you're tired, we can do this some other time. I know you had to work today." He sweetly gave me an out.

"No, that's alright. I did work, but it wasn't too bad. I've just had a lot on my mind, but that's done tonight. Tell me how your day went at the bank."

I sat, trying to follow his droning on about the thrills of banking, which in my book were zero. He seemed to like it, which I guess was a good thing, seeing as it was his career. I found the medical profession way more exciting.

It wasn't long before our waitress brought our meals and we got quiet, so we could enjoy the food. He didn't get the typical steak and baked potato with all the fixings you'd expect a man to get. That was me. He got salmon and grilled vegetables. It didn't look like it would be enough to fill me up, let alone him, but what did I know?

We weren't even a quarter of the way through our meal when the increase in the level of murmured conversations in the restaurant increased. Excited whispers broke out and tension suddenly filled the air. I looked up to see what had caused it and froze.

Striding toward me was a man with a determined and dangerous look on his face. I couldn't help but check him out as he stalked toward us. His eyes were blazing and his muscles were taut.

Ink came to a halt beside the table. His eyes bored into mine. I couldn't speak. I was in shock. He slowly turned his head to glare at Alex, who was staring at him, perplexed and slightly scared. I saw Alex gulp.

"C-c-can we help you?" he stuttered to Ink.

"Yeah, you can tell me why the hell you're sitting here eating dinner with my woman for starters. Then you can tell me why I shouldn't kill you where you sit," Ink said menacingly.

This loosened my tongue. "Ink, what are you doing here? You have no right to threaten Alex. I'm not your woman and I can go on a date with whomever I want.

It's none of your business," I hissed at him.

He leaned down until his face was only an inch from mine. I could feel his hot breath on my lips. The scent of mint, from the candy he liked to chew, filled my nostrils. "Like hell you're not mine, Alisse. Get your stuff and let's go."

Anger surged through me. He couldn't even allow me one night to forget about him. "I'm not going anywhere with you! Leave. I want to finish my dinner in peace. I'll be back at the compound when I feel like it."

He eyed me. I couldn't tell what was going through his head, but whatever it was, it was making him madder. Alex was sitting there stiff, and I could see he was uncomfortable. People were staring at us and whispering. I hated to be the center of attention, but I wasn't about to back down. I was over this, whatever it was. I had to get on with my life. I wanted someone special, like Chey had, and a family. Ink wasn't the one who could give that to me, so I wasn't going to waste my time mooning over him anymore.

Suddenly, Ink's hand came out to capture my jaw. He didn't hurt me, but he did hold me tight enough that I couldn't look away from him. "You and I are going to talk, tonight. Finish your dinner with this asshole, then get your ass home. Don't think about going anywhere else. Dante has orders to call me immediately if you do. If I have to come after you, you won't like it, Alisse." His eyes and his tone told me that he wasn't kidding around. Ink was on the edge of losing his cool.

I might not want to do as he said, but I knew when

not to poke the sleeping bear. Not saying a word one way or the other, I simply stared back at him. After maybe a minute, he snarled, then slammed his mouth down on mine.

He'd kissed me before and every time, he'd stolen my senses. However, this time, he was so damn aggressive and controlling, I could do nothing but submit. His tongue thrust inside my mouth and teased mine. His teeth repeatedly pressed into mine. When he stood up, I sat there dazed. He looked at Alex.

"Don't ever ask her out again. If you see her, go the other way. She's not available to you or anyone else. Understand?"

Alex nodded his head vigorously. I watched as Ink turned on his heel and marched out of the restaurant. Behind him, I saw Dante, Mayhem, and Crusher. They all had amused looks on their faces. I shot them scowls, which only made them smile harder.

After they left, the crowd continued to stare and talk. I fought to ignore them and I looked at Alex. He looked pale and shaken. While Ink was an intimidating man, I couldn't find it in myself to feel sorry for Alex. I didn't find guys who let others intimidate them attractive. He could have at least stood up for us verbally. It only confirmed what I'd already known. Alex wasn't the guy for me. However, I did feel like I owed him an apology.

"Alex, I'm sorry about that. Ink thinks that because I'm his club president's wife's best friend, he can tell me what to do. Let's forget him and finish this wonderful dinner."

"Alisse, I don't think you should be around a man like that. He's dangerous and if he's in a club, then he's obviously a criminal. If your best friend is married to a man like him, you should get new friends," he said piously. His attitude instantly pissed me off.

"Get new friends? Who are you to tell me that? As for what type of men Ink and the other Iron Punishers are, you have no idea. They'd give you the shirt off their backs if you needed it. They help people all the time. They may ride motorcycles, live in a compound, and have tattoos, but that doesn't make them outlaws or beneath you," I told him angrily.

He looked down his nose at me. "If that's how you feel and the kind of company you keep, I don't think we should see each other again."

"Good, we agree. I already made up my mind before Ink showed up to tell you we shouldn't go out again, but after the shit you just said, I'm more than certain."

His face got red and he came to his feet. He threw his linen napkin onto the table. Giving me a pissed-off look and one full of dislike, he turned and walked out, leaving me not only alone to finish my food, but to pay the damn bill. What a lowlife bastard. Determined to enjoy my food, I stayed and ate. I even got dessert. I refused to be run off by his behavior or Ink's. When I was done, I paid the bill with dignity, then got up and walked out, with my head held high.

In the parking lot, Dante was waiting for me on his bike. I'd driven myself to meet Alex and he'd followed me on his bike. His face was impassive as he watched me. I bet he texted Ink as soon as Alex left, getting joy out of knowing they ruined my date. Anger was still coursing through me. Maybe if it hadn't been, I might have been paying more attention to my surroundings. I might have noticed a dark shadow moving off to my left.

"Are you ready, oh jailer?" I asked sarcastically.

The bastard chuckled. "If that's how you see me, then yes, your jailer is ready. It's cold out here. Let's get you in the car and then home." He swung his leg over his bike to get off. I knew he was coming to open my car door. Before he took more than three or four steps, I heard a popping sound and a grunt, then I saw him fall. I knew that sound. It was a gunshot!

A shadow was detaching itself from the others, and I could see the shape of a man. He had his arm out in front of him. My heart escalated as I went into motion. I didn't waste time thinking about who he was or what he'd done to Dante, I just reacted.

Even if I was out on a date at a fancy restaurant, I hadn't come without my trusty gun. It was always with me. My hands shook a little as I shoved my hand into the secret compartment in my purse, made specifically for carrying my gun unnoticed. The man was walking toward me. I didn't bother to say a word. I yanked out my gun, aimed, then fired all in one smooth motion. One that I had practiced many times.

I heard him grunt, saw him jerk, then swear. I took aim again, but he must have decided he had enough, because he took off running into the night. I didn't let my guard down as I approached Dante. I had to see how badly hurt he was. I prayed he wasn't dead.

His moan of pain was music to my ears as I crouched next to him. He rolled over with difficulty and stared up at me with pain-filled eyes. "Get your ass inside! He might still be out there. Call Reaper and the guys. Tell them what happened. They'll come get you."

"Like hell I'm leaving you lying out here like a sitting duck, waiting for him to come back and finish you off. Where are you hit? Can you walk?" I was frantically running my hands over his torso, looking for a wound. He grabbed my wandering hand.

"Alisse, stop. You need to go inside. If anything happens to you, Ink will kill me. That's if Reaper doesn't get to me first. Whoever that guy was, he was after you. I'm fine. I have my gun and it's only a shoulder wound." He tried to assure me. My hand ran across something wet and sticky and he hissed.

I didn't waste my breath. I held my gun in one hand and took the one covered in his blood and called Reaper. I knew that he'd tell me what to do. Should I call the cops and an ambulance? The club usually didn't involve them unless it was absolutely necessary.

Reaper answered on the second ring. "Hey, Alisse, what's up? Are you on your way home? Ink is pacing the floor here at the clubhouse waiting for you."

"Reaper, I need you to come to the Grove. Dante has been shot, and I don't know if I should call the cops or not. He says it's only a shoulder wound, but I can't tell.

It's dark and we're outside in the parking lot. There's no cover and I don't know if I can get him inside without help," I told him hurriedly.

Reaper swore. "Son of a bitch! Get inside and stay there. Dante can protect himself. You're probably the target. We'll be there in ten minutes. Hold tight. Don't call the cops unless you have no choice. Someone might have heard the shot and called."

He didn't bother to wait to hear my agreement before he hung up. If he'd waited, he would have heard me tell him I wasn't leaving Dante alone. Pocketing my cell phone, I grabbed the arm of Dante's uninjured shoulder.

"I need you to help me get you behind this car, Dante. It'll give us cover. Then I want to look at your wound. Reaper and the others will be here soon."

He tried to argue and send me inside, but I ignored him. It was slow going, but I finally got him behind the car and then dug out the pen light I always carried with me. You never knew when it would come in handy. Holding it in my mouth, I eased the jacket off his arm with lots of cursing on his part. When it was off, I tore the hole in his shirt, making it bigger, so I could look at the wound. It was still bleeding more than I liked. Without my first aid kit, there was nothing I could do, other than apply pressure. I didn't have a rag, so I took off my jacket, which was made of thick cotton material, and pressed it to the wound. He hissed more. We sat there saying nothing as we waited to see what would happen next. I prayed they wouldn't take long and that the gunman was really gone.

Ink: Chapter 2

I was pacing a groove in the common room floor when I heard Reaper answering his phone. My ears perked up when I heard him say Alisse's name. I was still pissed about seeing her with that man and her refusal to leave with me. I almost dragged her out of there over my shoulder, but I figured someone would call the law and my ass would be in jail. My luck, she'd press kidnapping charges against me.

I jerked to attention when I heard Reaper say, "Son of a bitch! Get inside and stay. Dante can protect himself. You're the target. We'll be there in ten minutes. Hold tight. Don't call the cops unless you have no choice. Someone might have heard the shot and called."

I was at his side just as he hung up. He glanced over at me.

"What the fuck happened? What did you mean by target and Dante protecting himself?" I barked.

"Take a breath. We need to roll out to the Grove now," he told me, before he whistled to get the attention of the other guys in the room. They looked at him expectantly.

"Alisse just called to tell me that Dante was shot outside the Grove. She can't get him to cover. We need to go now. I told her to go back inside where it's safe."

Cheyenne gasped. I ran for the door, letting Reaper reassure his wife. I needed to go get Alisse and make sure she was alright. It only took me a couple of minutes to be on my bike and roaring out the gate. A few of the guys weren't far behind me, but I couldn't wait for them, even though technically, since Reaper and some of the other officers were going, they should be in the lead.

All the way to town, I prayed that she was safe and unharmed. I did send up a prayer for Dante too, but it was Alisse I was worried about the most. What the hell had happened? Had the Soldiers of Corruption taken their chance at us for payback? Was the gunman still there? Had she made it to safety inside?

I hardly slowed down when I turned into the parking lot of the restaurant. I scanned the area, looking for Dante or anyone suspicious. I had my gun in my hand. Movement behind a car drew my attention. My heart pounded harder when I saw that curly head of hair I loved, peeking a look over the trunk of a car. I rode straight up to her.

I barely bothered to stop, shut off my bike, and put down my kickstand, before I dove off my bike and was running around the trunk to her. I saw a look of relief on her face as I towered over her and a pale, sweaty Dante, who was grimacing in pain. She was pressing down on his shoulder with a blood-soaked sweater. I dropped to my knees. I could hear the others pulling into the lot.

Seeing that Dante was breathing, I didn't bother to

check on him. First, I had to reassure myself she was alive and unharmed. I gripped her face between both my hands, engulfing her. "Are you alright? Are you hurt anywhere?"

"I'm fine. Dante is the one to get hurt. Someone shot him. I don't know who it was. I couldn't get a good look at him. He ran when I shot him. He went that way." She pointed to the east. By then, the guys had joined us and were listening. All I could think about was her saying Dante was shot, and she shot the guy who did it.

"Are you crazy? You should be inside like Reaper told you, not out here where the fucker could come back and get you," I growled at her.

Her spine stiffened as she glared at me. "I wasn't about to leave Dante out here alone. He's been shot. He needs medical attention and I couldn't be sure the gunman wouldn't get a drop on him if he was dumb enough to come back. I had my gun. I was perfectly safe," she argued.

The urge to shake her was so great, I had to let go of her, stand up, and step back. Lash had come around and was kneeling beside Dante, checking him out. He had his medical kit with him. Lash was our medic when we needed him. He was the one to tell us if calling an ambulance or a trip to the doctor was necessary. I scanned the area, along with several of the others, as Lash worked on Dante. Alisse decided to ignore me and help him. Reaper came up to me. He put his hand on my shoulder.

"I know you're pissed she didn't listen. I am too,

but it seems like whoever it was, he's now gone. Let's get Dante patched up and back to the compound, then we can talk more and get the details. We don't want to attract attention. It doesn't seem like anyone heard anything and called the cops, otherwise they'd be here. You and I will stand guard while Lash and her work and the others search the area better, then we'll go."

All I could do was nod. It didn't take long for Lash to get him at least temporarily patched up. The decision was made to have him ride back in Alisse's car. She'd drive. We'd come get Dante's bike later. Two of us got him in her back seat then we got on the road home. All in all, it was maybe fifteen minutes tops. It was a miracle no one came out of the place while we were there.

The ride back seemed to take longer than ever, but eventually, I saw the gate ahead. Pulling into the parking area outside the clubhouse made my heart settle. The gate closed behind us, effectively keeping out those we were in danger from. My woman was back within the walls that would keep her safe. She wasn't going to leave this place again. Not unless I was glued to her side and was armed for bear.

I helped Lash carry Dante inside. The relief on his twin, Dillon's, face, when he saw he was alive, was visible. We took him straight to the medical room we'd set up recently for just this purpose. They had similar rooms in the Warriors' compounds and we thought it was a great idea. Dante was the first one to ever use it. We laid him down on the gurney we had in there.

The room filled up with the guys and Chey. She

looked pale as she hugged Alisse. Reaper took control, like he always did. The man was a natural leader. I could do it, but it wasn't my preference like it was with him. He was meant to lead men. I'd follow him anywhere, even into hell.

"Lash, how does it look? Does he need to go to the hospital?" Reaper asked him. He was watching Dante with his eagle eyes.

"I don't think he does. Luckily for him, it went straight through and looks like it missed anything vital. The bleeding is almost stopped, thanks to the pressure Alisse held on it. I need to clean it out and then put in a few stitches. He'll need some prophylactic antibiotics. I think Dr. Simpson will squeeze him in tomorrow or maybe just call in an order for us," Lash told him concisely.

"I can tell her what he needs. I bet she'll just call it in for us," Cheyenne said softly. Her and Alisse's boss, Dr. Simpson, had turned out to be a very pleasant surprise for us. She had experience with an MC and didn't look down her nose at us like we were a bunch of dirty criminals. I wasn't sure why she had that exposure, but we were thankful for it. She was quickly becoming a good friend to the club.

"Alisse, can you tell us what happened?" Reaper asked his wife's friend gently. He was watching her and Chey clinging to each other.

Alisse nodded. "Sure, Reaper. After I was done with dinner, I came out to leave and Dante was on his bike waiting for me. He went to get off it to open my car door and had barely started to walk toward me when I saw a shadow move. It looked like the shape of a man. That's when I saw Dante jerk and fall, then I heard the retort of the shot. I didn't think. I just drew my gun and shot at the shadow man. I know I hit him, Reaper. I heard him swear. He took off running. I think he was worried that the shots would attract attention. Once I saw he had left, I called you and waited with Dante until you got there. That's it. I wish I knew more to tell you."

She was very matter of fact about her retelling of the incident, but I could hear the notes of strain and fear in her voice. She'd been scared. Not giving a damn whether she liked it or not, I walked over to her, took her out of Chey's arms, and enfolded her in mine. I pressed her tightly against me, as I breathed in her scent and kissed her hair.

"Baby, I'm so fucking glad you're alright, but you should've gone inside where it was safe. He could have come back and brought reinforcements. We have no idea who it was or what he wanted," I admonished her.

"He wanted her. Before he decided to run, he was coming toward her. I think he was there to take her. Otherwise, why not shoot her?" Dante said hoarsely. The pain in his voice was evident. Lash had an IV in his arm and was injecting something into it. I hoped it was a pain killer. "I told her to go inside more than once, but she wouldn't listen. Damn woman." He growled at her.

She smiled at him. "You can boss me all you want, Dante, but I'll only do what you say when I think it's right. Leaving you there in the open without cover wasn't right. I got you behind the car and we were fine.

I kept watch while I held that pressure on your wound. I'm a woman. We know how to multitask, unlike you men," she teased.

Grumbles of protest echoed around the room. The tension lessened and I even saw Cheyenne smile.

"Ladies, why don't you head out the house so you can get some rest? Me and the guys have to have church and talk about this. Dillon, you can stay here with your brother and if anything changes, come get us," Reaper said quickly. I knew we'd be having church right away to discuss.

"Can't it wait until morning?" Chey asked him.

He shook his head. "No, Banshee, it can't. We can't waste time when something like this happens. However, you need to rest. This isn't good for you and the baby to stay up so late and worry. Alisse, will you make sure she rests at the house?"

"You can be sure I will, Reaper. Come on, Chey, let's go watch some sexy men on TV and snuggle in your big bed. If I fall asleep, Reaper will have to sleep in the guest room," Alisse said, as she threw him a mischievous look.

"You fall asleep and I'll be carrying your ass to your bed. I'm not sleeping anywhere but beside my old lady. Get outta here and let me do my job," Reaper said with a tiny grin.

Alisse went to pull out of my arms, but I held onto her. When she looked up at me, I lowered my head and I gave her a thorough, although gentle kiss. When I was done, she looked bemused.

"Go get that rest and don't be watching those shows with hot men in them. I'm the only one you're allowed to look at and think is sexy," I softly whispered in her ear. She rolled her eyes at me, but she didn't say a word. I let her go and watched as the two women left the room. As soon as they did, Reaper jerked his head and we all filed out to go into church, which was just down the hall from the medical room.

We all took our seats. It was Saturday night. Typically, we'd be partying and having fun. My single brothers most likely would be hooking up with one or more of the bunnies, or one of the hang arounds, who liked to come from town and the surrounding area. Since I laid eyes on Alisse, I hadn't touched a single one of them. She was the only woman I wanted to sink my cock into. If I couldn't have her, I didn't want a pale substitute.

"You know why we're here. Let's talk about who the hell did this. Was it the Soldiers of Corruption, do you think?" Reaper asked. I knew he had his own thoughts, but he liked to hear ours first.

"I don't think so," I told him.

"Why not?" he fired back.

"Because if it was them, there wouldn't have been only one of them. They would've come as a pack. You saw Serpent and his crew. No way they'd leave one guy to take us on. That's why I don't think it was one of them."

There were speculative mumblings around the

table. No one spoke up saying they thought it was them.

"Okay, we all seem to agree it was unlikely to be them. Who then? Why would someone come after Alisse and shoot Dante? Dante seemed convinced the man was coming for her and he didn't want to shoot her. Was he trying to kidnap her? If so, to what purpose?" Reaper asked next.

"Money? He thought since he had seen her with us that she was important and we'd pay to get her back," Mayhem suggested.

"To sell her. She's a beautiful woman, out with only one guard. She'd fetch a high price from the right buyer." Spawn threw in his two cents' worth. It caused a growl to bubble up and escape me. All my brothers shot looks of sympathy at me. Every one of them knew how I felt about her. I didn't make a secret of it.

Spawn shrugged. "I hate the idea too, but you know how much of that shit goes on around the country and the world. I can get on the dark web and search some of the sites I keep an eye out for. If they've posted anything detailing a woman looking like Alisse, I'll find it and let you know."

"Thanks, Spawn, I'd appreciate it," I told him with a chin lift.

"It could be someone looking to add to his stable of women. There are pimps who find their girls by force," Ratchet, our road captain, offered as a suggestion.

"It could've been just a regular old robbery too," Shadow added.

All the suggestions, while good ones, did nothing to help solve who it was or made Alisse or even Cheyenne safe.

"Regardless of who it was, we know we can't ease up on allowing the ladies to leave the compound alone. Also, it tells us, one guard isn't enough. Alisse should've never had to fire her gun. I don't want our women having to do that, even if they can," Reaper growled.

"Well, I don't want my Alisse doing it either," I added for good measure.

"Your Alisse? Does she know that? I mean, shit, she was out on a date, Ink," Crusher asked, with raised brows. I glared at the fucker. I knew he was trying to yank on my chain a little.

"I planned to make that clear tonight when she got back, then this shit happened. I can promise you, she is mine and I'll do whatever it takes to keep her safe. Good ole Alex will stay away from her if he knows what's good for him."

Mayhem laughed. "Yeah, he looked less than thrilled to see you. I thought at one point he was going to shit himself. He sat there and didn't say a damn word."

"Yeah, he sure left in a hurry after we left. I don't think it was even five minutes later that Dante reported he had left the restaurant and Alisse stayed behind to finish her meal. She's one classy lady who won't take shit," Maniac said with a warning in his voice.

"I don't plan to give her shit. I know she's too damn good for me, but unlike other men, I know it and I'll do everything in my power to earn my place by her side and keep her happy."

"That's what you do. I know Chey is too good for me, but I'd never let her go unless she was absolutely one hundred percent sure she had no feelings for me. Or if I thought she'd only be happy without me. Then I'd do it and watch her from afar for the rest of her life, making sure she was happy and safe," Reaper confessed.

I wanted to say I would do the same, but I didn't know if I'd be strong enough to watch her with another man and have a family that wasn't mine. I think it would likely kill me. Although, in the case of Alisse, I'd seen enough to know she wasn't immune to me. She was fighting us because of her ridiculous notion that I wasn't serious or able to commit. That was true in the past, but not with her.

As they rambled on more about who and why, I zoned out. I fell into one of my regular daydreams. One where Alisse was mine and we had our children around us. I knew without a doubt I wanted her to be my old lady, my wife, and the mother to my children. It was time I found a way to prove that to her. Tonight had shown me that there would be no more waiting.

"Earth to Ink," I heard Reaper say.

I glanced at him, to find him smirking.

"What?"

"I asked if there was anything else you wanted us to discuss tonight."

"No, we're just going in circles. Let's call it a night

and see what Spawn can find on his dark web search. I want to go check on Dante then Alisse."

Reaper nodded then dismissed us. I didn't waste time before checking on Dante. He was sleeping, so we left his brother to watch him. Lash would be nearby if he needed anything. Reaper was waiting for me in the common room when I came out. It was only ten thirty at night, but it felt much later than that.

"You ready to head over to my house?" he asked. Alisse was living with him and Chey. I wanted nothing more than to have her living in my house, our house. I couldn't ask her to do that, not until I got her to take my claim seriously.

"Yeah, I am. I need to see if she's still doing okay. I don't want to overwhelm her tonight, but tomorrow, she and I will be having a talk. There will be no more going out on dates with other fucking men."

"I hear ya. If Cheyenne had done that to me, I would've lost my ever-lovin' mind." The whole time we were talking, we were briskly walking toward his house, which was the only house directly to the west of the clubhouse.

We'd set up the compound so that houses could be built along streets running east to west. The main road into the compound was a north to south flowing one that went through the whole place and out a back entrance. We had plans to add more things like they had in Dublin Falls and Hunters Creek, such as the swimming pool. My house was on the east side of the clubhouse. The first one on the same street as Reaper's on the other side. Maniac, our VP, had his house on the next street south of Reaper's. They're neighbors, although there's quite a lot of ground between each house. The only others to have houses were Mayhem and Tinker. They lived on the same side as I did, only another street over. This left Ratchet, Crusher, Spawn, Lash, Sandman, and Shadow yet to build their houses.

We were quiet as we walked into his house, just in case they were asleep. The lights were on in the downstairs living area, so we headed in that direction. I could stand a drink. Walking into the living room, we heard the television playing and the ladies were curled up on the couch, eating popcorn, with their eyes glued to the screen. When I looked to see what they were watching, I groaned. It was one of those Viking shows. One of the ones with the half-naked men, with long hair and muscles. The kind I told her not to be watching.

Cheyenne smiled at Reaper when she caught sight of him. He made his way straight to her end of the couch. Alisse gave me a wary look from the opposite end. I didn't hesitate. I went straight to her and I scooped her up in my arms.

"What the hell do you think you're doing, Ink?" she shrieked in surprise. I sat down and settled her on my lap. She squirmed to get away, but I held her tight.

"I thought I told you not to watch this kind of show?" I quirked my left eyebrow up at her.

She gave me a mutinous look, one that thrust out her jaw and made me want to bite it. "I can watch whatever I want, Ink. You're not the boss of me."

"Oh, I'm not, am I? Well, we'll just have to see. You watch this and you'll have to suffer the consequences."

"What consequences?"

I lowered my head and whispered in her ear, so she was the only one who could hear me. Cheyenne and Reaper were avidly watching us. "I'll just have to take you captive and ravish you until you submit to me and fall madly in love with me, like they do on these shows. If you want to look at muscles and tattoos, baby, I'll gladly strip naked and let you. You can touch, taste, and play with anything you want, for as long as you want." I nipped her earlobe.

She shivered and as I gazed in her eyes, I saw her pupils dilate. Her breathing hitched. She was aroused by the idea. After several seconds of silence, she tried to recover.

"No thanks. If I want that, I can find it elsewhere," she said softly, so only I could hear her.

"If you try that, you'll find that fine ass over my knee with my hand spanking it until you beg me to stop. There will be no more dates with other men, Alisse. If you want to go out, I'll take you," I warned her in a low growl.

"You wouldn't dare spank me!" she hissed.

"Like hell I wouldn't. I'll drag your pants down and redden that ass. Then when you can't take it anymore, I'll slide my cock into your hot, tight pussy and fuck the rest of your stubbornness out of you," I continued to whisper to her.

She wiggled on my lap, which ground her pussy on my already hardening cock. That only made it worse. I knew the instant she realized what she was doing to me. Her eyes widened and she froze. Knowing there would be no better time than now, I stood with her in my arms. She wrapped her arms around my shoulders like she thought I'd let her fall. I was holding her bridal style. I looked at the amused face of Reaper and the concerned face of Cheyenne.

"We're going to go and let you guys get to bed. Talk to you tomorrow."

"Go? I'm not going anywhere. I live here, remember?" Alisse reminded me, as if I could forget.

"I know exactly where you've been living. You and I have some shit to talk about and I don't plan to do it here. My house is more private," I explained, as I walked to the front door. Reaper got up and came to open it for me.

"Put me down! Reaper, tell him to stop," she begged.

"Sorry, A, but I make it a policy not to interfere with my brothers and their women. You'll be perfectly safe with him. Don't forget to take your coat." He grabbed her coat off one of the hooks by the door and laid it over her. She still had on her shoes.

"I'm not his woman," she yelled, as I walked out the door and down the steps. I heard Reaper's laughter. I didn't waste time heading to my house. It was a little bit of a walk, but nothing terrible. The whole way there, she tried her damndest to get me to let her go, so she could go back to their house.

"Ink, you're acting crazy. We have nothing to talk about. Even if we did, it doesn't need to be tonight. I'm tired. I want to go to bed."

"I told you at the Grove, that when you got back, we'd talk. Well, I was going to wait until tomorrow after what happened, but after seeing that show you were watching, I decided tonight it is. If you're that tired, we'll lie in my bed while we talk."

"I'm not going to get in your bed with you!" She acted like she was shocked at my suggestion.

"Why not? We're both adults. Are you scared you can't control yourself and you'll attack me?" I goaded her.

"As if. I can control myself, just fine, I'll have you know. It's you who can't control yourself. I told you a hundred times, I'm not going to be a notch on your headboard, Ink. You have enough of those without me adding to it. If you're horny, go to the clubhouse. I'm sure the skanks have come out of the woodwork by now."

"And I've told you a thousand times, I'm not looking for a notch on my headboard. Going to the clubhouse to have meaningless sex with one of those women holds absolutely zero appeal to me. You're who I want. You're who I'll have, and if I die from blue balls waiting, I guess I'll die."

She snorted and gave me a disbelieving look. "Die of blue balls? Who do you think you're kidding? I know damn well you haven't been going without sex since I came here four months ago. I see the way JoJo and the others try to hang onto you. You might not do it when I'm around, but I'm no fool."

I stopped not far from my house and stared down at her. There was enough light from the moon that I could see her and the street. "Alisse, I haven't touched a fucking woman since the day I laid eyes on you. I don't know what else I can say or do to prove to you that you're the only one I want, and that it's not for a few nights, weeks or even months. It's forever. Just like it is for Reaper and Cheyenne and all our friends in Dublin Falls and Hunters Creek. Hell, even Agony has found himself a forever woman down in Cherokee. I burn for you night and day. I think about you when I should be working or listening to what my brothers are saying. I dream about you and the life I can so clearly see us having together. The children we can have together. Why won't you give me your trust?"

I began to walk again. As we mounted my steps, she shook her head. I caught a look of pure sadness on her face. "Ink, you're not capable of being with just one woman. You'd end up breaking my heart. We'd get together and as soon as you cheated on me, we'd be done and I'd be left to pick up the pieces. Even if we had children, I would never stay with a man who cheats on me."

I opened my door and walked inside. I kicked it shut behind us and kept going, headed for my bedroom. She was looking around as we went. Entering my room, I took her to the bed, sat her down on it and took off her shoes and socks. After those were off, I took off my boots and socks. I pushed her until she was flat on her back and I was hovering over top of her. She stared at me in alarm.

"Now, you're going to explain to me why in the hell you are so fucking sure that I'll cheat on you. You have no idea if I'm a cheater or not. You're making assumptions," I growled. She was pissing me off with this talk.

She stared at me for almost a minute without saying a word. I wasn't going to let her leave my room until she told me the truth. I had to know why she was so adamant this would happen. I'd rather cut out my own heart than hurt her like that. I wouldn't risk it. To have her then lose her over something as silly as easy pussy wasn't something I'd ever do to the woman I loved. Yeah, I said the L word. I'd known within the first month that I was head over heels in love with her.

She took a deep breath then she blew my world apart when she said, "I know because I know at least one woman you did it to and you hurt her something terrible. I thought you were in love with her and would never do that, but you did." I reared back in shock and waited for her to continue.

Alisse: Chapter 3

I watched as confusion overtook Ink's face. God, had he done it to so many women, that he couldn't recall them all? Anger bubbled up darker inside of me. I let him have it. As I did, I refused to acknowledge that a lot of my pain and anger was due to him shattering me and my dreams of a hero, who I found out had lead feet.

"Alisse, babe, I have no idea what the hell you're talking about. What woman did I cheat on and how do you know I did?"

I pushed him away from me. He tried to not let me move away from him, but I kept pressing against his chest until he moved off me. I sat up and shifted until I was as far away from him as I could get on the bed. I curled my arms around my legs, hugging them tight against me. Maybe that would help me not to fall to pieces.

After I was done with this ugly tale, I was done. I was going to insist that Reaper let me move off the compound. If they still believed it was too dangerous for me to be alone in Bristol, I'd move somewhere else. It would be better anyway. I knew that I could no longer live in the same town as him and risk seeing him. Watching as he had woman after woman traipsing through his life and bed would be torture.

"I was fifteen the first time we met. I saw you walk through the door and I admit, to my teenage heart, you looked like the most handsome guy I'd ever seen. I was jealous. You were laughing at something she said. For almost a year, I watched you together every time I was around and you always seemed to be happy and in love. I never thought once you'd cheat on her."

"Baby, you still have me confused. Where was this? You said when you were fifteen. How can that be? I don't remember you. Who was the woman you're talking about?"

"I didn't look like this then. I was fat and hadn't grown out of my gawky teenager stage. You didn't know I existed. I guess after cheating so many times, you probably can't recall who she was. Does the name Amber Lantz mean anything to you?"

He stiffened and his face grew dark. "Amber? You think I fucking cheated on Amber?"

"I don't think it, I know it. You almost killed her when you did," I snapped back at the anger in his voice. How dare he be angry when he was the one in the wrong?

"I never cheated on that lying whore," he snarled back at me.

I came up on my knees and got in his face. "Like hell you didn't! She came home crying the day she found out and she broke up with you. She told the whole family how she caught you cheating with another woman. That when she confronted you with it, you didn't deny it and told her that you were never going to be tied down to one woman. That she could deal with it or else."

In a flash, he was back across the bed and had me by the upper arms. He gripped me hard, but not enough to hurt me. He gave me a gentle shake. "Like hell I did! Tell me what all she said, then I'll tell you what really happened. How do you know Amber? Start there."

"I'm her little cousin. I doubt you remember Lissy."

His eyes widened, as he looked me up and down. "Oh my God, Lissy! You're Lissy. Why didn't you tell me this when we met again?"

"Why should I? I knew you wouldn't remember me. As for what she said, she came in the house with tears streaming down her face after being out with you. She sobbed out how she caught you cheating. She wouldn't name the other woman. My uncle was so pissed, he wanted to hunt you down and beat the shit out of you, only she begged him not to. She said she loved you and it would kill her if he did that. She was so upset that not long after that, within a month, she moved away to live in DC."

"Did she say anything else?" he ground out between clenched teeth.

"No, only that and that there wasn't just one woman you cheated with while the two of you were dating. That's why I'll never let anything happen between us, Ink. I'll never end up like her, pining for a man who tore my heart out. To this day, she still talks about you. She's never gotten married and every guy she's ever dated, never lasts. You ruined her life."

"Are you done?" he asked. His voice had gone scary soft. I nodded my head yes. What more was there to say? I sure as hell wasn't going to tell him that the crush that I had on him then had blossomed into love for me. That secret could go to the grave with me. He stared into my eyes, barely blinking as he started to talk.

"I remember you now. You were such a quiet, sweet, and pretty thing. You watched but didn't say much. I hated how your family seemed to ignore you and fawn all over Amber. I asked her about it and she laughed and said you were the ugly duckling of the family."

I hung my head. That was true. It was a joke in my family. All of them were really tall, slender, with perfect figures. They all had blond hair and blue eyes. I took after my dad, who had been mixed. I didn't look like them. The only one who never said it was my mom. She always told me I was beautiful and unique, but that's what moms do. They think their kids are beautiful even when they're not. I didn't say a word.

"It used to piss me off when she'd say that. I told her to stop. It's true we dated for almost a year. However, that's as far as the story goes that's true. I hate to be the one to tell you this, baby, but your cousin is a lying cunt."

I sucked in a harsh breath to hear him call her that. What the hell? First he called her a whore and now a cunt.

"I'll admit, she was my first and only serious girlfriend. I was dumb and twenty years old when we met. I'd casually dated some girls and I'd been sexually active since I was sixteen. When I met Amber, I thought I had met the love of my life."

Hearing him call her the love of his life made my heart hurt.

"However, as time went on, I began to notice things about her and the stuff she did that put my teeth on edge. I started to call her out on her behavior. Not ever in front of anyone, but when we were alone. The day we broke up, I'd had enough. I'd just found out from one of my buddies that she'd been sleeping with not one, but two of our other friends. Guys who I thought were my best friends. It had been going on for months."

I gasped, not believing what I was hearing.

He continued, "I confronted her with it. At first, she tried to lie her way out of it, saying they were just jealous of us and trying to cause trouble, but I showed her I had proof. The friend who told me said he'd suspected it for a while but had no proof. So, he watched and waited for a chance to catch them in the act. One night, they said they were too busy to hang out with him and he knew I was out of town that weekend. He waited outside her house and saw both guys pull up and pick her up. They went out to a vacation house the one boy's family owned. They had a threesome out there and he got the pictures to prove it."

My stomach cramped. He looked like he was dead serious.

"He showed them to me when he told me, so I would know he wasn't making shit up. I showed those to her.

When she saw those pictures, she confessed, but tried to tell me they didn't mean anything. It was just sex, but I was the one she loved. I told her I didn't love her and would never love her and I never wanted to see her again. That it was past time we parted ways and I'd been thinking about it anyway. She was angry as hell at me and kept begging me not to break up with her, but it did her no good. The following week was when I joined the Iron Punishers as a prospect. I'd been wanting to do it for a while, but Amber kept telling me not to do it. That she didn't like the idea of me being in an MC. I heard not long after we broke up that she moved away."

I sat there stunned and unable to form a sentence. The inflection of sincerity in his voice was hard to ignore. Could he be telling the truth?

He reached over and took a hold of my chin, lifting it so I had no choice but to stare into his eyes. "After that, I never let a woman get close to me again. I didn't date. I fucked then walked. Any woman wanting more, I didn't touch. I always made my rules clear and if they tried to change them later, I'd cut things off. I wasn't ever going to get serious again with a woman."

I jerked my chin out of his hand. I went to get up off the bed, but Ink whipped me around and pushed me onto my back again, so he could hover over top of me. "I said that's what I swore, but then this green-eyed, goddess came sashaying into the ER one day and threw that plan right out the fucking window. I knew as soon as I laid eyes on you, that I'd met the one woman I was willing to go the whole distance with."

"Ink, you don't need to—"

He cut me off. "Don't call me Ink. I want you to call me Austin when we're alone like this. It's what bikers do when they find their old lady. They have them use their real name."

"I'm not your old lady," I protested.

"But you will be. I'm not going to let you walk away from what I know is the best thing to happen in our lives, Whirlwind. I love you and I'm pretty damn sure you love me too. Your heart is safe with me. I'll never break it. I'll never throw it back in your face. Please, tell me you believe me and that you'll give me a real chance to prove to you that I'm not lying."

My head was whirling like the whirlwind he called me. My gut was churning. My heart was racing. Should I take the chance? I knew if I was wrong, it would tear me apart. He didn't say another word. All he did was watch me intently, as I fought to make a decision. In the end, I gave him what I could.

"Ink, there's nothing I'd love more than to give you a chance and for this to work out. However, I'm scared. You can crush me so easily. I hate you having that kind of control over me."

"You have just as much control over me. Don't you think I'd be crushed and devastated if you decided to leave me? I would."

"I'll try. That's as good as I can promise at the moment. I'll try. Why don't we spend time together and see what happens? But there are some rules if we do this, and they're not up for debate," I warned him.

"Anything. Tell me what they are."

"There will be no seeing other people. If I find out you went behind my back and slept with another woman, we're done. There will be no forgiveness. That's even if we're not sleeping together. I'm not ready to jump into bed with you, no matter how physically attractive you might be. That kind of intimacy with you would be too much right this minute."

"I can do that," he said quickly, without blinking an eye.

"You need to go and get tested to be sure you have nothing that could be transmitted to me, if or when we decide to become intimate with each other."

"I've done that already. Even though I've never been with a woman without a condom, I routinely check to be safe. You can never be too careful."

"Good, I want to see those results and I'll show you mine. The last ones are from three years ago, but I'll get a new one, if you want, even though I haven't been with a guy since then."

"You haven't had sex in three years?" he asked, incredulously.

"No, I haven't. I don't do casual hookups and after the last guy, I decided I was done trying to find something that wasn't out there. I realized the chances of me finding a man to spend my life and have a family with was not going to happen."

"Oh, baby, it's going to happen. That man is right

here in front of you. We'll make our forever together and have those kids we both want. I promise you that," he whispered, right before he laid a soul-scorching kiss on me. My body went up in flames instantly.

I tried not to moan, as his tongue played with mine and his teeth nibbled on my lips before sucking my lower lip into his mouth. My breasts tingled and my nipples beaded up while my panties grew damp from the slickness spilling out of me.

A small moan escaped, which seemed to only egg him on. His hands slid down my arms and ribs, to settle on my hips. He dragged me closer. I could feel his erection pressing into me. He felt so big. The ache between my legs got worse. In order to save myself, I tore my mouth away from his.

"Ink," I protested. His glare had me backtracking. I'd give him this, for now. "I mean, Austin. We need to stop."

"I don't want to, but if that's what you want. I know you have to be tired after tonight. I'll let you use the bathroom first then I'll take my shower. You can wear one of my shirts to bed, although I'd prefer if you were naked," he said with a wink. He eased back away from me. As he did, I saw him adjust himself. I couldn't help but stare at the bulge in his pants. I had to rip my eyes away from it. He smirked at me.

"I'm not staying here. I'm going back to Chey and Reaper's. They'll be expecting me."

"They know you're with me. I want you to stay with me. I won't press you for more than you're willing to give me, baby, but I need to feel you in my arms. I need to know you're safe. Hearing Reaper say someone was shooting near you almost gave me a heart attack. I was terrified you were hurt or dead. I'll sleep on top of the damn covers and you can get under them, if that makes you feel safer. Please."

To see this strong, dominant, alpha male begging me made my insides turn to mush. Although I knew the smart thing to do was to go back to my best friend's house, I capitulated.

"Fine, I'll stay, but you have to keep your hands to yourself. I'm dog-ass tired and I need some sleep."

"Scout's honor."

"You were never a scout," I told him. All he did was grin at me, his naughtiness oozing out. While I got the shower started, he dug out a shirt for me to wear. I would've preferred a pair of clean panties, but the shirt was so long on me, it was almost a short dress. I took a quick shower then waved him inside once I was done. Ten minutes later, after I laid there in misery, listening to the water and imagining him naked and wet, he came out wearing sweatpants, but no shirt. He crawled into bed and snapped off the bedside light. I rolled on my side, facing away from him.

"Goodnight," I said.

His arm reached out and pulled me against his chest. His mouth nuzzled my ear as he said, "Goodnight, babe."

I thought I'd never be able to fall asleep, but I was

wrong. The warmth and comfort of his arms had me dropping off in no time.

I blinked my gritty eyes open to take in the hazy sunlight coming through the window in his bedroom. The curtains weren't all the way closed, which let in some light. I stifled my groan, as I stretched. I lifted Ink's arm slowly off my waist, so I could slip out of bed to use the bathroom. I had to pee something awful. I thought I had made a successful escape, until he asked hoarsely, "Where are you going?" His arm came back around me.

"I need to use the bathroom."

He let go of me reluctantly. I scrambled to the bathroom. I was almost ready to wet myself. The relief on my bladder was tremendous. Once I was done, I wiped, washed my hands then went back out to the bedroom. I should get dressed and leave, but the bed was so comfortable and it was calling me. Giving up the fight, I went to get back in it. Ink held up the covers, so I could lie underneath them. Instantly, his arm was tugging my back against his chest.

"Go back to sleep. It's still early. Later, I want us to go get breakfast. Does that sound good to you, babe?"

"That sounds wonderful."

I couldn't keep the smile off my face as I fell back into a slumber. A few hours later, his alarm went off, waking us both up. I snuggled into my pillow. He got out of bed. A smack to my ass cheek had me sitting up and glaring at him. He was grinning at me. "Come on, woman. Time to go eat. I'll give you ten minutes to get ready. If you're not, then I'm taking you as-is."

"In-Austin, you can't take me out of here in a t-shirt! I need clean clothes, my toothbrush, a hair pick, hair product, and my makeup."

"You can stop at Reaper's long enough to change into clean clothes. As for a toothbrush, I have an extra one you can use. And you don't need any damn makeup or gunk in your hair. You're too beautiful even without it. That's just gilding that your lily doesn't need."

"My hair will go wild if I don't." It was already curling all over my head. My hair was the bane of my existence.

He reached over and tugged on one of my curls, letting it bounce back in place when he let go of it. "I fucking love your curls. Don't do a thing to them. Come on, live dangerously."

I grumbled but got up. Ten minutes later, we were walking through the front door of Cheyenne and Reaper's house, so I could change my clothes. They were in the kitchen. Reaper was drinking coffee. I knew Chey was drinking her decaf tea. They smiled at us and I could see the speculation in their eyes.

"Babe, go get changed. Do you want me to see if they want to go with us?" he asked, pointing to the couple. I nodded my head.

I had no idea what he said while I was gone, but when I got back, he informed me they were getting ready to go with us. We had to wait about ten minutes for them to come back. I tried not to fidget as we waited.

Being in broad daylight somehow made me more nervous about what I'd agreed to last night. I turned on the television. I couldn't tell you what I watched. Ink seemed content to sit there holding my hand and not saying a word. When they rejoined us, Reaper suggested we stop in to see how Dante was doing before we left. None of us were opposed to that idea.

At the clubhouse, it was still quiet. The guys must still be in bed after a long night of partying and sex. Luckily, no one was lying around the common room naked. When we tapped on the medical room door, Dillon called out for us to enter.

I was happy to see that Dante looked a smidge better than he did when I saw him last night. He had some color back in his face. He assured us that he was fine. We only stayed a few minutes to chat then we told them where we were going. They told us to enjoy ourselves.

Since Cheyenne was pregnant, the decision was made to go in Reaper's truck. It was an extended cab with plenty of room for the four of us. I sat in the back with Chey, so Ink could have the extra leg room in the front. She gave me quizzical looks all the way to town. I knew she was dying to interrogate me about what happened last night. I'd have to tell her later when we were alone.

I was thrilled to see Reaper pull into Annie's. Annie was his mom's best friend's younger sister. I knew her from my days of coming to Bristol to stay with family. As we entered her diner, she greeted us with a big smile and hurried over to hug us.

"Welcome. To what do I owe the pleasure of you four this morning?" she asked, as she led us to a secluded booth in the back. Even at this hour, the diner was relatively busy. Annie had the best home cooking in town. They'd be hit with even more people after church was over with.

"We woke up starved for some of your amazing cooking, Annie," Chey told her with a smile.

"I always love to see you come in here. What will it be for drinks? Let's start with those."

We gave her our drink orders and she gave us the menus. Although I'd been in here numerous times, I still liked seeing it and deciding what to get. The problem was, she didn't just have a few good things. The whole menu was excellent. It was hard to decide. I was waffling between a cowboy breakfast or a pancake and waffle one.

Ink leaned over to speak softly in my ear, sending shivers of awareness down my spine when his breath rushed over my ear. "What're you going to have, baby?"

"I can't decide. It's between the cowboy breakfast or the pancake and waffle platter. What're you having?"

"I'll have the cowboy platter. Why don't you get the other one and we'll share?"

"You'd do that? Most people hate to have others eat off their plate."

"It doesn't bother me. I'd gladly share anything I have with you." The look of desire in his eyes made me want to kiss him, but I held back. We were in public and I wasn't sure if I wanted anyone knowing we might be entering into a relationship. At least not until I was sure.

"Okay, then we'll share. Only don't hog more than your share or I'll stab you with my fork," I teased him.

"You wouldn't do that, would you?" he asked in surprise.

"Oh, yes, she would. One time we split dessert, which was fine with her, until I started to take more than my half. She left prong prints on the back of my hand for a week," Cheyenne told him.

"She's not lying, I did. But the ho was eating my half and it was chocolate cake. She should know as a woman, you don't mess with another woman's chocolate," I pretended to whine. Both men burst out laughing, as Chey gave me a look, promising she hadn't forgotten to pay me back for that. It happened about six months ago.

Annie brought our drinks then took our orders. I noticed she was waiting on us, but none of the other tables. I pointed this out to the other three when she walked away for a second. "Why is Annie only waiting on our table and no one else?"

"Probably because I'm her favorite person in the world and she loves me," Reaper said with a smile.

"No, it's because I have to make sure my pseudo grandbaby gets fed and it has nothing to do with you. You're just the sperm donor. It's because I love Cheyenne and Alisse," Annie said, from behind him.

Reaper grabbed his chest. "Annie, you wound me!"

"Like I believe that. Okay, tell me what's going on with the two of you?" She pointed to me and Ink. I was about to tell her nothing when he answered her.

"I'm working on convincing her I'm the man for her and no one will ever love her or make her as happy as I will. I'll need all the help I can get, Annie. Will you help me?" He batted his lashes at her and stuck out his lip, like a little kid pouting. The look was so comical on a grown man like him, I couldn't help but giggle. Chey laughed too.

Annie's mouth dropped open in shock. She didn't say anything for several seconds then she got excited. "Are you telling me that another Punisher is off the availability list? You're really planning to settle down with one woman?"

"Cross my heart and hope to die, yes, I swear. She stole my heart the moment I saw her again."

"Again?" Reaper, Cheyenne, and Annie all asked at once.

"Yeah, again. I found out last night who Alisse is. I knew her by another name years ago." That's all he said. I could tell the women were dying to ask more, but they didn't. Annie got called away by one of her waitresses a few seconds later.

We chatted about work and the past week. Cheyenne and I were working on Mondays and Fridays, the two busiest days of the week for our doctor. Luckily, she only saw patients until noon on Fridays, then we had the rest of the day to catch up on other things before the weekend. I was hoping this Soldiers of Corruption shit would resolve soon. I couldn't afford to work only part-time forever. I was living off my savings to make rent on the place I wasn't even staying in right now. I also had a car payment, insurance, utilities, etc. All the usual bills most adults had.

"Do you think I might be able to go back to work full time soon?" I asked the guys. I knew the answer was going to be no, especially after last night, but a girl could hope.

"No, I don't. I'm sorry, Alisse, but it's still too dangerous, especially after last night. Why? Are you bored?" Reaper asked me.

"A little, but mainly it's because I can't afford to live off my savings forever, Reaper. I don't make enough by working just those two days a week to cover all my bills. My rent isn't cheap. You know how it is. Nothing is cheap these days. Don't get me wrong. I'm thankful to you and the club for putting me up because I'm Chey's friend and all, but it was never supposed to last this long."

"We didn't just do it because of Cheyenne. We did it because we knew you were Ink's and he wanted you protected, as much as I want my old lady protected. Why don't you give up your lease like Chey did? It would save you a ton of money," Reaper suggested.

"You knew I was Ink's?"

"Hell yeah, they did. I made no bones about it, baby. My brothers knew I wanted you and would do whatever it took to keep you safe. I agree with Reaper. You should give up the lease," Ink said.

"Well, nice to know everyone knew before I did. And we haven't settled the question of me being yours yet. As for giving up my apartment, I can't. There's no guarantee I can get it back or one as nice after this threat is over with."

Ink stared at me hard. His hand was holding mine. We were sitting side by side in the booth, like Reaper and Chey were on the other side.

"Babe, I know we're still working things out, but I told you, we'll work it out. You're going to be with me. There's not going to be a need for you to get an apartment. You'll be living with me at the compound in the house."

He was just like Reaper. He'd used similar tactics to get Cheyenne to give up her place.

"I'm not doing it, so forget it. I'll be alright for a while longer. I'll hang onto it."

"I could pay your rent," he volunteered next.

"No way! I'm able to take care of myself. Can we drop this and talk about something else?"

I could tell by the look on his face, he wasn't going to let this go forever. I had a reprieve, but Lord knew for how long. The rest of our outing was relaxed as we enjoyed the food and conversation. It was a very relaxed me who went back to the compound two hours later.

Ink: Chapter 4

Back at the compound after breakfast, we found the rest of our brothers were finally awake. They were congregated in the common room. Some were eating some pastries that one of them had gotten and drinking coffee. Others were talking or playing pool, a favorite pastime for most of us. When the four of us entered, the comments and questions started.

Ratchet was the first. "Why the hell did you guys sneak out without telling us? I might have wanted to come have breakfast," he groused, as he stuffed a donut almost whole into his mouth.

"Yeah, you look like you're starving. How many of those have you had?" I asked him sarcastically.

He patted his flat stomach. "A few, but I'm a growing boy. I need real food."

"Yeah, well, keep eating like that and you'll need a dump truck to move your ass. Of course, that's probably wishful thinking on my part. Why is God so cruel? Men can eat anything and everything and not gain an ounce and all I have to do is look at food and my ass gets bigger," Alisse bemoaned after teasing Ratchet.

"Your ass looks just fine to me, sweetheart," Ratchet popped off to her.

I narrowed my eyes on him. He was fighting not to grin. "If you know what's good for you, you'll keep your eyes off her ass and any other part of her anatomy. If you don't, I'll beat your eyes shut, so you can't look," I growled at him.

"What about my hands?" was his instant retort back.

"If you touch me, Ratchet, I'll be the one to break your hands. You won't need to worry about what Ink does to you," Alisse told him calmly with a serene smile.

"Fuck, she's mean. You sure you wanna woman like her?" he asked me.

"I'm positive."

"So, does this mean the two of you are now official? No more of us watching you circle around each other? Because I have to tell you, it was getting old. Everyone knows you're into each other like those two sickening fools," Tinker added with a grin.

I hugged her close to my side and held onto her hip, so she couldn't move away from me. I placed a kiss on her pouty lips. She shuddered. I didn't take it as far or do it as long as I wanted, but it gave me a taste of her. Kissing her was like swallowing warm spices to me.

Whistles and hoots rang out. Her cheeks were flushed when I pulled back. I looked at my smiling brothers. I knew every one of them was happy for me. They might tease, but they knew she was mine. "Does that answer your question? She's still trying to say we're not definite, but I'll wear her down."

"Hell, that's going to be fun to watch. We should take bets on how long she lasts," Lash piped up.

"There will be no betting. I swear, you'd bet on anything, wouldn't you?" Alisse asked with a roll of her eyes. It was true, we did often bet each other on the strangest things. The newest thing was what the sex of Reaper and Cheyenne's baby would be.

That didn't keep any of them from shouting out their bets. I even added mine, which was a week. She elbowed me. However, the best one was when Cheyenne shouted hers, which was eight hours. This had everyone laughing and Alisse giving her bestie a death glare.

After a few more minutes of this, they started to settle down. She popped up on her toes to say quietly in my ear, "I'm going to go see how Dante is doing and if he needs anything. I'll be back."

"I'll come with you," I immediately offered.

She shook her head no. "No, I won't be long. Stay here and keep an eye on these nuts. Although, you might be the king nut, so that might not be the best thing." As she went to walk away, I smacked her ass, just to get that look from her. I watched as that ass of hers jiggled as she walked away. I could feel my erection growing.

"Get your head out of the gutter. So, I take it that last night went well after you went back to your place?" Reaper asked, as he handed me a beer. He'd sat Chey down at one of the tables and gotten her a flavored water while we'd been teasing.

Giving him a chin lift in thanks, I took it and I answered him, as we sat down with Cheyenne. "It went more than okay. I got her to agree to give this thing between us serious consideration. She's still scared that I'll hurt her. She thought I was a cheater and she couldn't trust me. I have to show her that I'm not."

"Did she say why she thought that?" he asked. I glanced at Chey. I wondered if she had known the whole story. From the look on her face, she didn't. I hoped Alisse wouldn't get pissed at me for telling them.

"I knew Alisse when she was a teenager. Only she looks different now, so I didn't recognize her. She was called Lissy then. I dated her older bitch of a cousin, Amber. I found out last night, Amber lied to everyone about why we broke up."

"Let me guess, she said you cheated on her," Reaper said with a note of disgust in his voice.

"Got it in one. Yeah, she did. Alisse had a crush on me and it totally gutted her that I supposedly did that to her cousin. Only, I wasn't the cheater. Amber was. I broke up with her. Right after that was when I joined the club as a prospect."

"I wondered at the time if it was because of a woman. You had this wariness about you when you joined."

"Didn't we all? I mean, none of us ever thought we'd meet a woman we'd want to claim and keep forever, did we? I never thought I would, not after Amber. You only ever were serious about Chey," I pointed out.

He laid a kiss on her lips. I watched them give each other loving looks. Before, I had been amused by those looks and maybe a tad envious, but now I was happy that I could do the same to my woman.

Speaking of my woman, Alisse dropped in the chair beside me. "What're you talking about over here? Did I miss anything? Dante's sleeping by the way."

"I was telling these two about how we knew each other."

She groaned. "Yeah, that was something to hear. I never thought Amber was an angel, but I also never thought she was a liar."

"But you do now?" Chey asked her.

"I can see that some of her odd behaviors that never made sense to me, do now. She was always such a goody two shoes around the family. I mean, they thought she was perfect. I could never compete with her, not only in behavior but in looks or anything else, according to my mom's family. It was tough growing up like that. Thank goodness, we didn't live in Bristol all the time, or I'd have never had a break from it."

It pissed me off to no end that her own family had treated her as less than perfect. Anyone who was around her for even an hour could tell she was not only beautiful and sexy, but smart, loyal and an amazing friend.

"They were dumbasses forever saying the shit they did and for acting that way, Alisse. You're so far from an ugly duckling, it's laughable. You're smarter and more beautiful than Amber ever was. She would never be a friend like you are to Cheyenne. Your family better hope I never meet them, or they'll get an earful from me," I snarled.

"You're so sweet to say that, Ink," she said softly, before she gave me a peck on the lips. I didn't let her get away with that. I grasped the back of her neck and held her tight, so I could kiss her the way I knew we both needed and wanted. No polite kissing shit here with our family. A tiny moan escaped her when we broke apart. I couldn't help the smirk I got on my face. She punched me lightly in the gut.

"I can't believe anyone, let alone your family, ever called you an ugly duckling," Chey said, sounding appalled. Reaper was frowning.

"Believe it. I was lucky my mom didn't ever say that. She would defend me, but then again, she was my mom. My dad was seldom around my mom's family, but when he was, he'd get pissed and tell them off."

"Why was your dad not around them much? It sounds like you visited often," I asked. We hadn't gotten into this last night.

"He knew they didn't like or approve of him. They thought Mom had married beneath the family and my dad being mixed only made it worse. They're a bunch of racists, I hate to say. Me not being tall, blond and blue-eyed, only made me stick out more to them. I know they didn't like people seeing me with them whenever the family was out and about."

"Cocksuckers! They ever do that shit in front of me

and I'll beat the men and tell the women what fucking bitches they are. You never have to worry about me thinking or acting like that. I'm always proud to be seen with you and I will be the same with our kids, no matter who they look like. Personally, I want them all to look like you."

Her mouth dropped open like she was in shock. I could tell she'd never had anyone say that to her. I had to fight not to kiss her again.

"Ink is right. You're all those things and no one has the right to make you feel bad about yourself. I've been jealous of your skin tone, that body, and those eyes of yours since I met you. You make it hard to be your friend," Cheyenne told her.

"Bullshit, but thanks for saying that. You know you're gorgeous. Anyway, I'd rather not talk about how my family treats me. Ink, as for meeting them, it's not likely. I tend not to associate with them much, now that I'm an adult. Occasionally, I go to a family event because I think my mom would've wanted me to. Despite how they are, she did love her family."

"Speaking of your mom, it sounds like she's gone. I'm sorry, baby. What about your dad?"

"Dad died when I was seventeen. He had an undiagnosed heart condition. Mom passed when I was twenty-two. Honestly, I think she died of a broken heart. She never got over losing my dad. They were so in love with each other."

"You never had any brothers or sisters?"

"No, my mom had to have a hysterectomy after she had me. They would've loved more." I heard the sadness in her voice. Wanting to get her mind off that and onto something else, I changed the subject. I decided to tell her about my family.

"Well, you had two loving parents, which I'm so glad you did. I don't have any siblings, or at least none that I know of. With my dad, it's possible I have some half-brothers and half-sisters running around out there. He wasn't much of a father. He drifted in and out of our lives. Mom was there but only sort of. I was taking care of myself by the time I was nine. Honestly, when the two of them passed when I was eighteen, it was a relief. They weren't close to either of their families, so I didn't have a relationship with them. The only family you're getting out of me is this bunch of assholes." I pointed around the room as I said it. I couldn't help the smile I had on my face. They were the best family.

"Honey, I'm sorry. I did have great parents. My dad didn't have any family that he knew of. He was raised in an orphanage. He and my mom met their freshman year of college and by the time they hit the one-year mark, I was born. It was tough, but they still somehow got their degrees."

"Okay, enough of this depressing shit. You both have this awesome family now, so you don't need any of those shitheads. Let's relax and talk about something fun," Reaper interjected. That brought the conversation to a halt. He could see how much it was upsetting her. That's how we ended up spending the rest of the day laughing and hanging with the club, talking about other things. Overall, it turned out to be a really good day. One I wanted to repeat every day.

I looked around the shop. Punisher's Mark was the club's tattoo shop and my baby. Unsurprisingly, my road name came from my occupation. I was a tattooist. I'd gotten my first tat at fourteen. Yeah, it was without parental approval, but the guy who did it, didn't give a shit. I fell in love with them then. From that day forward, I hung out at his place every chance I got. He showed me everything he knew and at sixteen, he let me start to do drawings and hang them on the shop's wall. The guy had even let me use him to practice on. His name was Harry.

By the time I turned eighteen, I was apprenticing at his shop. It was the only real job I'd ever had. Now, fourteen years later, I was known as the top tattoo artist in Virginia. I had people come from all over to have one done by me, which still blew my mind.

Luckily for me, the club had seen my talent and bought out Harry's shop when he decided to retire and move to Florida. It was because of my tattoos that I met Reaper and then the rest of the club. They were clients first, who had encouraged me to join the club. I'd been running it for them since day one. That was ten years ago. As the manager, I made a bigger cut of the profits than my brothers did. That was the deal at any of the businesses we owned. There was the standard cut then the extra on top for the ones doing the extra work.

Usually, I loved going to Punisher's Mark and

getting lost in a day of work, however, today wasn't one of those days. All I could do was think about Alisse and wish I was back at the compound with her. If I hadn't had a couple of big appointments, I would've rescheduled them so I could've stayed home.

I had more freedom than a lot of people. I could pick my projects and hours. If I wanted to take time off, I did. I rarely did it, but the option was there. I wouldn't abuse it, but I could see that I'd likely be taking more time away from the shop than I ever had in the past. With Alisse in my life, I wanted to enjoy our time together.

I had three other tattooists, one piercer, plus a receptionist who worked for me. Tammy, Elliott, and Chuck were the artists. Sunshine, and yes, that was her real name, was our resident piercer and Greta, our receptionist. They rounded out my crazy work family. They drove me crazy at times, but I wouldn't trade them for anything.

Initially, I wouldn't have said that about Sunshine. When she first came to work for us, she'd wanted to hook up. She wasn't a bad looking woman and in other circumstances, I wouldn't have objected, but one of my rules was, I didn't shit where I ate. I never slept with anyone who worked for the club. She hadn't been happy, but she got over it and we went on to become friends.

Greta had never been an issue. She was married to Chuck and he would've ripped my head off if I'd ever thought of doing anything with her, which I didn't. I wasn't someone who slept with married women. I believed if you were married, you stayed faithful to that person. Probably not what most people thought a biker would think, but it was in my case and the case of my club brothers.

I was staring off into space when Sunshine came up and elbowed me in the arm. "What's up, boss man? You've been distracted all day. I mean, more than usual. In fact, what the hell has been up with you for the past four months?"

I looked around to find myself the center of attention of the whole crew. We were having a lull in customers. Knowing that I wouldn't get off telling them it was nothing, not after she called me on it, I decided to tell the truth. They'd find out soon enough anyway.

"I was thinking how I wish I was home, so I could be spending the day with my woman, rather than here looking at your asses," I told them with a grin. Looks of astonishment lit their faces before the questions began.

Sunshine was the first to say something. "What the hell? Since when do you have a woman? I mean, one who isn't simply a warm body for a night? You are meaning someone important, right? Not one of your bunnies or bar hookups?"

"Yes, I mean someone important. She's going to be my old lady and wife. So, when you meet her, treat her with respect. Her name is Alisse."

"Damn, I had no idea. Congrats, man. I can't wait to meet the woman who brought your ass to heel. What's she like? How did you meet her?" Elliott fired off.

"She's Cheyenne's, Reaper's old lady, best friend. She's been staying at the compound with us. She's amazing. You'll see when you meet her. She works with Chey at Dr. Simpson's office."

They'd all met Cheyenne. I hadn't talked about Alisse to them because I'd wanted to have something that was all mine. We lived in each other's shit so much, it was hard not to know everything about each other.

"When are you bringing her to meet us?" Greta asked, as she smiled at her husband.

"Whenever she'll say yes. She's going crazy right now, having to stay at the compound and only getting to work a few days a week. Maybe later this week."

"Why not today?" Elliott asked.

"She works on Mondays and Fridays. Besides, I'm not sure I want her to meet you just yet. I can't have you scaring her off."

This got the expected response of derision and questions about what was wrong with them. I loved pulling on their chains like this. I was laughing at them when my cell phone rang. I took it out of my cut and saw it was Reaper calling. I held up a finger, so they'd get quiet then I answered.

"Hey, Pres, what's up?"

"Ink, how soon can you get back to the compound? We need to talk."

The seriousness in his tone had me stiffening and a knot forming in my stomach. Something was wrong. My first response was to ask him, "Is Alisse alright?"

"She's fine. I need to talk to you and the guys. I got

some news today about the Soldiers. I want us to have church."

I sagged in relief that she was okay, although the knot didn't completely unravel, hearing he wanted to talk about the Soldiers of Corruption. Any mention of those bastards put us all on edge.

"I have one more small piece to do. He should be here any minute. If we stick to what we discussed and he likes what I drew, I can be there by four thirty, maybe five. Is that soon enough, or do you need me to reschedule?"

"Nah, that should be fine. The others have to tie up stuff at work too. I just didn't want anyone to stay over tonight. The sooner the better for this shit is my thoughts. I'll send out a text to have everyone be here and in church by five thirty. See you then. Bye."

"Bye," I told him, right before he hung up. He was getting better at not just hanging up. Cheyenne was having an influence on him. In the past, he'd just abruptly hang up the phone.

Everyone was watching me with worried looks on their faces. They didn't know specifics about what was going on with the Soldiers of Corruption, other than we were on extra alert because of someone having their nose out of joint. We'd had to warn them when things started with that club to be on alert and we'd upped the security at our businesses.

"Is everything alright, Ink?" Chuck asked. He was the quiet one, who usually liked to stand back and observe. He was a huge hulking guy covered in tats, who was intimidating as hell. He was the kind of guy you wanted to have your back.

"Everything is fine. Reaper just wants us all back early for church. This isn't our usual night, so he wanted to be sure I wasn't working over."

"Is it about that trouble you've been having?" he asked next.

"Yep. Alright, let's get back to work. Greta, if my client isn't here in the next five minutes, please call and make sure he's still coming."

They took this as the dismissal it was. They weren't offended. They knew I wouldn't share club business with them. Fortunately, Greta didn't have to call my customer. Three minutes later, he came strolling through the door. I got luckier when he loved the drawing that I'd done off what we'd discussed over the phone and he didn't want any changes to it. I got down to business right away.

After he paid and left a couple of hours later, I started to clean up. Sunshine came into my room. "Hey, I can do this. You go ahead and head home. Good luck with your meeting."

"Thanks, Sun. See you tomorrow." I gave her a pat on the shoulder then told the others goodbye and hit the road. The ride was a fast one and I enjoyed what was left of the January sun. It was cold, but not as cold as it would be once the sun went all the way down.

I got back in time to grab a drink and dropped a kiss on Alisse's mouth as she walked through the door with Cheyenne, Dillon, and Ratchet before heading into church. I wish I'd had time to speak to her, but it was time to find out what was new. All I said was I'd see her after church. I saw looks of worry on both women's faces.

Taking my seat, I tried to be patient as Reaper got started. He didn't waste time jumping into it.

"You all know I had news today about the Soldiers. I've been talking to Gabe, Sean, and Griffin. They've been checking into them and that club in Ohio we found out about from Serpent. It looks like they're going to be the first target. There's been enough time since we took out Serpent that it shouldn't raise too much suspicion."

"When do we make our move? Who's going in?" Mayhem asked.

"Hold on, we're not going yet. We need more information and the Dark Patriots think they might be able to take the lead on this. At least they hope so. I gave them two weeks to have something figured out, or we'll go on our own. We can't keep watching over our shoulders forever. Slither and Ogre are out there and I don't trust them. They have to know that we were the ones to make Serpent and the others disappear. They can't prove it, but it would be too much of a coincidence for it to be anyone but us. They have to know they're dead, even if no bodies have been found."

He was right. We'd made sure the bodies wouldn't be found, but they'd be idiots if they didn't suspect us. Who else could it be? Of course, with how drugged up Serpent had been, a drug deal gone wrong wouldn't have been out of the realm of possibility, if Slither would bother to acknowledge his kid had a drug problem. Having numerous guys then end up dead in one of the clubs they infiltrated might raise their suspicions. We were slowly chipping away at them. It wasn't as fast as we'd like, but we couldn't rush this and risk fucking up and missing some of them. This was a long game kind of situation.

While we were all more than willing to go in and take care of them ourselves, if we could find another way, we would. I hated the thought of leaving our compound vulnerable. I wanted my whole club to be here to guard the women and our livelihoods. I knew Reaper would be thinking the same thing. We wanted to protect our family and those who worked for us. If we went to do the job, then we'd have to call in reinforcements here. We had friends who would do it, but we didn't want to ask unless we had to.

"Fuck, I hate that we have to wait, but I understand. How likely do you think it is that Sean and the guys can pull this off?" Maniac asked.

Reaper had served in the SEALs with Sean, Gabe, Griffin, and their dead friend, Mark. That was how the club had met the Dark Patriots. We met them several times and I liked them. They were solid guys you could always count on.

"Did Sean say how he thought they might be able to do it?" I asked.

"No, he said he didn't want to say more until he knew for sure if it was a go. I trust he'll tell me as soon as he can. They know how urgent this is. Which brings us to making sure we have a backup plan in place, in case we do have to go in either alone or with them. We need things to be covered here at home."

No one argued with that. So, for the next hour, we talked about who would stay or go if that were to happen and who we'd ask to come help cover our area while we did it. It was a given that Terror and his guys down in Dublin Falls would help. After all, Reaper's brother-in-law, Viper, was one of the Warriors.

Bull and his guys in Hunters Creek would be more than willing, but they lived further away, so we decided to see if Jinx and his Ruthless Marauders would be available, since they were in Knoxville. They'd come to help when we needed it with Serpent. They were less than two hours away.

We'd upped the electronic security at the compound and our businesses since the start of this whole fiasco with the Soldiers. More cameras and better alarms were added. We would make periodic, staggered patrols, so no one could predict when we might be checking up on our businesses. So far, knock on wood, we hadn't had any major issues, which added to our anxiety, rather than lessening it.

By the time Reaper called the meeting to an end, I was exhausted and all I wanted to do was go spend time with my woman at my place. Or I should say our house since I was already thinking of it that way.

Last night, I had again convinced her to stay all night with me and not go back to Reaper's house. I was planning to see tonight, if I could get her to agree to bring at least some of her stuff to my house. I was hoping to not sleep alone again. Having her in my arms gave me a sense of contentment I'd never had in my life. I slept deeper and longer.

Walking out of the common room with the others, I was happy to see she was still there. She and Cheyenne had gone and changed out of their work scrubs and into regular clothes. They were lounging on one of the couches and were laughing. She smiled at me when she saw me, which made my knees feel weak. God, I could never tell the guys that, or they'd call me a pussy.

Reaper and I didn't waste a second before we headed over to them. I tugged Alisse to her feet and gave her the kind of kiss I'd wanted to give her earlier. Out of the corner of my eye, I saw Reaper was doing the same thing to Chey. Alisse responded beautifully and was as eagerly devouring my mouth as I was hers. I was a panting mess by the time we took a break.

"Hi, baby. That's the kiss I wanted to give you earlier. Are you hungry? I can see what we have at the house to throw together or we can order in. Whatever you want." I was easy to please. I wasn't the best cook in the world, but I was decent. I knew after these past few months, she was better than I was. However, I knew she had to be tired from working and I didn't want her to think I expected her to work all day then come home to cook for me. I might be a caveman in some ways, but I liked to think I was a modern one.

"Hi, handsome. Thank you for that kiss. I am hungry and I bet you are too. Chey and I were just talking about what we should make for dinner. It's getting late. She suggested we throw some burgers and stuff on the grill. It's quick and easy. Plus, yesterday, Dillon picked up the grocery order and we haven't put away the meat in the freezer yet. Or if you'd like something more, we should order, since nothing has been thawed out." She was nibbling on her thumbnail, like she was worried I wouldn't like her suggestion. I took it away from her teeth and kissed it.

"I could go for that. What about you, Reaper?" I knew he'd been listening.

"I think that sounds great. Why don't we see if the others want in on it? Babe, if I get the guys to do the peeling and chopping, would you make those homemade fries?"

"Sure, ask everyone and if they peel then I'll make them. We have that industrial fryer in the kitchen. That makes it quick and easy to make them," Cheyenne agreed.

In no time, we were all at work to get dinner cooked. It was all-hands-on-deck for this. Those not cooking did prep work. By seven thirty, everyone was sitting down to eat the burgers, fries, and hotdogs we'd cooked. It wasn't anything fancy, but it tasted great. For dessert, they'd gotten out two giant cheesecakes they'd hidden in the freezer. Around here, if you didn't hide it, shit would be gobbled up.

I was content to watch her laugh and chat with the others as the evening wore on. When it got later and I knew we needed to head to bed, I whispered in her ear,

"Babe, I want you to stay with me tonight. Please."

She didn't argue. She got up, said goodnight, told Chey she was getting some stuff from the house then let me lead her out—another small victory on the road to making her mine.

Alisse: Chapter 5

My week had flown by faster than they had for a while. I was still only working two days a week, but I'd been busy doing other things. One of those things was moving my belongings from Cheyenne and Reaper's place over to Ink's house. It seemed stupid to keep my stuff there when I was spending every night at his house. I'd get up in the morning and find I'd inadvertently forgotten to bring something with me the night before. So, on Thursday, while Ink had been at work, I moved my stuff. He'd been encouraging me to do it.

The look of happiness on his face, when he got home and he realized what I'd done, had been worth the sweating I did. Sure, I could've asked Dillon to do it for me, but he was busy and I didn't feel right telling the prospects what to do. Dante was still on the mend from his gunshot wound. He was up and about, but healing. He was in no shape to lift stuff. He was the other major thing that had kept me busy. I had to nag him, along with Chey, not to overdo things. He tried to wave off our concern, but we wouldn't let him. He bitched that it was like having two moms. I was quick to remind him that I was only two years older than him and he was the same age as Cheyenne. He shrugged at me when I did, the asshole.

Tonight, seeing as it was Saturday, I knew to expect that the bunnies and probably some of the hang arounds would be by the compound. They tended to come on weekends or when the guys asked them to. It wasn't anything I could control and I couldn't really get too pissed off about it. After all, other than Reaper and Ink, none of the guys had a girlfriend or wife. Yeah, I was including Ink in there since he'd constantly referred to me as his all week.

However, if one of those bitches dared to lay a hand on him, I'd have something to say. Before, I hated it when I saw one of them flirt with him or he'd talk to them. JoJo, one of the bunnies, had been the worst. I stormed out one night when he smiled at her. There was something about her that rubbed me extra wrong. Paula and Desi were less catty, if that made any sense.

Ink had told me early in the evening that we'd leave before things got crazy, but I told him I didn't want that. I didn't want him to feel like he couldn't stay and have fun with his brothers because of me. If I was jealous or feeling insecure, then I'd have to deal with it. I had to learn to trust him. If he proved I couldn't, then it was better to learn that now rather than later.

Cheyenne, being a true friend, told Reaper she wanted to hang out later tonight too. I knew she was doing it to back me up. It was after ten o'clock and the music coming from the stereo was loud. Some nights, the guys would get up and play for us, but not tonight. They were all drinking, but no one was drunk, not even close.

I was at the dart board with Ink, Crusher, and Tinker. We were playing against each other on teams. The guys had been impressed when I first showed them that I had skills at this game. My hand and eye coordination were spot on. I played a lot of darts in college. In fact, I was so good that Crusher and Tinker both tried to claim me as their partner rather than Ink, but he said no.

I was laughing at how pathetic those two were looking, after Ink and I had just won a game, when the door opened. Cold air rushed in and in came the three bunnies. I was glad to see there didn't appear to be any others with them. That would leave them plenty of men to choose from, eleven to be exact, if you counted the two prospects. It looked like some of the guys might be out of luck, unless they went to town or more women showed up later.

I had noticed over the months that the bunnies were territorial of the guys. They didn't like it when other women from town came to party with the club. They saw them as belonging to them. In a way, I could see that. They were here mainly to provide sexual favors in exchange for the club providing them protection. Unlike some clubs, they weren't paid and didn't live onsite. I think Reaper, having raised his little sister here, might have had something to do with that. As long as they kept away from Ink, I wouldn't bother them.

I didn't bother to pay much attention to who they sought out. I was with Ink and we were having fun. I might not have noticed at all where they were, if I hadn't turned around fifteen minutes later, after going to retrieve my darts, to find JoJo sidled up to Ink. My temper instantly flared. I could tell he was trying to get her to leave him alone. I watched and listened for a minute.

"JoJo, go bother someone else, will ya? I'm busy playing darts with my old lady. I'm not interested in having a drink or anything else with you now or ever. I've been telling you that for four months. When will you get that through your head? Alisse is my woman." I could hear the weariness and anger in his voice. I hadn't realized he'd been telling her this the whole time I'd been at the compound.

I watched as her face flushed with anger and she put her hand on her hip, thrusting it out. I wanted to yell over and tell her to put on some clothes before she caught pneumonia. I guess she thought the way she was dressed and standing made her look sexy. To me, it looked pathetic. Don't get me wrong, she had a nice body, the bitch. She was skinnier than I was, which I kind of hated. Her face was worn looking even though I knew for a fact, she was younger than me by a few years. None of the bunnies were even thirty yet. I found that out from Chey, who I think asked Reaper. I got immense satisfaction out of the fact my face had zero lines and didn't look like leather. I was snapped out of my pleasant and catty thoughts by her words.

"You're really going to claim that bitch? Come on, Ink. There's no way she can satisfy you like I can. You know you love my mouth. She's not club. She's not gonna be able to understand you or the things you do. She can't expect you to be faithful. You're a biker for God's sake. Better she finds that out now." She rolled her eyes.

I was speechless at first. Crusher and Tinker were eyeing JoJo then darting looks at me. Ink was glaring at JoJo. Deciding to take the bull, or in this case the heifer, by the proverbial horns, I hurried over to them. I wrapped my arm possessively around Ink's waist. His hand came up to pull me even closer and his lips landed on my hair. He liked to do that when he couldn't reach my mouth.

"JoJo, I suggest that you do as Ink says and move along. There's nothing here for you. I'm sure the other guys wouldn't mind your attention. For the record, I don't have to have grown up in a club to know what Ink needs or wants. He has no problem telling and showing me. As for your mouth, well, the less we talk about that the better. I doubt you can suck start a motorcycle, but I bet I can. Lastly, he knows if he wants me, and he says he does, that touching you will end that. Not every biker is a cheater. I would've thought you learned that from hanging with the Warriors."

I made my voice as condescending as I could. After a lifetime of being on the receiving end of it, I knew how it was done. Usually, I wouldn't act that way, since I hated to be treated like that, but in this case, I let it fly.

Her face went beet red and she stepped closer to me. I was ready for her. My dad had taught me how to protect myself, just like he did my mom. Not only could I shoot, but I could throw a punch and knew enough other self-defense moves to hold my own. Or at least be able to get away, which was the point. I'd fought with men, so fighting her wouldn't be a problem.

"Who do you think you're talking to like that, bitch?" she shrieked. I saw the others turn to look at us and someone lowered the music.

"I believe it's clear who I'm talking to, bitch. I'm talking to you. Leave Ink alone and we won't have a problem. Keep it up and you won't like it. I can guarantee you that. Look at Paula and Desi. They're not over here trying to hang off him. They have class." Now that he was officially mine, I wouldn't walk away in a fit of anger.

I knew what she was going to do before she even started to move. Ink must have guessed too because he tried to push me behind him. I didn't go. Instead, I moved forward and away from his hand on my hip. JoJo came flying at my face with her claws extended. She was going to scratch my eyes out.

Now, that's not a bad move, but not one I'd fall for. Slapping her hands down and away from my face with my non-dominant hand, I threw a punch with my other one, all in one motion. She never saw it coming. She still didn't know what happened after my punch landed, because she hit the floor on her ass and was out like a light. I heard swift intakes of breath from all around me.

Suddenly, the laughing and talking started.

"Jesus Christ, where the hell did you learn to throw a punch like that, Alisse?" Crusher asked. I could hear awe in his voice.

"Damn, I think I just went hard. That was sexy as fuck," Ratchet said with a laugh.

89

"You go, babe" I think it was Spawn who said that. There were others remarks, but there was only one person I wanted to hear say something. I turned to stare at Ink. He was standing there looking down at JoJo then up at me. I couldn't tell by the look on his face if he was pissed or not at me. Just as I was starting to get worried, he reached out, grabbed me, jerked me against his chest, and kissed me. His tongue, lips, and teeth feasted on my mouth. I moaned in pleasure.

By the time he stopped, I was a quivering ball of mush. Fire was racing through my body. My core was clenching and my nipples were hard nubs, begging for his touch. His eyes were hot with desire. He bent down and hoisted me over his shoulder and started for the door. As he went, he hollered to the others.

"Make sure JoJo knows that I meant what I said. She doesn't want me to let Whirlwind loose on her again. Now, I have something I need to address with my woman. 'Night." Laughter followed us out the door. I hung over his shoulder, rubbing up and down his firm back. I couldn't reach his ass, but if I could, I'd have my hands on it too.

"Are you taking me to punish me for doing that?" I asked him, trying to sound casual.

"No, I'm taking you to punish you for making me so fucking hard. I feel like I might shatter any second. Shit, you might want to hide when we get to the house, otherwise, I might be chasing you around, begging you to let me inside of you. That was so fucking hot, baby," he said hoarsely.

I moaned then confessed, "You won't need to beg, Austin. You might be the one who needs to hide. I feel like tearing off your clothes and riding you until we're both too sore to do it anymore."

He stumbled for a second then his stride got longer. In no time, he had me through the front door of his house and shut the door. I didn't have time to take a breath before my feet hit the floor and he had me pinned up against the door. His mouth attacked mine, as his hands tore at my clothes. I stepped out of my shoes while he removed my clothes. Our hands tangled as we both tried to unclothe the other.

I'd never been this desperate for a man. Sure, I'd had decent sex in the past. I'd more often than not, gotten off, but never had I been this ready to have a man's cock inside of me. Ink broke our kiss long enough to yank off both our shirts. While he was doing that, I was frantically tearing at his belt and zipper to get his jeans undone. He already had mine undone and pushed to my knees. I stepped out of them and then dropped to my knees on our pile of clothing. I yanked his jeans and underwear down to his knees then to his ankles. He stepped out of them, as I got my first look at his cock.

Yes, we'd been sleeping together for a week, but he always had on pants. I guessed from the bulge in his pants that he was packing more than your average-sized cock, but nothing had prepared me for this. He was super-sized. So big that I wondered if he'd fit. His cock was long, I'd guess at least nine inches. It was thick, thicker than my wrist. Veins stood up all down his length. The huge mushroom-shaped head was a dark purplish-red color and was covered in precum. It also had decorations. Down his entire length were multiple bars. He had a Jacob's ladder.

I couldn't stop myself from tasting him. I stuck out my tongue and swiped it along the head, lapping up his essence. His cum was salty with a touch of tanginess. I eagerly licked more, taking a moment to tease his slit with the tip of my tongue. He moaned and fisted my hair.

"Fuck, if you do that, I won't last, Alisse. I want you too much."

I smiled up at him and whispered, "Good," before I opened wide and took him in my mouth. His hips jerked, causing his cock to press in deeper. I was right. He was almost too big. I had my mouth as wide as it could go, and he was stretching it, looking for more room. It made it hard to swirl my tongue like I usually would, but I adjusted my technique.

Maybe I'd been trying to piss off JoJo when I made the blow job remark, but I had my prior sexual partners tell me I sucked cock like no one they'd ever been with before. I think part of it was because I genuinely loved to do it. I got enjoyment out of it. In Ink's case, I knew that I loved him and I wanted to give him the most pleasure possible. I fisted his base and added in strokes, being careful of his piercings. I'd never been with a guy who had any. Working to take more and more, I teased as much as I could as I pumped his cock and teased his sac. I gently massaged his sac before moving my fingers back to press on the area between his balls and asshole, his taint.

He shuddered. His thrusts were getting faster and deeper. As he hit the back of my throat, I took a deep breath, worked to relax and let him slip down my throat. I swallowed over and over. I gagged but kept going. His finger bit into my scalp.

"Jesus Christ, you have to stop, baby. I'm going to explode," he warned me.

I slipped my finger up to coat it in the wetness from my mouth. It was running down his balls. Getting it soaked, I slid back to his taint then past it to his puckered ass. He tensed. I waited to see if he told me not to do it. "I don't know if I'll like that or not, but do it," he hissed finally.

I rubbed the outer ring until I felt him relax then I eased the tip inside. His tight rings of muscle tried to keep me out, but I kept thrusting in and out, until I pushed past. As soon as I did, I homed in on his prostate. His groan of pleasure and his cock jumping in my mouth told me he liked it. It only took maybe a minute of stroking his cock and prostate as I sucked him deep, for him to come. A scream was ripped from him as he shot load after load of cum down my throat. I swallowed as fast as I could, so I wouldn't miss a drop.

When he was done, he slipped out of my mouth. I eased out my finger. He collapsed to the floor on his ass and stared at me in a daze.

"Motherfucker, I've never come that hard in my life. What the hell did you just do to me, woman? You weren't kidding. You can suck start a motorcycle," he gasped.

I couldn't help the laughter that bubbled up in me. As I laughed, he leaned forward and kissed me. His tongue delved into my mouth. I knew he could taste his cum, since I still could. He didn't seem to be put off by it.

After he was done kissing me, he pulled away and told me, "Give me another minute then it's your turn. If I thought you could do it, I'd ask you to carry me up those stairs. Fuck! The guy is supposed to leave the woman like this, not the other way around."

That only made me giggle. He gave me a rueful look. True to his word, a minute later, he got to his feet and helped me to mine. He swung me up, so I had no other choice but to wrap my arms and legs around him. He easily carried me up those stairs. His mouth kept playing with mine as he did it and his cock rubbed against my soaking wet pussy. I had wetness down to my inner thighs.

In the master bedroom, he laid me gently down on the bed. He didn't immediately get on it with me. Rather, he went to the bathroom and came back with a wet washcloth that he used to clean my fingers. Once he was satisfied they were clean, he pressed me flat and crawled between my legs.

"I don't know where to start. I want your mouth, your breasts, and your pussy all at once," he growled.

"I love all those choices, but if I have a say, I need your mouth on my pussy before I go insane, Austin. I need to come. I need to come before I die," I pleaded.

I wasn't lying. It did feel like I would die if he

didn't. He gave me a wolfish smile before he started at my mouth and teased his way down my body. No matter how hard I pushed his head down, he took his time licking, kissing, and sucking on my mouth and breasts. By the time he made it to my pussy, I knew one lick was all it was going to take. He spread my lips wide with his thumbs and swiped from my clit to my entrance. I screamed as I came, bucking my hips off the bed. He held me down, and thrust his tongue inside me to flutter it, as I came. Wetness gushed out of me. He greedily lapped it up.

As I started to come down from the high, he moved up to suck and bite my clit. He purred as he did it and shook his head from side to side as he thrust two fingers inside of me. I was instantly coming again. He worked me without pity as I came and came, losing track of how many times I orgasmed. The intensity got higher. The final time he made me come, it was by not only sucking on my clit and finger fucking my pussy, but he also slipped a finger into my ass like I'd done to him. The room got dark as I screamed and fought to breathe.

Eventually, I regained enough of my senses to find I was lying boneless on the mattress. He was smiling at me.

"You're a God. I submit," I whispered hoarsely. I was hoarse from the screaming.

"Oh, I'm not done yet, Whirlwind. That was just the opener. My cock needs to be inside your tight pussy," he growled. I gasped, as he raised up on his knees and I saw he was rock hard again. He pumped up and down his length, making me want to cry. I wanted him but I couldn't move.

"I can't," I cried.

"Yes, you can. Are you on birth control? We didn't talk about that when we looked at our results," he observed. He was right. We had shared our test results with each other earlier this week, but never talked about birth control. I nodded yes. He didn't need to worry about that. Seeing me nod, he hooked my legs over his forearms, lifted my ass off the bed and lined the head of his massive cock up with my entrance. He never looked away as he slowly pressed inside. In and out he went, working that huge cock into my pussy. The sensation of his piercings rubbing my inner walls was indescribable. He was stretching me so much, it stung, but I wouldn't ask him to stop. I needed him too much.

By the time he was all the way buried inside of me, I felt like I would burst, I was so full. He slowly pulled back then thrust forward. In and out he went, twisting his hips, dragging his Jacob's ladder across my nerve endings. Every once in a while, he'd circle my clit with his thumb. That wasn't all he did. He also sucked and nipped on my nipples. In no time, I was racing toward another orgasm and this one was going to be even bigger. My nails bit into his forearms.

"I'm close," I whispered. This must have been what he was waiting for because he sped up and took me harder, deeper, and faster. I screamed until I couldn't breathe as I came. I clamped down on him so hard, he hissed and swore. He dragged his cock back and forth a couple more times then roared as he jerked and filled me full of his warm cum. The last thing I recalled before I lost touch with everything around me was thinking, I'd die without him.

Ink: Chapter 6

I watched Alisse sleep. She looked so innocent and content, curled up on her side, in the bed next to me. Last night literally blew my mind. Don't get me wrong, I'd had a lot of women give me blow jobs and I'd eaten lots of pussy and had sex more times than I could count, but not once had any of those women come close to making me feel like being with her last night did.

She made me feel like I was having an out-of-body experience. Her mouth on my cock had been mind-blowing. She hadn't lied when she made her remark to JoJo. I shied away from thinking of how many men she'd been with to perfect that technique. I hated the idea she'd been with anyone but me. Was it a double standard? Hell yeah, but I couldn't help but wish I was the only one to have ever been with her. She'd call it more caveman bullshit.

However, it wasn't just the blow job that blew my mind. She'd done that finger in the ass thing that I never imagined in a million years I'd let a woman do, and it had driven me wild. I wouldn't be objecting if she wanted to do that again. The biggest surprise for me was what it had felt like when I was inside of her. She had felt like no other woman I'd been with. I knew it was more than just the fact she was the only woman I'd had without a condom. She was the only woman I'd ever been with who I loved. God, did I love her.

I was afraid to tell her that this soon. I didn't want to scare her away. She was still skittish and not without reason. She'd believed her bitch for a cousin. After all, why would you ever think your family would lie, right? I could wring Amber's neck for saying that shit. If she hadn't, Alisse and I might have been together months ago.

She wiggled deeper into her pillow, like a puppy rooting. It made her ass wiggle, which made my half-mast cock go to a full-on steel pipe. I stroked up and down my length as I stared at her, drinking in her beauty, as I decided where to start. After the first-time last night, we rested then we went at it again. If I hadn't known how tired she was, I would've done it a third time, but I could see she was exhausted, so I restrained myself. That restraint was gone.

Easing myself down some in the bed, I slowly eased her top leg back, so I had a clear pathway to her pussy. I softly petted the soft curls she had guarding her treasure. My mouth started to water as I recalled how good she tasted last night. Checking to make sure she was still asleep, I squeezed between her thighs and opened her lips wide with my finger and thumb.

Her lips were so damn pink and plump. Her clit was hidden but it wouldn't stay that way for long. Sticking out my tongue, I licked her from her entrance to her clit. I could taste myself on her. It didn't turn me off. In fact, the thought of it being the two of us together made me even harder, if that was possible. She moaned but her eyes stayed shut. She shifted a little on the bed, which made her legs open wider.

That single taste sent me over the edge. I opened my mouth wide and assaulted her pussy with my tongue, teeth, and lips. She gave a shriek as she shot up in the bed. Her hand landed in my hair and she tugged, but I didn't stop. The bit of pain only spurred me on.

"Oh my God, Austin!" she cried out.

I lifted my head long enough to smile up at her and say, "Good morning, Whirlwind." As soon as I said that, I got back to having my breakfast. I licked her from top to bottom then bottom to top. I teased her entrance by thrusting my tongue in and out of her, mimicking what my cock would soon be doing. I sucked hard on her clit, then batted it around with the tip of my tongue. She shuddered then her fingers relaxed in my hair and she started to push my face into her pussy harder. I couldn't help the smile that came over me. Yeah, my baby liked to have her pussy eaten. Good, because I already knew it was going to be a very regular occurrence.

As I worked her toward her first orgasm of the day, but by far not her last, she got louder with her whimpers and pleas. I added my fingers to her pussy, so I could thrust in and out of her tight hole. She was releasing her cream all down her thighs. My goatee was covered in it. This would be my new beard oil, I thought with a snicker. She trembled, stiffened then came crying out, as she flooded my mouth with her essence. I lapped up every drop.

When she came down from her high, she whispered to me, "What was that snicker about?"

I grinned at her as I lifted my mouth away from her. "I was just thinking of how your cum is now my new beard oil."

"Eww, Austin, that's gross. Who would want to walk around smelling like my pussy?"

I sat up and frowned at her. "I would and there better be no one else smelling like it. If I could bottle this scent, I'd make millions."

She rolled her eyes at me. "You're nuts. First of all, no one else is going to be getting the chance to use it for that. Second, no one would buy it. Guys are so damn weird. Third, in case you forgot, that's probably not all me down there."

"I didn't forget. We fucking smell and taste amazing together, baby. And there would be plenty of people who'd pay for this. You taste like heaven. I'll never get enough. Get ready for you to be serving this as my breakfast every morning. That doesn't count the snacks I'll want throughout the day and night."

She flopped back on the bed and laughed, shaking her head. I couldn't let her get away with that. As she laughed with her eyes closed, I grabbed her hips, flipped her over on her stomach, yanked her to her knees and sank into her, all in one big move. She cried out and bucked back into me, which only drove my cock deeper into her tight pussy. I groaned at the feel of her hugging my cock so damn snug.

"Oh God, you're so big," she moaned.

"All nine inches just for you, baby. How do you like

my ladder? Does it feel good?"

I knew the women I'd been with in the past had mostly loved it. A rare few had complained about it being too much. In their cases, I hadn't cared if it was or not. As long as we both got off, that was fine by me. They weren't sticking around for encores, unless they were bunnies, then they took what they got. In her case, if she said it was too much or she didn't like it, I'd take the fucking thing out. It had been a bitch to get and let heal, but she was what was important. I knew I'd have no problem getting the best sensations out of being with her, even without it. I'd gotten it done in the first place on a dare.

She didn't answer me at first. I pulled back and slowly sank back inside. She shuddered. "Baby, do you like it? Does it hurt?" I asked. I hoped like hell I wasn't hurting her. She hadn't complained or acted like I was last night.

She shook her head emphatically. "No, it doesn't hurt. It feels amazing, Austin. I just can't think when you're inside of me. My brain short-circuits or something."

I smiled as I thrust again, this time going deeper and a little harder. Last night, we'd been in such a fevered rush, I'd taken her hard and fast both times. This time, I wanted to take my time. I wanted her to feel how much I loved her, even if I couldn't say the words yet.

"Good. That's what I want to hear. If I do anything you don't like, tell me. I'll stop. I want you to enjoy every damn thing we do together, baby. There's no enduring it. If you don't like my ladder, I'll get rid of it."

Her head whipped to the side and she stared over her shoulder at me in shock. "What? You'd take it out if I didn't like it? Honey, that had to have hurt and taken forever to heal. Why in the world would you do that?"

"Because if it doesn't make you feel good, then it doesn't do a damn thing for me. You're the last woman I plan on riding my cock, Alisse. I'll do anything it takes to give you the pleasure you want and deserve." I thrust in and out slowly again and again. Her eyes went soft and dreamy.

"Don't you dare take it out. It feels so amazing, I can't even describe it. What about you? Does it make sex feel better to you, or would you like it if I had piercings too?"

I held back my moan of pleasure as her pussy momentarily tightened around me. I shook my head. "No, there's nothing you need to do to make this feel better for me. You are hands down the best I've ever had, Whirlwind. That mouth of yours should be insured and your pussy is unbelievable. God, we need to stop talking before I come."

She tightened around me again as I told her what I thought of her mouth and pussy. More heat filled her eyes, as she suddenly slammed her hips back to meet my thrust. "Only if we can insure your mouth and cock, handsome. Harder, Austin. I need you to take me harder and faster," she moaned.

I gritted my teeth to keep going at the same slower pace. Nothing would make me happier than to go faster and harder, but I wanted this to last. "Nope. You deserve for me to take my time. This isn't a race to see how fast I can get off. If you want to, then go for it."

"Oh, so if I want to come over and over, you'll just keep going slow and holding back, will you? Wanna see about that? I bet I can make you break," she said with a smirk.

Giving her a wolfish grin, I said, "Game on, baby. Do your worst."

I started the struggle of a lifetime. She started by trying to speed us up on her own. She tried to slam her hips back to meet my thrusts, but I held tight to her hips and prevented her from doing that. When she realized she wasn't going to get me that way, she started to talk dirty to me.

"Oh, Austin, yeah, baby, right there. Fuck me harder. I need your cock filling me up with all that delicious cum. You know you wanna flood me with it, don't you? I want you to fuck me. Fuck me like you mean it."

I had to grit my teeth to keep from doing what she asked. I fought to slow my thrusts down even more, although it might end up killing me. I reached around to tease her clit. She moaned and jerked.

"I am fucking you and meaning it. When the time comes, I will fill this tight pussy up until you drip all day, baby. Talking dirty isn't going to make me break," I warned her.

She kept trying for a few more minutes. Once she realized I wasn't going to break, she changed tactics, but not before I made her come. As I was sliding in and out, nice and deep, but slow, I rubbed her clit in a circle with one hand while I twisted her nipple with the other. She tightened around me like a fist and came, crying and shaking. I had to close my eyes and think about working on my bike to keep myself from coming. I was having a harder time not coming than I was pretending.

When she finally eased up her hold on me, I took a deep breath and opened my eyes. Her head was lying on the mattress. I licked up her spine, causing her to shiver. As she lay there, I decided she needed to come again. Hopefully, I'd be able to keep from blowing my load. I wanted her to have at least a couple of orgasms before I got my release. If she was any other woman, I'd have made sure she got her satisfaction at least once, but it didn't matter if it was multiple times. I hadn't been a total selfish lover in the past, but they hadn't meant anything to me other than a hole to get off in.

Teasing her soaking wet slit, I got my fingers nice and slick with her cum then I ran them around to her ass. Last night, she had her finger in my ass. It was my turn to find out if anal play was something she liked done to her. If it was, then there would be another way I'd be claiming her soon. Some guys might not enjoy it, but I did. If she did too, then I'd have more ways to ensure her pleasure. If she didn't like it, then I'd be fine without it. I didn't have to have it. There were lots of other things we could try.

I teased the outer rim of her asshole. At my first touch, she tensed a little. I waited to see if she would tell me no. When she didn't then started to relax, I took that as her confirmation to proceed. I slowly breached her puckered hole. She hissed a tiny bit. I knew it had to sting. I had big hands and my fingers were thick.

"Do you want my finger in your ass, baby? Do you like this?" I whispered.

She gasped then nodded her head, as she pressed back on my finger, driving it a tad deeper. "Yeah, I like it. It's just that your finger feels so big. Don't stop."

"If you think my finger is big, you should feel my cock. Have you had a cock in this ass, baby? Do you like that? Do you want that?" I asked, as I thrust deeper. My cock was sliding in and out of her pussy just a little faster and harder.

She moaned before she answered me. "I have. It was alright. To be honest, the guy I did that with wasn't all that patient. It hurt more than it felt good. If that's how it usually is, then I'm not sure I want that, unless you do."

"Alisse, if you don't like it or want it, then I don't. However, it sounds like that asshole was too busy worrying about himself. If he had done it right, you should've at least gotten more pleasure out of it than pain. If you don't like it, I'll stop." I went to withdraw my finger, but she stopped me.

"No! No, I don't want you to stop. You're making it feel better than I've ever felt before. I want to at least try with you, Austin. I want to try everything with you at least once."

Hearing her confess that ramped up my need to come. The thoughts and images that came to mind were so many that I felt my cock expand. She whimpered and thrust back on my cock and finger.

"That's a dangerous thing to say, babe. Anything could get you into trouble," I warned her.

"Then bring on the trouble," she said, as she tightened herself around me. By this time, I'd managed to work a second finger into her ass. My control slipped and I began to thrust in and out of both her holes harder, faster, and deeper. It didn't take more than a minute for her to detonate. She screamed and shook as she gushed. Her hands fisted the bed sheets and she wailed into her pillow.

Feeling her milk my cock and fingers, I knew I couldn't hold back. I let loose and pounded into her as I chased my own orgasm. It only took me a few hard thrusts before I shouted and poured out my load, as I grunted and filled her with cum. I felt like I came forever. When she relaxed fully underneath me, I eased out of her and collapsed next to her. We panted as I held her sweat-slickened skin against mine. I ran my fingers up and down her arm and ribs.

"Baby, I think my brain exploded."

"Mine too. I can't move, Austin. Do we have to get out of bed today or can we just stay here?"

"We can do anything you want. If you want to stay in bed all day, then we will. Can't promise I'll be able to keep my hands to myself."

"I'm not asking you to."

"Good. Now, why don't we go get cleaned up and

then find something to eat. We're going to need our strength." She laughed as I dragged her out of bed and into the bathroom. We took our time cleaning each other. By the time we were done, both of us were hot and bothered, so we had to get in another session before heading to the kitchen.

It was only Wednesday and I was wishing the week was over. I wanted to be at home with Alisse. While I loved my job, I wanted to be with her; however, I had a lot of appointments scheduled this week. It was after the holidays and people were getting their ink before spring and summer got here.

Most of them were repeat customers, which I liked. Not only did it mean they liked what I did last time enough to get more, but I knew their style and what they would most likely want. However, my next one was a new one. I wondered what it was he or she wanted to get. There was nothing noted by the name, only that a two-hour slot had been taken. That was unusual. Greta typically would have noted something down. I went to find her.

"Greta, this next one of mine doesn't say what the person wants. Is it a guy or a girl? Did they say what they were looking for?"

"I'm sorry Ink, he didn't say. I asked, but all he said was it would be small and he didn't know yet. I tried to get more out of him. He didn't sound that friendly to be honest," she told me with a frown on her face.

I shrugged. "Oh well, I guess I'll see. Don't worry about it. Let me know when he gets here. Thanks." I walked off to prep my room.

When he walked in ten minutes later and I was called to the front, it was all I could do not to tell him to get the hell out of my shop. Standing there staring at me was the guy who had taken Alisse out to dinner the night I'd gone after her. The one who'd looked like the yuppie in a tailored suit with the perfect hair and manicured nails. I fought not to be ugly. There were other customers in the shop and I didn't want them to think I acted like an asshole toward people. That was a good way to ruin your business. Taking a deep breath, I gave him a curt nod.

"Alex, would you like to follow me or do you need to look at some pictures? If you need to look, be aware that depending on what you pick, I might not be able to finish it today. You only asked for two hours when you made your appointment."

He eyed me up and down. I could tell by the look on his face, he didn't like me. Well, too bad. I didn't like his ass either. Finally, he answered me. "No, I don't need to look. We can go to your spot."

Greta rolled her eyes at me, as I turned and strolled down the hall to my space. He followed me. After he sat down gingerly on the tattoo chair, like he thought it would bite him or had germs on it, I closed the door with a snap. He jumped, which gave me great pleasure. I took a seat on my stool at my workstation.

"I need to ask a few questions. First, have you ever

gotten a tattoo before? What is it you want? Where? Do you want color or black and white?" I fired off my questions one after the other. Typically, I'd wait for the customer to answer the first question before asking the next one. I liked to put my clients at ease. In his case, I didn't give a fuck.

He looked around the room, taking in the pictures I had on the walls and my equipment. When his eyes met mine, I knew he wasn't here to get a tat. He had something else in mind.

"I've never had one of those disgusting things, nor do I ever want one. I came to see you about Alisse."

I crossed my arms and stared at him, making sure to give him my best dead-eye look. I saw him squirm a little which made me happy. "What about Alisse? I don't appreciate you taking up my valuable time for a chat that has nothing to do with my business."

He snorted. "Valuable time? How valuable do you think it is? All you are is an uneducated, uncouth, ruffian, who is in a motorcycle gang. I came here to tell you that you need to stay away from Alisse. She's a lady and too good for the likes of you. She's going to be my future wife."

Anger flared through me, but I made sure he couldn't see it. I smirked at him. "My time is very valuable. I have people sometimes wait months just to have a piece of art done by me. I may not have a college education, but I'm far from uneducated. As for being a ruffian, well, that might be true, but Alisse doesn't seem to mind. Does she know about this delusion you have that she's going to be your future wife?"

His face flushed red. He sat up straighter in the chair. I saw his fists clench. I remained relaxed. I knew he had no idea I could explode into action at the first sign of him taking a swing at me. I was hoping he would. Although, a guy like him would probably be too worried about messing up his manicure or busting up his knuckles. Mine had seen plenty of fights and I had the scars to prove it. You just couldn't see them underneath the tats on my fingers.

"It's not a delusion. I knew as soon as I saw her that she would make the perfect wife. If you hadn't interrupted our dinner that night, I'd have gotten my ring on her finger."

I stared at him in shock. Was this guy for real? "A ring? Correct me if I'm wrong, but you only met her a couple of days before that date. That's what she told me. How the hell were you going to ask her to marry you? You don't know her. Alisse told me that you were mad that she was friends with Cheyenne, associated with us, and walked out on your date with her, leaving her to pay the check. That doesn't sound like a man who wants a woman to me," I sneered at him.

"I made a mistake. I shouldn't have done that. As soon as she returns my calls or texts, I'll make it up to her, which is why I'm here. I know you're interfering with that somehow. I want you to leave her alone. As much as I hate to do it, I know only one thing works with men like you. So, how much will it take for you to walk away and never speak to or see her again?" He pulled a fucking checkbook out of his jacket pocket.

I leaned closer to him and narrowed my eyes. "Listen, motherfucker, there's nothing you can give me that will ever make me walk away from that woman. She's the woman I love and I'm going to be the one who marries her ass, not you. I suggest you stop calling and texting her, or I'll make you. Forget her name and number. She's mine. Now, get your sorry ass out of my shop before I throw it out." I stood up to tower over him.

He scrambled to his feet and shot me an alarmed look.

"Y-y-you can't threaten me! If you lay a hand on me, I'll call the cops," he sputtered.

"This is private property. You're now trespassing. You'd better leave before I call the cops and have you arrested." I stomped past him and jerked the door open. Standing aside, so he had to squeeze past me to get out of the room, I waited for him to leave.

He threw me terrified looks as he practically ran out of the room. I followed him all the way down the hall to the front desk. Greta, Tammy, Sunshine, Elliott, and Chuck were standing there watching us with raised brows. Seeing that no one else was around I pointed out the door.

"Get the fuck out and don't come back. Remember what I said. Stay away from Alisse. If you don't, you won't like what I do," I warned him. He ran out the door, as if the hounds of hell were after him. As soon as the door closed, the questions flew.

"What the hell was that about?"

"What did he want?"

"Who is he?"

"How does he know Alisse?"

I held up my hand to stop them. "He's a guy she went out to dinner with a couple of weeks ago. I put a stop to it and he flounced off. He was here to tell me to stay away from her and to pay me to do it."

"What the hell? Is he insane? No one in their right mind would come up in here and do that to you. Even if you weren't part of the Iron Punishers, you could squish him like a pissant," Elliott said in astonishment.

"I guess he's not as smart as he thinks he is. Forget his dumb ass. Make sure if he calls again to tell him we won't accept his appointments. If he tries to come in here, call the cops. I doubt he'll be that dumb again, but you never know."

"What're you going to do? Are you going to tell Alisse? Which brings up the question, when do we get to meet her? I have to see what she's like to have two such different men wanting her," Tammy said with a grin.

"Since he was my last appointment and wasted my time, I'm going home now. I'll tell her what the dumbass did and see what the hell these calls and texts are about. She didn't tell me he was doing that. As for bringing her here, if you can behave yourselves, I'll see if she wants to come with me tomorrow. Only you'd better be on your best behavior."

There was a chorus of "I will." Grabbing my helmet,

I told them later and headed out to my bike. I needed to talk to my woman and find out what the hell she'd been hiding about this guy and why. The whole way there, my anger burned higher. That son of a bitch had no right to interfere in my relationship with Alisse. And she had better have a good reason why she didn't tell me he was bugging her.

Alisse: Chapter 7

I heard Ink's bike pull up outside the house. I couldn't help the smile that spread across my face as I hurried to greet him at the door. I'd missed him and I couldn't wait to kiss and hug him. The day seemed to have dragged on forever.

I flew into his arms as the door opened. He caught me and wrapped an arm tightly around me, as I raised up and kissed him. The kiss went on for a long time and made my toes curl. By the time he pulled away from me, I was panting and my panties were damp.

"Welcome home, how was your day?" I asked him in a rush. I caught sight of his face. He wasn't looking happy, despite the kiss we'd just shared. In fact, he looked pissed off. What in the world?

"What's wrong?" I asked, as I tried to back away from him. He held me against him, not letting me put another inch of space between us. His fingers dug painfully into my hips. His eyes bore into mine. I saw anger burning in them.

"Wrong? Why would there be anything wrong? I mean, just because I found out that my damn woman has been getting calls and texts from another man and she never told me... That doesn't mean anything, right? Would that be what you would call wrong? If so, then yeah, I guess there is something wrong," he snapped.

My heart sped up as it sank. How did he find out about that? I was hoping he'd never find out. I'd hoped that Alex would give up once he realized that I wasn't going to answer any of his calls or texts.

"How do you know about those?" I whispered. The anger on his face was scaring me a little.

"How? When your date came into my fucking shop under the pretense of wanting a tattoo then proceeded to warn me away from you and even offered to pay me to stay away. I didn't know you and he were going to get married!" he snarled, as he let go of me and gave me a tiny push, as if he didn't want to touch me. I stumbled back.

"He did what? And what do you mean, he and I are getting married? Have you lost your mind? I'm not marrying him. I don't know him. We only went on that one date and he left it early. You know that!" I said, slightly hysterically.

"You heard me. He booked an appointment for a tattoo then when he arrived, he told me how I needed to stay away from you, since I was an uneducated, uncouth ruffian and you were a lady. He intends to marry you and doesn't want me in the picture. Only money works with men like me. He wanted to know how much it would cost him. Why the hell didn't you tell me he's been calling and texting you, Alisse? Don't you think I should know that? If I'm your man, I should know these things. You don't keep shit like this a secret."

He looked like he was ready to punch something. I'd never been scared of Ink, but I was starting to wonder if I should be. I shoved hard against his chest. I think it was more the shock of it than the actual shove that made him take a step back. I backed further away from him quickly, putting the couch between us. I watched as his eyes widened then narrowed.

"Alisse, why are you behind the couch? Surely, you don't think I'll hurt you, do you?" he asked me in a low growly tone.

"I don't know what you'll do, Ink. I've never seen you like this. Maybe we should talk about this after you calm down," I said in a hurry. As he clenched his fists and closed his eyes, I took off. I ran down the hall and into the bathroom. I heard him yell my name, but I didn't stop or look back at him. I slammed the door closed and locked it. I was shaking so hard, I could barely stand, so I huddled in the corner as far from the door as I could get. *What could I do?* I thought frantically.

He pounded on the door, making me jump. "Alisse, open the goddamn door! I'm not going to hurt you. How the fuck could you think that? Come out here and talk to me."

Typically, I was what I considered a badass woman who stuck up for herself and others. I'd go toe-to-toe with almost anyone. Hell, I carried a gun and wasn't afraid to use it. I've learned self-defense over the years. But a huge man like Ink, who looked as pissed as he did, scared me shitless. It made me think back to when I was little and the shouting and hitting.

My dad had never hit my mom, but my uncle, Amber's dad, wasn't such a nice guy. More than once, when we visited my mom's family, I'd seen him fly into a rage and tear up things as well as hit people, including his wife. For some reason, he never hit Amber. The family had all backed off and left him alone when he got like that, usually after drinking. I couldn't ever recall anyone trying to stop him. It used to terrify me, and my mom would tell me to hide under the bed in the guest room where we stayed. She never told my dad about those times and told me not to either. I knew if he knew about them, he'd never let us go see her family again. I thought I'd gotten over that fear until Ink brought it back tonight. Tears ran down my face as I feverishly thought about what I could do.

"Alisse, baby, please open the door. I'm sorry I scared you. I'm not mad at you. I'm pissed at that jackass Alex." His tone was much calmer, but I wasn't convinced he meant what he said. My uncle had played that same trick more than once. People had fallen for it, only to come out and he'd get his hands on them. The black eyes, bruises and a few times, broken bones had testified to that being a lie.

With my brain tripping over itself and not being able to rationally think, I did the only thing I could. Luckily, I'd tucked my cell phone in my bra strap since I didn't have pockets in my pants. I yanked it out and shakily hit the dial button for Cheyenne.

She answered, sounding cheerful. "Hey, girl, what's up? I figured you'd be all over Ink by now. I thought I saw him come home. I know how you can't resist that man."

"Chey, I need you to send Reaper to the house, please, hurry," I whispered.

She got quiet and serious fast. "What's wrong?"

"Ink came home pissed and I'm scared. I'm locked in the downstairs bathroom. He wants me to come out, but I can't," I sobbed.

"Oh my God, he's what? Okay, hold on. I'll get Reaper. He'll be right there, honey. Stay on the phone with me." I could hear her rustling. As I waited, I could hear her talking to someone, but it was muffled, like she had her hand over the speaker.

I jumped when Ink knocked on the door again. "Whirlwind, please, you're scaring me. Say something. Please."

"Please go away, Ink." I pleaded. I thought I could hear bikes in the distance getting closer. "Chey, are you still there?" I whispered.

"Yeah, I'm still here. Reaper and Mayhem are on their way. What's he saying?"

"He wants me to come out. He said I'm scaring him."

"Stay there. Don't come out until Reaper says it's okay."

The roar of bikes got closer then I heard them stop outside and the engines died. The thunder of boots was heard clearly in my hiding spot, then the shouting started.

"Reaper, Mayhem, what the hell is going on? Why're you busting in my house like there's a fire? Is there something wrong?" Ink barked at them.

"Yeah, there's something wrong! Your old lady called mine, scared to death and told her she locked herself in the bathroom. Alisse is scared of you, Ink. She said you were pissed," Reaper growled.

There was a moment of silence then Ink swore. "Fuck! She did what? Goddammit, Reap, you know me. I'd never touch a hair on her head. Yeah, I'm pissed but I wouldn't hurt her. Alisse, baby, open the door. Come out here so we can talk. I'm not going to lay a hand on you," he pleaded with me. I fought not to give in to what sounded like pain in his voice. What if I did and then after Reaper and Mayhem left, he went off again?

"Ink, why don't you and I go outside and let Reaper talk to her?" Mayhem suggested calmly.

"I don't want him to talk to her. I need to talk to her. I need to fix this. I swear to God, I never meant to scare you, baby. I'm pissed, but only at Alex. Sure, I was upset you didn't tell me he was bugging you and I want to know why you didn't, but I'm not going to hurt you."

"Ink, man, go with Mayhem. Let me handle this," I heard Reaper say in a firm tone. It was his president's voice, not his friendly voice.

There was silence again then I heard Ink mutter, "I'll go, but don't take forever. I need to talk to her." The thump of boots faded away.

"Alisse, honey, it's alright. You can come out now.

He's outside."

"I'm going out to Reaper," I told Cheyenne. I didn't give her time to reply before disconnecting the call. I stood up on shaky legs and stumbled to the door. It took more than one attempt to get the door unlocked. When I swung it open, Reaper was there to pull me into his arms. I went to him and started to cry. His rubbed his hands up and down my back.

"Shh, you're alright. Calm down. Tell me what the hell happened. I know Ink can be scary when he gets pissed, but surely you don't think he'll hit you, do you?"

I couldn't answer him. I didn't know what to think. Flashes of my past kept flickering through my mind— the echo of fists meeting flesh and cries of pain. My heart racing in fear, afraid if he found me, I'd be next. My legs gave out. Reaper swept me up in his arms and carried me. I have no idea where. All I knew was I couldn't stop bawling and shaking. I heard raised voices, but I couldn't understand what was being said. It was like I was under water. Finally, in order to get some peace, my brain shut down and everything faded away to nothing.

Ink:

I paced outside on my front lawn. I couldn't believe that Alisse locked herself in the bathroom and called for help. How could she think I'd ever lay a hand on her? I looked at Mayhem. He was watching the door with a frown on his face. He stood between me and it.

"Jesus Christ, what the fuck happened? Sure, I'm pissed, but why the hell would she ever think I'd lay a hand on her? She knows this club doesn't believe in that shit. I don't understand."

"Ink, I don't know. You look scary when you get mad. Maybe she's never seen anyone like that. Maybe she's had a bad experience. Or maybe you and her don't know each other well enough yet for her to know your behaviors and how to handle them."

I was fighting to calm myself down, so I could talk to her when Reaper got her to come outside. I thought I had it under control, until my front door opened and Reaper came out, carrying a limp Alisse in his arms. I shoved past Mayhem and ran up to him. I looked down at her to find her eyes were closed and she looked deathly pale. I tried to take her out of his arms.

"Give her to me! What the hell happened?" I yelled. He held onto her, much to my displeasure.

"Ink, let me carry her. If she wakes up and sees you doing it, she'll probably freak the fuck out again. Let's get her to my house and see what the hell is going on. I think it's better if we're not in your house when she wakes up."

It took all my willpower not to argue and tear her away from him anyway. I stayed on his heels all the way to his house. Mayhem was ahead of us. He opened the door. As we walked in, Chey came out of the kitchen and gasped then ran up to us.

"Oh my God, what did he do?" she cried out. She shot daggers at me with her eyes.

"Do? I didn't do shit! Reaper came out carrying her. She was like this. I'd like to know what the hell happened."

Reaper took her into the guest bedroom and laid her down on the bed. He looked over at me. His face was hard and worried. "I don't know. She came out crying. I tried to tell her that you'd never hurt her. All of a sudden, she collapsed. I held onto her so she wouldn't hit the floor and brought her outside. Fuck, tell me exactly what happened. What did you say and what did she say? Babe, go get a cool washcloth, will you?"

Cheyenne reluctantly left to do as he asked. I didn't wait. I launched into a recount of the entire encounter with Alex at the shop and then what happened once I got home and brought it up to Alisse. Chey joined us and listened as she laid the cool cloth on Alisse's forehead. The whole time I spoke, I held onto Alisse's hand and rubbed it. When I got done, I glanced around at the three of them. They had puzzled looks on their faces. It was Cheyenne I addressed.

"Chey, you're her best friend. What the hell was this? I was loud and I was angry, but I would never hurt her."

She shook her head. "I don't know why she reacted like this. She's usually a little defender, you know that."

"Do you think we should call a doctor or maybe Lash? I'm worried about her being unconscious," I asked, as I rubbed her arms. She was showing no signs of waking up.

Mayhem had his cell phone out and was texting. "I'm getting Lash's ass over here. This is bullshit. Something is wrong. Alisse isn't afraid of anything I've ever seen," he grumbled, as he sent it.

I leaned down to whisper close to her ear. "Baby, it's Austin, please wake up and talk to us. You're scaring the shit out of us. I can't deal with you scaring me like this. I need to know what I did wrong so I can fix it. I'm sorry. I love you." As I poured out my heart, she gave a tiny moan then her eyelids fluttered, like she was going to open her eyes.

"That's it. Open those beautiful eyes, Whirlwind. Come on, you can do it," I encouraged her, as I gave her hand a squeeze.

Slowly her eyes opened. They were clouded with confusion as she looked around at the four of us staring intently down at her. She tried to sit up, but I held her down. I didn't want her to risk fainting again.

"Why are you all staring at me? What happened?" She looked at the room. "Why am I in your house, Cheyenne?"

"Do you remember calling me or Reaper coming to the house? How about Ink coming home?" Chey asked her quickly.

It took several seconds for the confusion to clear and then she stiffened. Her eyes darted to me. I saw fear creep back into them. I immediately tried to put a stop to that.

"Baby, don't look at me like that. I would never, never hurt you. Shit, do you think if I did, my brothers would let me live? I'm so damn sorry that I scared you. I was pissed at Alex and upset that you didn't tell me he's been hounding you with calls and texts. I shouldn't have gotten so mad in front of you. Now that I know it causes you to react like this, I'll never do it again."

"Alisse, tell us why you got so scared. I know it has to be more than just how Ink acted. You looked like you'd seen a fucking ghost when you came out of the bathroom before you fainted," Reaper told her sternly.

She didn't answer immediately. I saw her swallow. Finally, she looked at me. "Can I sit up please and have a glass of water? I'm thirsty."

I eased back but instead of letting her sit up on her own, I gently lifted her into a sitting position. Cheyenne went to get her a drink. There was a brief knock at the front door, then Lash came striding in. He had his medic bag with him. He came straight over to her. I moved out of the way, so he could sit down beside her.

"Hey, sweetness, I hear you fainted. Let me check you out and see what's wrong. Stare at this light." He held up a lit penlight and shined it in her eyes. She did as he asked, but she spoke to him as she did it.

"I'm fine, Lash. There's no need for you to come over here and do this."

"Oh yes, there is. When I hear one of my sisters fainted and I know my brother is probably losing his mind because his old lady did that, I'm going to come make sure you're alright. Did you get dizzy? Feel faint before you passed out? When was the last time you ate? If I didn't know the two of you just got together less than a week ago, I'd ask you if you could be pregnant."

She gasped. "No, I'm not! And it's not my blood sugar. I had a snack two hours ago." She took the glass that Chey brought back and gulped down the water.

"Hey, take it slow, We don't want you to choke or throw that up. Okay, so no dizziness. Tell me what was happening before she fainted."

I quickly gave him the bare facts. His brow pinched together in consternation when he heard what had happened.

"Shit, I can't believe it. Ink can be a hothead, that's for sure, Alisse, but he's not a woman beater. Tell us what was going through your mind when this was happening."

She got paler when he said that. I inched closer to her and reached around him to take her hand again. She tried to pull away, but I wouldn't allow her.

"Tell us, baby. I can tell by that look on your face, you had thoughts. What were they?"

She glanced down at her lap. Not making eye contact, she explained to us what her uncle used to do. Instantly, rage ripped through me. Son of a bitch, she had a goddamn flashback. She had trauma and I had no idea about it. Lash finished checking her heart and listening to her lungs as well as checking her pulse. He moved out of my way. He gave me a nod, letting me know she was alright.

I picked up her hand and brought it to my mouth. I kissed each of her soft knuckles. She watched me. "I'm so damn sorry that you saw that growing up, baby, and that my anger made you think of that bastard. A real man doesn't hit his family. I might get pissed but if I want to hit something to relieve the anger, I'll go to the gym and punch a punching bag or worst-case scenario, I have punched a wall before. I only punch people when they do something to deserve it, like hurt someone else. You will never do anything to deserve my fists."

She startled me when she lunged toward me and threw her arms around me. "I'm sorry," she cried, before her mouth landed on mine. I took control of the kiss as soon as she let me. I kissed her deeply and for a long time. I told her how I was feeling through that kiss. When we were done, both of us were a little dazed and the others were smirking at us.

"I think she's fine. If you're feeling okay, Alisse, why don't you and Ink go home and you can talk calmly about what had him so pissed off? If she needs anything, just call me," Lash said, as he packed up his stuff.

"Babe, will you come with me?" I asked her. She nodded. I didn't let her get to her feet, even though she tried. Instead, I picked her up in my arms to carry her like Reaper had. She kept apologizing to the others as we strolled out the door. They told her repeatedly, she had nothing to be sorry about. It didn't take me long to reach our house. I took her straight to our room and laid her down on the bed. I curled up with her and held her tightly to me.

"Tell me about the calls and texts. I promise not to get pissed."

"It's silly really. I knew you disliked him after that night we went to dinner. Hell, I didn't like him much either after he said that stuff about Cheyenne and the club. So when he kept sending me the texts and leaving messages, I ignored them, hoping he'd take the hint and stop."

"What did these messages say?"

She reached into her bra and pulled out her phone. I couldn't help but smile. It killed me every time I saw her do that. She handed me the phone. It was open to her text messages. I quickly scanned them. Most of them were just repeats of essentially the same thing.

Alex: Alisse, I'm sorry the other night ended on the note it did. I need to talk to you about making it up to you.

Alex: I need you to call me. We need to talk.

Alex: Why won't you answer me? I know that we would be perfect together. You don't need someone like him.

Alex: You'll get hurt hanging around a man like that. You're better than that.

They went on and on. I could see that he sent several a day almost every day since that night. Fury bubbled up inside of me, but I fought hard not to let it show. I couldn't afford to let her see it.

"I knew you'd be upset, so I didn't tell you. I wasn't really hiding it. I was avoiding you possibly hunting him down and beating his ass," she confessed.

"If I did, he deserves it, Alisse. He's hounding you. This behavior is harassment. After what he pulled today at my shop and then these, if he calls or texts more, or comes back to the shop to waste my time, I will be paying him a visit and he's not going to like it."

She grabbed my hand. "You can't! He's not worth going to jail for, Austin. He's the kind of asshole who would have you arrested."

At least she was back to calling me by my name. Earlier when she called me Ink, I wanted to protest.

"Babe, if I beat his ass, he'll be too scared to call the cops. Promise me. Promise me that if he calls or texts, you'll tell me right away. And I'll promise, if I have to pay him a visit, I won't go to jail."

I stared intently at her. Finally, she sighed then nodded her head. "Okay, I promise, but if you do go see him, you have to tell me too. This is a two-way street."

"I promise. The other thing is, I need you to promise if I start scaring you again, you will immediately tell me. It is never my intent to make you afraid of me, Alisse. I love you and I will never hurt you. The shit you saw growing up only makes me hate your family more. I never liked Amber's dad when we dated. He came across as an asshole. She never hinted that he was abusive." Hearing him say he loved me, didn't seem possible.

"Probably because she was daddy's little girl. She could do no wrong and he never took his temper out on her. It was mainly my aunt. Sometimes, he'd go after one of my other male family members if they tried to intercede. I don't recall seeing him hit any of the other women, although he did scream at them."

"Did your mom ever say why she kept visiting? Did she miss them that much?"

"I think she was trying to regain the closeness they had growing up. Only they were too bigoted to accept her and me because of my dad. He stopped going when I was little. He refused to put up with them. He tried to tell Mom not to take me, but he knew if he forbade it, she'd be miserable, so he didn't. She knew if I told him about my uncle, he'd put a stop to our visits. I don't want to make it sound like they were all hateful all the time. Sometimes they were fun and I had a good time. I got to play with my cousins and spend time with my extended family."

I inched closer and smiled at her, as I leaned closer. "And you got to meet the man you're going to spend the rest of your life with. Don't forget that. A man who is crazy for you and would love to lay you out on this bed right now and show you how much he loves you. Let me help erase all that nastiness from before, baby. Let me make love to you," I whispered, before capturing her mouth. Her moan was enough of an answer for me.

Ink: Chapter 8

After the scare last night with Alisse, then the make-up sex, I wasn't going to mention her coming to the shop with me to meet the crew. However, it came up this morning as we were making breakfast. I told her that when she was ready, they wanted to meet her. She got excited.

"I'd love to meet your employees, Austin. What about today? Is it a good day for me to go with you? If you have a lot of tats to do, I can entertain myself. I have my book reader and I can read or something. I've been wanting to see what the shop is like."

"Whoa, you don't have to go today. Baby, you had a hard night. Don't you want to rest?"

She had shaken her head no. After talking a few more minutes, she had me agreeing. That's how an hour and a half later, I was pulling into the parking lot at Punisher's Mark with her wrapped around me on the back of my bike. The weather was decent today and she wanted to ride with me. She knew I hated to ride in cages unless it was absolutely necessary.

She patted her hair down after she took off her helmet and looked in the side mirror on my bike. I saw her grimace.

"Babe, you look beautiful."

"I want your friends to like me and not think you're with a crypt keeper."

I laughed. "Alisse, it would take you having a total transformation to even start to look like the crypt keeper. You're gorgeous. Now, stop it and let's go inside."

She hung back as I held her hand and entered the shop. Greta was at the desk. Her head came up and she smiled, ready to greet me like usual, when she spotted Alisse. She jumped to her feet and came rushing out around the counter. She flew toward us and pushed by me to take Alisse in her arms.

"Oh my God, he brought you! Why didn't you tell us she was coming today?" she chided me. "We'd have spruced the place up. I'm so glad to meet you, Alisse. I'm Greta. I run the counter for Ink. I'm the receptionist slash cashier."

Greta's excited voice brought the others out to see what was going on. Soon, Alisse was mobbed with hugs and greetings. I stood back smiling as she stood there looking stunned. I saw Elliott give my woman an appreciative once-over. I elbowed him.

"Keep your eyes off her and put your tongue back in your mouth. She's taken and I'll kill any man who tries to take her from me."

"Hey, man, you can't blame me. She's gorgeous with a capital G. I don't know how you lucked out. I know she's yours and I have no doubt you'd gut me if I ever went after her. However, you can't expect me not to at least enjoy the scenery. That's impossible, you lucky bastard."

I couldn't help but grin at his observation. He was right. She was eye catching and impossible not to stare at. I caught myself doing it all the time, especially when she was lying next to me in bed asleep.

"As long as all you do is look, then I might let you live."

"I can see why that shithead who was in here yesterday wanted to run you off." Chuck came over to tell me. His gruff exterior was almost cracking a smile as he watched Tammy, Sunshine, Greta, and Alisse chatting. Our first client wasn't due for another hour.

"Yeah, he wants her bad. We talked about it and if he keeps up the calls and shit, I'll be paying his ass a visit."

"If you do, I'd love to be there. The nerve of him is unbelievable," Chuck grumbled.

In no time, Alisse was dragged to the back employee break room and served coffee. It wasn't that cheap shit either. We liked the good stuff that had lots of caffeine. The one we drank was touted as the strongest coffee in the world. All I knew was that it tasted like coffee, not like a watered-down essence of coffee. I got both of us a cup and sat down with them, as the others got their drinks. Elliott didn't drink coffee. He drank those disgusting energy drinks that made my stomach curdle. Chuck's addiction was Mountain Dew. Greta had to monitor him, to make sure he didn't drink more than two a day. If she had her way, he wouldn't drink any.

"Alisse, tell us about yourself. Ink has been very cagey. All he's told us is your name, that you're best friends with Cheyenne and you work with her. Oh, and that you're his," Tammy stated.

"Well, there's not a lot to tell. I work with Chey at Dr. Simpson's office. I'm a medical assistant like her. I should've gone back to school to be a nurse, but I thought I'd work a year as a MA then go back. That was six years ago. I'm originally from Blacksburg, Virginia. My mom's family was from around here. I moved back here five years ago. That's really all. Oh, and I'm twenty-seven."

"Baby, you never told me you wanted to be a nurse. You should do it."

"Ink, it's too late for me to do that. I can't afford to work full time and go to school. At a minimum, it would take me another two years to get my associate's degree in nursing. I like what I do. I still get to work with patients."

She said that, but I could see the longing in her eyes. She wanted to be a nurse. I made a vow to her right then and there. No matter what it took, she would pursue her dream. Hell, she didn't need to work, not now that she was living with me.

"Well, then it's a good thing you're going to live with me at the compound. You don't need to worry about working full time and that will leave you time to take those classes."

Her mouth fell open in shock. I smiled back at her.

She wouldn't argue about it in front of others. I knew she'd wait until we were alone. "Ink, we'll talk about this later," she dismissed me.

They asked her more questions before she found out what each of them did at the shop. It wasn't until the first customer came in that we were able to break away. I took her on a tour of the shop then into my room. I shut the door. She looked around with interest. Finally, she came over to me.

"I need to ask you something. I'm not sure if I want to know the answer or not."

"Go ahead, ask."

"Have you and Sunshine ever...you know... been together? Is she the one who gave you your ladder?"

Her questions surprised me. Maybe not the ladder one, but the first one did.

"No, she didn't do my piercing. I had that long before she came to work here. Why in the world would you think we hooked up? I don't mess with our employees. That shit almost never works out and you end up losing a good employee when it's all over. No, I've never slept with Sunshine or Tammy."

"I didn't mean to upset you. I just got this vibe off her, like she wasn't as thrilled to meet me as the others. I saw her looking at you when you weren't paying attention. I think she likes you and that got me wondering if the two of you ever did it."

I tugged her into my arms and held her close. I kissed her softly. When I raised my head, I responded to her observations. "I won't lie. She did at first want to hook up, but I told her that wasn't happening. She backed off after I did that. She's been here three years. I've never caught her looking at me funny. I think you're imagining it. She's dating someone the last I heard. She has no reason not to like you, baby."

"So you've never slept with anyone here. What about the other businesses the club owns? Those wouldn't be your direct employees. Christ, I can't believe I'm asking you this! Never mind, it's none of my business. I'm sorry. Can we talk about something else? When is your first customer due?" Her discomfort with the conversation was evident.

"Look at me," I ordered her. I waited until she did it then I kept talking. "That rule goes for all our businesses. The women I've been with were either club whores or women from town. I'm not proud of it, but sometimes I picked them up in a bar. What I didn't do, is ever take any of them to my house. You're the only woman that's been in that bed and my house like that and you're the only one who will ever be there. You're my old lady. That's forever."

She passionately kissed me. When she was done, I was hard and looking around to see if I could get away with fucking her right here. A glance at the clock told me I had thirty minutes until my first appointment. I could hear the others talking. We'd have to be quiet. I nibbled on her earlobe, making her shudder.

"Do you think you can be quiet enough that I can take you here and now without the others knowing it? I wouldn't want to scare off our customers," I teased her.

She looked startled then a look of desire came over her face. Her breathing increased. I could see that her nipples were hard even through her bra and top. I lowered my head to bite down on one of those pert nipples through the fabric. She moaned softly.

I undid the buttons and zipper on her jeans, so I could slip my hand down the front of her pants and inside her panties, where I found her pussy soaking wet. It was my turn to moan. I rubbed back and forth, getting my fingers coated in her juices, before I took them out and sucked them clean one at a time. I savored her taste.

"Oh God, Austin, you're making me crazy. I'm so hot for you," she moaned in my ear. I walked to the door, locked it, then came back to her. She was sitting on the tattoo chair.

"Strip and lay across that chair. This is going to be faster than I like, but I'm not going to be able to make it through the day without this," I growled. I watched as she stripped off her clothes then laid her sexy naked body across the chair just like I asked. Her round ass was high in the air and I could see her pussy peeking out between her legs. I took my boot and gently kicked her legs open wider, until her pussy lips parted and I could see her clit and all that wonderful, glistening cream spilling from her pussy.

I dropped to my knees and dove in. I ate her pussy from behind, making sure to give her clit lots of attention. She buried her face in her hand, to hold in her moans and cries. I sucked on her pussy then would flick my tongue up and down the entire length of her slit. When I made it to her entrance, I thrust my tongue inside her and fluttered it around. Her hips jerked. Knowing she was close already, I slipped two fingers into her tight pussy and I finger fucked her.

I licked up to her asshole, where I rimmed her puckered entrance. Her whole body spasmed. When I went back to sucking on her clit, I nuzzled her back door with my nose. I made sure to rub my goatee all over her pussy. She loved it when I did that. It made her shiver and gasp. I used my hands to keep her from closing her thighs around my head.

In a matter of minutes, she stiffened, bit down on her hand and came. I licked and thrust the whole time she came, wanting to make it last as long as possible for her. When she finally relaxed and went limp, I stood up and quickly tore open my jeans. I didn't get naked. I just shoved them and my underwear down to my knees, freeing my cock.

I pumped up and down the length a couple of times. Precum was oozing from my slit and covered the head of my engorged cock. It was dark red and the veins were standing out. Gripping her hips in both hands, I jerked her ass back up in the air and thrust into her pussy in one long, continuous thrust. She moaned as I slid through that tight glove until I had every inch of my cock buried in her pussy. I was kissing her cervix. Pumping in and out of her, I started slow then I planned to speed up. Leaning over to whisper in her ear, I told her what I wanted.

"One of these days, I'm going to fill you so full of my cum, that you'll have no choice but to have my baby. I'll plant my fucking seed deep. I can't wait to see you all swollen with my child. Your tummy all round, this ass even more lush and those breasts heavy with milk to feed our child. Fuck, that's going to be sexy as hell."

She trembled as she looked over her shoulder into my eyes. I saw surprise and want there. "You really think a pregnant woman will be sexy?"

"My pregnant woman will be. You all ripe will be fucking hot." I closed my eyes as I imagined that. Some might think it was gross, but the image of Alisse like that made me hornier. I sped up, thrusting faster and deeper into her.

I made sure my piercings scraped over that spot in her pussy that I knew would drive her wild. She was gritting her teeth, trying not to scream or make other noises. I kept sharing my fantasy. It was one of hundreds I had about her.

"I want to see you like that more than once, Alisse. How many babies do you want?"

Her breath hitched, then she quietly moaned, "I don't know. I always thought I'd like two or three. What about you?"

"Three sounds good. When do you think we can start on the first one? I don't want to let Reaper and Cheyenne get too far ahead of us. I'd like it if our kids grew up together as best friends." I slammed into her hard. She gave me a wide-eyed look.

"H-H-how soon? I don't know. We're just getting started, honey. Don't you think we should wait?"

"No, I don't. I want one now. I've been praying your fucking birth control doesn't work and that I already knocked you up. You're going to marry me and have my babies soon," I growled, making it sound like an order.

I waited for her to tell me to go to hell. I knew I sounded like a controlling asshole and I expected her to put me in my place. Instead, she shuddered, jerked and then her pussy tightened down on my cock like a vise and she came. Her whole body spasmed as she buried her face in her arm to stop from crying out. That pushed me to thrust only a couple more times then empty my load inside her. As the cum squirted out of me, I prayed that it would find her egg. God help me, she would kill me if I got her pregnant now, but I didn't care. I had been telling the truth.

Reaper had told me how he fell instantly for Cheyenne and knew out of the gate he wanted her to have his baby as soon as possible. Some guys would have told him he was nuts. I didn't because I thought the same thing when I saw Alisse. Only in my case, it took me four months to get her in my bed. I had lost time to make up for. Cheyenne was already ahead of us.

I kept gliding in and out of her even after I stopped coming. I wasn't ready to disconnect. If I could live inside her, I would. Eventually, I knew I had to stop and clean us up. Regretfully, I pulled out and watched as my cum slid out of her. I couldn't help but push it back inside of her. Luckily, in my room, I had a sink. I grabbed wet paper towels and cleaned her up. Once she was clean, I wiped off my cock, washed my face and goatee then tugged up my pants. I waited to fasten them, so

I could help her get redressed. When she was covered, I gave her a slow passionate kiss. Our tongues tangled together. Breaking away before we went too far and I lost my mind again, I buttoned and zipped my jeans.

She was staring at me.

"What's wrong, baby?"

"Were you serious about what you said or were you just playing with me?"

"You mean about having a baby?"

She nodded her head yes.

"No, I wasn't kidding. I'm dead serious. As soon as you give me the green light, no more birth control and we go for it. It might take a while to get there. I hear some people can take months to get pregnant. I don't want there to be a huge gap between our kids and Reaper's kids, if we can help it. They'll be each other's best friends and will look out for each other."

"Austin, I don't know what to say. I mean, I think we need to settle in a little before we jump into having kids. What if we don't work out? What if you decide being a one-woman man isn't for you?"

"Is that what you're worried about, me deciding you're not the one for me? If it is, you can forget that shit. I know you're the one."

"Most people date, move in together, get engaged, married, then have kids. You just want to jump to living together then bam to the kids' part."

"No, I want to date at the same time we live together

and the baby, the engagement and marriage are coming. I just need to decide when to spring that on you. I don't want to scare you off," I told her, with a wink.

Her mouth hung open. I gently pushed her jaw up to close it.

"I hate to disrupt this discussion, but it'll have to wait until later. I need to get ready for my client. What are you going to do while I work? Do you want to watch me give him a tat?"

"Won't he mind that?"

"Nah, he's a regular for me. He'd love to have a beautiful woman watch him get inked."

That's how the rest of the day went. All my clients were more than happy to let her watch and ask questions. She talked and joked with them. When we weren't with them, she talked with Tammy, Chuck, Greta, Elliott, and Sunshine, although I noticed she talked the least to Sunshine. Time actually flew by. Before I knew it, it was the end of the day and we were saying goodbye to the crew. They all begged her to come back soon. I was a very content guy who rode home that evening with his woman plastered to his back.

Back at the house, we worked on throwing a simple dinner together. It was grilled chicken breasts, a salad filled with all kinds of vegetables and as the side, she whipped up some cheesy, garlic potatoes that were to die for. I ate more than I should've, but it was too good to pass up.

After dinner, we took a walk around the compound.

I pointed out the areas we were planning to put the playground and build up the barbeque area. Also, I showed her where we wanted to put a swimming pool. She was excited about it all. We were going to be like Dublin Falls and Hunters Creek soon.

They resembled small housing communities more than they did an MC compound. If it wasn't for the walls, the gate, and the razor wire at the top of the walls, no one would ever guess it wasn't one. They were serious about protecting their families. Just like I knew we were. Reaper and I were leading the way. I had no doubts more of my brothers would find their women and hopefully soon.

Alisse:

After spending all day at Punisher's Mark, you'd think I'd be exhausted and ready to go to bed. I wasn't. I couldn't forget what Ink said to me at the shop when he was making love to me. His talk about wanting to have kids and that an engagement and marriage was coming, I didn't know what to think of that. I knew that Reaper and Chey had moved at warp speed when they met. They met, she got claimed, engaged, pregnant, and married in less than three months.

Ink and I had only slept together for the first time a week ago. I was practically living with him and he claimed me as his woman, his old lady. I might not have a property cut like Cheyenne to go with it, but something told me, I would. I tried to ignore the tiny nagging thought in the back of my mind that taunted me with doubts.

It liked to tell me that Ink would grow tired of me and kick me out of his bed and life. That he'd realize I wasn't who he wanted to spend the rest of his life with. It whispered that he claimed me in name only as his old lady, because he didn't intend to give me a property cut or ask me to marry him. It was stupid, I know, but it wouldn't go away.

After we watched some television, he took me to

take a shower then he made love to me until I was weak. Now, I was lying next to him with my head on his chest, trying to sleep and not think.

"Baby, I can hear you thinking. What's wrong?"

I didn't want to tell him about my doubts, so I brought up our earlier talk.

"I was thinking about what you said today at the shop when we were together. You mentioned all those fantasies of yours about having a baby. Were you serious? What else do you fantasize about?"

He rolled me onto my back, so I had no choice but to look up at him. His face was serious as he answered me.

"Whirlwind, you are the love of my life. I know that without a doubt. I am dead serious about wanting to have a baby with you as soon as you tell me yes. It's my dream. Just like I dream about slipping my ring on your finger and standing up in front of our friends and becoming man and wife. I don't want to scare you, but I have lots of other fantasies too."

"Really? You think all that's going to happen soon?"

"I plan on it, yeah. Tell me about your dreams. You said you wanted to be a nurse, but it's too late. It's not. You don't need to work full time. I want you to stay here with me in this house. We can let your apartment go. You go see the counselors to see what you need to do to get started on your RN classes."

"If I did all that, then the baby would have to wait, Austin. I can't work part-time, be up all night with a baby and go to school. I'm a multitasker, but I'm not that good."

"You won't be doing it all. If you get pregnant, then don't work at all. Concentrate on school. I'll be here to help you with the baby. I know breastfeeding is said to be the best, but if we bottle feed the baby, then I can get up at night or whenever to feed the baby so you can sleep. Same goes for when you need to go to classes or study. If I have to work, we'll bring in someone we trust to watch the baby for us. It's doable."

I sat up and stared at him. "You've really thought about this, haven't you?"

"I have. I've been waiting to talk to you about it since earlier. I want you to pursue all your dreams, baby. I won't hold you back. I only want you to let me be there with you as you go after them. Let me help you to soar. I'm living my dream. I have a great club of brothers, a job I love, and a woman who completes me. All I need now is that family and you with my last name. I think Alisse Kavanagh has a great ring to it."

As crazy as it might sound, everything he was saying was making my heart leap for joy. I wanted all that too. I launched myself onto him, pushing him on his back. He went easily and folded his hands behind his head. He smiled up at me. I straddled him and ran my hands up and down his muscular chest and arms. I loved the feel of the hair on his chest rubbing against the palms of my hands, or across my nipples.

"Well, who could say no to that? I think you've almost got me convinced."

"What will it take to convince you all the way?" he

asked with a growl, as I licked his nipple then I bit down on it. He hissed, but it was a hiss of pain mixed with pleasure.

"Why don't you show me one of those other fantasies you have running around in your head?"

"You mean one of the ones where I do such naughty things to you that you get more pleasure than you've ever had in your life and you beg me not to stop, then beg me to stop, only I won't until I've wrung every drop of your cream, screams and pleasure out of you? One of those? Okay, I can do that."

I shrieked in surprise when he flipped me off him and onto my back and he straddled me. By the time I fell asleep hours later, I could barely move and my whole body felt like it was one big, boneless noodle. I had his marks of possession all over my body. His cum filled every hole and my pussy and ass were sore. Yeah, he sure had some great fantasies. I only prayed I could survive them all if they were all like this.

Ink: Chapter 9

Today was the day. The day I'd get my property cut on her as well as my ring. It would be the happy note we needed after the craziness of the past week and some change. Last week, Reaper and Cheyenne went to visit the Dark Patriots to go over what was needed to take down the rest of the Soldiers of Corruption in the clubs they'd infiltrated over the past few years.

Besides getting their help with this job, Reaper had been broadsided with unexpected news. His old Navy SEAL buddy and deceased Dark Patriot co-founder, Mark, wasn't dead. He'd been undercover for five years in one of the biggest outlaw MCs in the country. He'd been declared dead and he'd stayed that way, so he could bring them down from the inside. However, it was also discovered that Sean, Gabe, and Griffin had known he was alive after the first year and they kept it hidden from everyone else, including Mark's sister, Cassidy. To say that she was pissed would be an understatement.

Thankfully, despite the hell of these past five years and his battle to make it up to his sister and friends, Mark had volunteered to be the one to help us, by going into the Legion of Renegades MC and working to bring the Soldiers in it down. The others tried to talk him out of it, but his reputation as Undertaker, enforcer for the Tres Locos, had been too perfect not to use.

Undertaker had promised Reaper he'd make sure to take out that club and help with any of the others, in order to ensure that Cheyenne and other innocents were safe from the Soldiers and their evil ways. They'd left there to come home and fill us in on what the plan was. Hopefully, the main leaders of the Soldiers, Slither and Ogre, would be eliminated soon. If we could cut off the head, maybe the rest of the snake would die.

With all this going on and the fact Reaper knew I was anxious to fully claim Alisse, he suggested the club go out tonight to party and celebrate. Everyone had been more than happy to say yes. Even though we could and usually had parties at the clubhouse on Friday and Saturday nights, it was still fun to go out sometimes. Our bar of choice was The Deuce. It wasn't owned by us, although we were hoping to buy it one day from its owner, Darren. He'd promised us that when he was ready to retire, we'd get first dibs on buying it. Until then, we'd be happy to spend time there whenever the mood struck. It had great bands on the weekends and was a very popular place.

However, before we went out, there was one thing I had to do. I had to get my name on Alisse, so that everyone would know she was mine. That meant we all had to meet in the common room before heading out to the bar. We planned to go early, so we could get seats, otherwise, we might end up standing. That wouldn't be fun.

When Alisse came out of our bedroom, my breath got caught in my chest. She was stunning. Not to say she wasn't beautiful on any other day, she was, but tonight, she looked even better. I don't know if it was the glow on her face or the subtle makeup she'd applied, or the sexy top with those skintight jeans, but whatever it was, it was amazing.

I couldn't help but pull her into my arms and lay a hard kiss on her. She responded immediately, which led to us both panting when the kiss ended. "Why don't we say to hell with tonight, and we'll stay home?" I said hoarsely.

"No, Austin, we can't do that. Everyone is expecting us to go. I want to go and get out of the house and the compound. I love you, but I need to have some social interaction other than with you and the guys."

I knew she was right. She and Cheyenne had been more than patient with the restrictions we put upon them when it came to not leaving the compound. On the two days they did leave, it was straight to work then straight home. They didn't get to stop anywhere or do anything else. It got old really fast.

I pretended to pout. She smiled. "Fine, if you insist, but you owe me," I grumbled, as I let her step away from me.

She patted me on the ass and winked. "I bet I can think of a way to make it up to you when we get home."

"Oh, I can think of a few ways you can do that. I hope you're ready for it," I said, as I raked her from head to toe with my eyes. I let the passion and hunger I was feeling show on my face. She shivered and I saw her nipples pebble underneath her top. Unable to resist, I gave her one more kiss, while I teased my thumbs back and forth over her nipples. She moaned and rubbed her thighs together.

Finally, I broke the kiss and moved away. "Time to go. Come on, baby, the others are waiting for us at the clubhouse." I took her hand and led her to the door. We stopped long enough for her to grab her jacket and her purse then we were out the door.

Since it was going to be nighttime and it was cold out, I had arranged for her to ride in the car with Cheyenne. Dante was driving it. The rest of us were going to ride our bikes. We were mostly impervious to the cold and rode our bikes in every kind of weather. Hell, I'd even been out in the snow on mine. Riding in the rain sucked, but I'd done it more than a few times.

I rode over to the clubhouse with her on the back. It was a short hop and skip to get there. As we walked inside, I was happy to see that everyone was here. We wove our way through them to the bar where Cheyenne was sitting with Reaper by her side. He gave me a chin lift when he saw me and nodded. I knew that meant he had what I wanted. The ladies hugged like they hadn't seen each other in ages, rather than a few hours ago.

Seeing we were all here, Reaper waved his hand to me. I climbed up on the bar, which startled the ladies. Alisse gave me a surprised look filled with questions. I gave an ear-splitting whistle to get my brothers' attention. They all turned to stare at me and the silence after the noise was deafening.

"Before we go out to have our night of fun, there's one thing I have to do first." I saw the looks of comprehension come over the guys' faces. Cheyenne was smiling. Alisse was still looking puzzled. I held out my hand to her. She took it and I pulled her toward me. Reaper helped to hoist her up on the bar with me. She grabbed my cut as she staggered into me. I held her tight, so she wouldn't fall.

"Alisse, you know that I've already laid claim to you as my old lady." She nodded her head. I continued, "However, in order for everyone to know that you belong to me and that I'll be the one defending you if they ever lay a hand on you, you need something visible to show them."

Her eyes widened. I saw the beginning of comprehension come across her face. I held out the hand not holding onto her and Reaper put a cool leather garment in it. I held it up so she and everyone else could see it. She snatched it out of my hand and spread it wide. On the back were the words *Property of Ink*, which I'd been dying to see on her. On the front, over the left pocket, was her club name, *Whirlwind*.

"Will you put it on me, Ink?" she asked softly.

"I'd love nothing more, Whirlwind."

She held out her arms, so I could slip it over her shoulders. She hugged it close and rubbed her hands down the soft leather. It fit perfectly and looked great on her. I tugged her into my arms and kissed her, as the room erupted in whistles and shouts of joy. Eventually, I let her go and jumped down from the bar. I lifted her down. Cheyenne gave her a hug as Reaper shook my hand. After several minutes of handshakes and congratulations, Reaper told us all to get our asses outside, so we could get on the road.

I walked her to the SUV and opened the door. I tucked her inside, making sure she put on her seatbelt while Reaper saw to Cheyenne. I gave her a quick peck on the mouth. "Babe, I'll be right behind you. See you in a few minutes."

"Okay, ride safe."

I closed her door then got on my bike. Starting it up, I pulled up to the back of the SUV. Those of us who were officers were riding in the front with Reaper, while the rest rode behind the SUV. Reaper circled his hand in the air and we took off. The ride to town was a quick one. We drove into the parking lot of The Deuce in no time. The lot was already half full and it was only seven thirty.

We found spots to park. When I did, I hurried to get over to the SUV, but Dante had beaten me to opening Alisse's door. She did stay in the car and allow me to be the one to help her out. Even though we were all here and celebrating, I didn't forget to keep my eyes open and to scan the surrounding area for signs of trouble.

There were a few other bikes in the parking lot. They weren't ones I recognized, so we'd have to see who they were when we got inside. Most of the time, it was solitary or civilian riders. At times, we did get riders from other MCs who stopped in town, but most of them knew to ask permission before stopping or riding through our territory. It was only common courtesy to do so. It had been a while since we had any of them or had trouble.

We flanked our women as we escorted them inside. The blast of warmer air was welcome after the bite of the wind outside. I scanned the interior, looking for those bikers and any threats while Reaper got the attention of one of the waitresses. Halfway through my scan, I saw them. From the looks of them, they were a bunch of civilian riders. None of them wore colors, but they were dressed in jeans, boots and a few had on plain leather cuts.

"I see them, brother, don't worry. I'll keep an eye on them," Mayhem whispered in my ear. I hadn't known he was near me.

"Good. I don't think they're a threat, but you can never be too safe."

One of the waitresses came over and gestured for us to follow her. As we passed the bar, Darren, the owner, threw up his hand at us. We gave him chin lifts and hand raises back. He had a look of relief on his face. He knew with us in here, there shouldn't be any shit happening tonight. We tended to protect businesses, even if they weren't our own, when we were out. We liked to keep the peace and if that didn't work, we liked to end the fight.

We helped to put three tables together to make one long one that all of us could sit at. I hung Alisse's jacket on the back of her chair after I slid it in for her. Once we were settled, our waitress, her name was Clary, asked what we wanted to drink. She was young, I'd say in her mid-twenties at the most. She was very pretty in that girl-next-door way. I saw more than one of my club brothers checking her out. She blushed a couple of times when they made flirty remarks to her. I was surprised that she didn't flirt back. After getting all our orders, she hurried over to the bartender.

"Don't you dare be flirting with her and trying to get in her pants, you guys. She's too innocent for you," Cheyenne told them with a glare.

"Too innocent for us? You mean she's innocent like you were when Reaper decided to claim your ass. Hell, you're still innocent in a lot of ways, Chey. What if she's the one for one of us?" Ratchet fired back at her.

"I wasn't that innocent when Reaper met me. I knew what MC life was," she protested.

Reaper nipped at her neck and said loud enough for all of us to hear, "You might have known some things about MC life, but you were innocent and you know it. You proved that the first time we slept together, baby."

We all laughed, even Alisse, as Chey elbowed Reaper in the gut. He laughed and rubbed his hand over her belly. You couldn't tell she was pregnant yet. The baby wasn't due for another six months. I noticed Reaper loved to rub his hand across her belly whenever he got the chance. I wondered if I might get the chance to do that to Alisse one day soon. I sure hoped so. I hadn't lied to her when I told her I wanted her to have my babies.

We sat and chatted until our drinks came. As the night progressed, we laughed and had even more fun. The place kept filling up with more bodies. I wasn't drunk nor was I not paying attention. We were all still on alert in case trouble found us, in whatever form that might be.

Right after nine o'clock, the band started to set up. Good, I knew the women were wanting to dance. Even if she was staying sober, Chey was bouncing in her seat to go out on the dance floor. Alisse was more subdued, but no less eager. I was surprised to see she wasn't drinking anything alcoholic. When I asked why, she said she wasn't in the mood for it. I left it alone. If she didn't want to drink, she didn't have to. I made sure that between every beer, I drank at least one full bottle of water.

My brothers had kept up the gentle teasing of Clary. She was good natured and smiled at them. She didn't get offended or flirt back. By the time the band started playing, the place was full. We had a clear view of the dance floor, so we could see the women when they took to the floor. We'd asked for these tables for that very reason.

I had to admit, Alisse and Cheyenne had rhythm. That was more than I could say for a lot of women up on the floor. Their hips and asses shook to the beat and Alisse's body was making my cock stand up and take notice. Here I was, in a roomful of people, most of them I didn't know, getting a hard-on for my woman. Damn, if it kept up, I might have to drag her off into the dark and do something to make it go away.

Even over the loudness of the band, the crash of something caught my attention. I swung around to see that the table of the civilian riders had made the noise. One of the guys had tipped over his chair while he was still in it. He was lying on his back, as his friends laughed at him. I couldn't hear what he said, but it was clear he was swearing at them. Finally, a couple of them helped him up and sat his chair up. It looked like they'd had more than their fair share to drink.

"Those guys had better stay off their bikes tonight. They'll be a menace on the road," Maniac stated to the table at large. All of us had turned to look at them when we heard the crash.

"Yeah, I hope they're smart enough to not ride home," Reaper added.

My brothers and I were drinking, but not enough to be dangerous or even legally drunk. When we got closer to going home, we'd switch to all non-alcoholic drinks. Dante wasn't drinking at all. As the driver for the women, he was to stay sober. No way we'd endanger them.

An hour later, I realized that I wasn't being as observant as I should have when I was approached from behind by someone. My first clue that someone was there was when a sultry voice said my name. Only it wasn't my road name. I whipped my head around and was momentarily left speechless. Standing there, looking at me expectantly, was Amber, Alisse's cousin, and my long-ago girlfriend. She was smiling like she thought I'd be happy to see her. When I didn't say anything, she spoke again.

"Austin, it's me, Amber. It's been a long time. How are you?"

"I know who you are. The name is Ink now, not

Austin. What're you doing here? I heard you moved to DC several years ago."

She moved closer and placed her hand on my shoulder. I shrugged it off. I didn't want her touching or talking to me.

"Why're you acting like this? It's been forever since I've seen you. I'm in town visiting family. I came for a night out and imagine my surprise when I saw you across the room. I had to come say hi. From the looks of you, you're now in a motorcycle gang, is that right? Wow, I never imagined that of you." She licked her lips as she hungrily raked her eyes up and down my body.

"It's a club not a gang and yes, I've been a part of the Iron Punishers since right after we broke up. No offense, but I have nothing to say to you. Why don't you rejoin your friends or whoever you came with and leave me alone?"

Her gasp of outrage only grew worse when Alisse chose that moment to come back from the dance floor to take a break. As she pressed past Amber to take her seat, she looked at her with interest. I saw the moment it registered with her that the woman standing beside my chair was her cousin. Shock quickly bled into a look of anger. She stopped to stare at Amber. Amber must have felt her eyes on her because she glanced up and froze. I wanted to laugh at the look of surprise on her face.

"Lissy, what are you doing here? And with these bikers? Does the family know you're hanging out with bikers now?" I could hear the snideness in her voice.

"Hello, Amber. I don't know or care what the family knows. As for me hanging with bikers, I guess technically I am. Although is it hanging when you're the old lady of one of them?" She turned so Amber could see the back of her property cut.

Amber gasped and whipped around to stare at me. "You said your name is Ink. Does that mean…"

"Yes, that means Alisse is my old lady. In biker terms, she's my wife. I took one look at her and fell head over heels in love with her. She'll be my legal wife soon, as well."

Alisse took her seat, making sure to press up against me. I wrapped my arm around her and hugged her tightly to my side. I placed a kiss on her mouth. I made sure it was a passionate one that would leave no doubts in Amber's mind that Alisse meant everything to me. By the time I broke off the kiss, Amber was gone.

"Where did the bitch go?" I asked Crusher. He was across from me.

He pointed. "She joined that group of drunk civilian riders over there. The ones that's been here all night. I saw her come in a little bit ago, but I had no idea she was Alisse's cousin. Fuck, glad I know now. I won't be going near her with a ten-foot pole. She's been flirting with that table and making eyes at men all over the damn place."

I glanced over to the table he was talking about. I saw she was there, hanging onto one of the guys. She was whispering in his ear, as she glared over at us. I gave her a smirk then turned my back on her.

"Baby, are you alright? I know it had to be a shock to see Amber after all this time."

"It was a shock, but I'm alright, Ink. I have no idea why she's here or brought up the family. Why would they care if I'm dating a biker or not?"

"Who knows? I think she was making a dig at you. But why are you shocked she's in town? Your family is here. Her parents still live here, right?"

"They do live here, but it's been years since she's come to Bristol to see them or the rest of the family. After she left, she stayed away. I know my aunt and uncle went to see her a few times, but she refused to come back here. We all thought it was because of you breaking her heart, but I know that's not true anymore. Maybe she was worried she'd run into you. What did she say before I came over?"

"She came up behind me and called me Austin. When I looked around and saw who it was, she said hi and asked how I was. I told her my name was Ink now and asked what she wanted. She acted like she had no idea why I was being cold toward her and said she was here visiting family and was out for the night. She was surprised to see me in an MC. That's all she said before you came over."

"I don't understand how she could have enough gall to come up and speak to you after what she did. Is she that self-centered that she didn't realize you'd want nothing to do with her after what happened? It was all I could do not to punch her in the face and tell her to stay the hell away from you. Cousin or no cousin, if she comes over here again, I'll deck her ass. It makes my blood boil to remember what she did to you."

I gave her a hard kiss before telling her, "You're turning me on talking like that. Keep it up and we'll be making a trip to the back."

She laughed and gave me a kiss.

"God, you two are as bad as those two. All this lovey-dovey shit is making me sick. I need another drink," Sandman playfully groused.

This made Cheyenne, who'd returned to the table with Alisse, and my woman tease him. When Clary came by to check on us, he put in an order for another beer. I got a soda for me and one for Alisse. While Clary was getting them, the women excused themselves to go to the bathroom. I waved my hand at Dante and Dillon. They both gave me a chin lift and followed the ladies. We weren't taking any chances. If they weren't here to do it, then I'd have gone with them or one of my brothers.

When they came back, they took time to drink some of their drinks then went back up on the dance floor. I was waiting for the band to play a slow song, so I could dance with Alisse. They played two slow songs back-to-back every hour or so.

It was Maniac who got my attention and directed my eyes to the dance floor, which I'd only looked away from for a minute. As I turned to look at what he was indicating, I stiffened, seeing that a man was up in Alisse's face. As I came to my feet and started across the floor, it registered it was one of the men from the table of civilian bikers. The man that Amber had been whispering to in his ear. What the fuck did she tell him?

Alisse was scowling at him when I came up to them. I had to strain to hear him over the band, but he was yelling loudly, so it wasn't terribly hard to hear him. He was wavering on his feet and his speech was slurred. He'd obviously had too much to drink.

"What kind of slut steals her cousin's man? You're a whore. Why don't you leave him alone? He doesn't love you. How could he after being with her? She's beautiful and you're just some mongrel half-breed."

I heard enough. I latched onto the collar of his shirt and I swung him around to face me. His t-shirt tore in my grip. I got in his face. "Listen to me, motherfucker. If you don't want to be eating my fist and losing all your teeth, then I suggest you sit your ass back down at your table and stay the fuck away from my woman. No one stole me. I broke up with that whore Amber years ago. Good riddance too. The best day of my life is the day I ran into Alisse again. There's only one woman I love and it's this woman. I'd better never hear you refer to her as a mongrel or half-breed again."

I shoved him away from me, as I tugged Alisse close to my chest. She hung onto my cut. I could feel the tremors running through her body. I couldn't tell if they were due to fear or anger. By the look on her face, I wanted to say anger.

He staggered and bumped into some other people on the dance floor. They shoved him away and gave him looks of disgust. His bloodshot eyes glared back at me. Instead of him going back to his table, he stumbled back toward me. I pushed Alisse behind me as well as Cheyenne, who I snagged gently by the arm. I felt several presences behind me. When I looked over my shoulder, I saw it was my brothers. I knew they'd keep the women safe.

When I glanced back, the man had gotten close enough to speak so I could hear him. He was still wavering on his feet. His face was flushed red. "Who the fuck do you think you are to touch me? I'll say whatever I want to that cunt. Amber told me all about her and how she took you away from her. You left her pregnant and without her family."

The pregnant word surprised me, but I didn't let it show. If she'd been pregnant, there was very little chance it was my baby. I hadn't slept with her for a month before we broke up and I would bet money, the guys I caught her with weren't the only ones she was sleeping with at the time. Thank God, I'd always worn a condom, even though she tried to get me not to, on more than one occasion.

"The only cunt or whore or slut around here is Amber. She's a cheating bitch. And if she was ever really pregnant, I can guarantee you, it wasn't mine. She spread her legs for a lot of men, even when she was with me. So, if you're fucking her now, I'd watch it and wear a condom. No telling what you might catch off her. No one stopped her from seeing her family. If she didn't, it was because she was too embarrassed to see them. Why don't you take her ass and go?"

Our confrontation had attracted a lot of attention. I didn't want to get into an actual physical fight in here, but if he started it, I'd finish it. Words were one thing, but fists were another. I caught sight of Darren. He anxiously watched us. His bouncers were standing near the dance floor. I gave him a headshake, signaling to him that their help wasn't needed.

Darren had seen us in action enough to know if there was trouble in here, we'd take care of it for him. It was one of the reasons he liked us to come in and drink. We didn't let things get out of hand. More than one drunk had been thrown out by one of us over the years.

The stupid drunk dumbass in front of me, didn't take my advice. I saw the punch coming a mile away before it got near my face. I easily moved my head to one side, making him miss me. The punch made him stagger and almost turn a quarter of the way around. I didn't waste time. I grabbed him and jammed his arm up behind him in a half-nelson hold. He yelled out in pain. Holding his arm in place, I started to march him toward the door. As we came closer to the table where he had been sitting with his friends, they all came to their feet. I saw Amber standing behind them. My brothers quickly went over to them.

"If you don't want to end up in the hospital, I suggest you take your buddy and leave. We don't want to fight, but we will if we have to. I can promise you, there's no way you can win against us," Mayhem told them calmly. There were six of them, seven, counting the guy in front of me, against thirteen of us. We'd fight them fair, one-on-one, and still win.

They must've been more sober or smarter than the guy I had a hold of because they didn't argue. As they got their coats, I saw Amber sneaking off out the front door. People parted to let us pass. At the door, one of the bouncers held it open for us.

"Thanks," I told him, as we passed him. The air outside was frigid. I walked my guy to the middle of the parking lot, where their bikes were parked. I looked around to see if I could see Amber, but she was nowhere in sight. I pushed him away from me as I let go of his arm. He stumbled then turned to look at me bleary-eyed.

"I suggest you call a ride. You're too drunk to safely ride. You'll kill someone or yourself."

"Fuck you. I'm fine to ride. This isn't the last you'll see of me, you filthy biker scum," he yelled. One of his friends hurried over to him and grabbed his arm.

"Shut up, Moe. These guys can kill us without breaking a sweat. I don't know what that bitch, Amber, told you, but it's not worth getting killed over. Let's go." He turned to look at me and the guys. "Sorry, he's drunk and doesn't know what he's doing. We'll make sure he gets home. Goodnight."

"He's too drunk to ride," I said.

"I know. I came in my car. I'll drive him home and bring him to get his bike tomorrow." He didn't waste time, dragging Moe to a car parked on the other side of their bikes. His other friends got on their bikes. None of them took their eyes off us, until they were well out of the parking lot. As soon as I knew they were gone, I waved over Dillon and Dante.

"I want you to take turns watching the bikes. I don't trust them not to come back and do something to our rides. Hate to do it. I know it's cold out here, so take it in shifts of fifteen minutes or so. I doubt we'll be here much longer."

"Hey, don't worry about us. We'll be fine, Ink. Go finish having fun. Alisse hasn't gotten a chance to fast dance with you yet," Dillon said with a grin. I flipped him off. He knew there was no way I'd fast dance. He laughed.

Heading back inside, I took Alisse off the arm of Spawn. The ladies had followed us out to the parking lot but stayed well in the back where they wouldn't get hurt. "Babe, I think I owe you a dance. It won't be a fast one, but a slow one, I can do."

She smiled up at me. "I'd love that. Then after that, I'll be ready to go whenever you are."

I nodded. I was ready to go too. Not only because of Moe and Amber, but because I had plans for her when we got back home. Plans that I didn't want to postpone.

Alisse: Chapter 10

I didn't say much in the car on the way back to the compound. Chey tried to engage me in conversation, but I was too busy thinking about what Amber had done and what that guy, Moe, had said. In particular, what he said about Amber being pregnant when Ink broke up with her. She hadn't stuck around long after they split and I hadn't seen her for a couple of years after that. Could she have had a baby? If so, was she hiding it for the rest of the family or had she given it away? Or was it all a lie?

At the compound, Dante let me out at our house. Ink had driven his bike into the garage and parked it. He came over and helped me out and thanked Dante. I said good night to him. We'd already dropped Cheyenne off at her and Reaper's house first. He hurried me inside, out of the cold.

As I took off my jacket and boots, he hung up his cut and took off his boots. Taking me by the hand, he led me to our bedroom. When I stepped through the doorway, he turned me around to face him. He had a concerned look on his face. He grasped my face between both of his hands.

"Baby, tell me what's wrong? I can tell something is bothering you and I think it's more than that stupid jackass at the bar. Are you still upset at seeing Amber and her talking to us? If so, forget about her. She's not important."

I didn't know how to ask him what was plaguing me. I didn't want to upset him, but I needed to know, for my peace of mind. After a minute of silence, I gave up trying to figure out how to sugar-coat it and I blurted it out.

"Do you think Amber was pregnant when you broke up with her? If so, do you think it was yours?"

Sighing, he let go of my face, took my hand and led me over to our bed. He sat me down on the edge of it. He kneeled down in front of me. I couldn't tell by the look on his face if this was going to be a good or bad discussion.

"Whirlwind, I have no idea if she was or not. It's possible, I guess. However, whether it was mine or not, I doubt it. We hadn't had sex for at least a month before we broke up. Before that, there was never a single time I went without a condom with her. She tried to have me do it, but I wouldn't. If she was pregnant, I'd lay money on the father being one of the men she was sleeping with besides me. I'm sure there was more than just the two I found out about."

His conviction was easy to hear. I sagged in relief. I hadn't realized how much I needed to hear his words.

"I feel like such a bitch asking you that, Austin. I'm not a hateful person, but I want to be the only one to have your children. The thought of Amber ever having one of your babies, makes me sick. I've never heard a peep out of my aunt or uncle about her being pregnant or having a baby. Surely, if it was true, I'd have heard it. If she was pregnant, where is the baby now? Would she have aborted it or given it up?"

"I don't know if she would have had it or not, baby. She doesn't strike me as the motherly type. If it'll make you feel better, I'll ask Spawn to do some digging. Believe me, if she got an abortion or had a kid, he'll find out. As for the father, if there is a child, I'm willing to take a test to show that it isn't mine."

"I'd like to know. And if there is a child and for some reason we find out it is yours, what will you do?"

He sighed and stood up to sit beside me on the bed. I buried my head in his chest. He rubbed up and down my back. He kissed the top of my head.

"Babe, if by some rare chance the baby is proven to be mine, then we'll talk about what we want to do. While I'd want to have a presence in the life of my child, I don't want to do anything that will hurt you."

"I wouldn't ask you to ignore the child if it was yours. It might hurt me to see them, but the child would still be a part of you. I'd want you to be a part of his or her life. Our children would grow up knowing they had a half brother or sister out there. I wouldn't expect us to hide it."

He tipped back my head and holding my chin between his finger and thumb, he kissed me. It was a kiss filled with passion, ownership, and love. As his tongue teased and dueled with mine, I pressed my lips against his harder. He withdrew his tongue, so he could nibble on my lips. I felt my back hit the mattress as he laid me back, coming over top of me to straddle me as he kissed the hell out of me.

When we came up for air, we were both panting and I was feverish. I wanted to tear off my clothes and demand that he take me right that second. I was so turned on, that my panties were soaked and my nipples were rock hard.

I grabbed the back of his t-shirt and tore it up and over his head. He helped me by lifting his arms. I tossed it to the side then scrambled to get to his belt. I fumbled as I tried to undo it before tackling his button and zipper. His hand landed on mine.

"Slow down, we have all night, baby."

"No, we don't. I need you inside of me now, Austin. I can't wait. Please," I begged him.

Seeing my distress, he helped me to undo his belt and jeans. As he stood to take them off, as well as his underwear and socks, I didn't waste time in removing my shirt. I'd gotten my jeans undone, by the time he was naked. He tugged them down my legs, taking my panties with them and dropped them on the floor. My socks only took him a couple of seconds to get rid of.

I spread my legs, so he could see how turned on I was. I was soaking wet. He groaned then swiped his fingers through my wetness, bringing them to his mouth, where he sucked them clean.

"Alisse, no one tastes as sweet as you, baby. I love how you taste. I could feast on you for hours."

"Austin, I'm so happy you love it, but I can't wait for you to do that right now. I'm dying here. Take me," I pleaded. I was cupping my breasts, twisting on my nipples. I was so close to coming just from that.

He growled then grabbed my hips and jerked me to the edge of the bed. Before I could say anything, he flipped me onto my belly and yanked my hips up higher. A second later, I felt the head of his cock press against the entrance of my pussy then he powered inside of me. He did it hard and fast.

The stretch from accommodating his girth made me cry out. It burned a little as he entered me. It did every time we made love. He hissed as he bottomed out inside of me.

"Fuck, you feel so goddamn tight and wet. Did I hurt you?"

"You didn't hurt me. It just burned a little. Don't stop."

He didn't stop. He took me hard and fast. His cock hammered in and out of me. I came within a minute of him being inside of me. It was a hard and long orgasm, which he prolonged with his thrusts. When I came down from that one, he didn't even slow down. He kept pounding my pussy. I was crying out in ecstasy.

"Best fucking pussy I've ever had in my life. I love this pussy. I could fuck you all day and all night, baby. Come for me again. I want to feel you strangling my cock," he snarled.

I came as he commanded. This one went one even

longer than the last one. By the time I was done with it, I felt like I was floating. However, he was still hard and hadn't come yet. Suddenly, he withdrew, flipped me over, lifted me off the bed and carried me to the wall. He pushed my back against it. I wrapped my arms and legs around him to keep from falling. He guided his cock back side of me and went back to fucking me like a demon. His eyes bored into mine.

"I love you, Alisse, I fucking love you and don't you ever forget it."

"I love you too, Austin."

His fingers bit into my hips as he kissed me while his hips kept slamming into mine, driving his cock deep. I had to tear my mouth away from him to breathe. He nibbled down my neck. I felt another orgasm coming. I panted out, "I'm close again."

He sped up and went even deeper, which I thought was impossible to do. Just as I clenched down on him, he said to me in a husky whisper, "Marry me, baby."

I looked at him in shock and wonder. Since my orgasm chose that moment to hit, I screamed out my answer, "Yes!"

He yelled my name, "Alisse", then he came grunting and jerking. His warm cum filled me. His groans were loud. He kept coming. When we were done, he staggered to the bed and laid me down gently. He collapsed beside me. His hands rubbed up and down my arm. His eyes were staring into mine. I saw the love shining there.

"Did you mean it?" He asked me.

"Mean what? That I'd marry you? Of course I meant it," I told him, as I caressed his cheek.

"Then I guess that means you need a ring, doesn't it?" He sat up and reached into his side table drawer. He brought out a small black velvet box. The kind that a ring came in. My heart sped up. He opened the box as he went down on his knees. He took out the ring and held it out to me. I sat up and automatically held out my left hand, so he could slide the ring on my finger.

It sparkled in the light of the lamp. It was an oval diamond, which was surrounded by a halo of smaller diamonds. I loved it. I admired it on my hand before leaning toward him, to give him a kiss. His mouth eagerly kissed me back.

After we stopped kissing, he got back up on the bed with me. He sat up with his back to the headboard and cuddled me between his legs. "I can't believe this," I whispered.

"Can't believe what? That I asked you to marry me? I told you I was going to do it. I was planning to do it tonight, but maybe not at the same time as you were sucking the life out of me. That was the spur of the moment there," he teased me. He laughed when I elbowed him in the ribs.

"Sucking out your life, was I? I'll remember that next time."

"Baby, you can suck anything of mine anytime you want to. I'll gladly let you."

I turned over to stare up at him and saw the joy and laughter on his face.

"I just bet you will. What would you have done if I said no?"

"I'd have kept making you come until you changed your mind. It didn't matter how many days, weeks, or months it took. I'd get you to agree to be my wife eventually. I want to claim you in every way possible, Alisse. Now, we'll be official in the biker world and the regular world."

"I'm more than happy to call you my old man and husband, Austin. There's nothing I want more, unless it's to have your children."

His hand came down to rub across the side of my belly. "Speaking of babies, how would you like to start on the first one soon?"

"How soon?" I asked, barely able to breathe. Was he asking because he was caught up in the moment or did he really want to start a family this soon? I know he'd mentioned it before but still.

"Tomorrow."

His answer stunned me. It took me several seconds to gather my scattered thoughts to respond to him.

"If you mean that, I think we can do that. Tomorrow is too soon but I'm due in about two weeks to renew my birth control shot. Would you like me not to do it?"

"I'd fucking love it, if you didn't renew it. I want to see you round with my baby. I want to hold our child in my arms. I'm ready for the whole family thing, babe, as long as you are too. If we're lucky, we'll have a baby by the end of the year."

"Well, maybe, it might take some time for me to get pregnant. After being on birth control, it can take a while for some women to start producing eggs again. We'll have to see. You know what that means. I'll have to put the nursing degree on hold."

I wasn't terribly upset at the idea. It was a minor irritation to wait, but if I got babies out of it, then it would be worth it. This past week I had checked into what it would take to get my associate degree in nursing. I was pleasantly surprised to see I had done all the prerequisite classes and only would have to take the core classes. That was two years' worth of full-time schooling. There were loans I could get to pay for it. I'd been excited when I told him what I'd found out.

"Baby, you don't have to put it off or not for long. You said there's a waiting list. Put your name on it. When the time comes, we'll see where you're at with the pregnancy. I still want you to do it. I'm not going to make you give that up."

"I know you won't. Okay, I'll put my name on the list. And I'll stop the shots. Anything else I need to do?"

"Yeah, tell me how soon I can get you down the aisle and your name changed to Kavanagh? I don't want to wait a second longer than I have to."

"Well, aren't we in a hurry to get shackled? Let me think about it. I bet I can figure out something. I don't want to wait forever and there's no reason we have to.

I don't want an elaborate wedding that costs the moon and is a waste of money. Something simple, intimate and only for us and our closest friends, will be fine with me. We'll invite the bulk of people to the reception. Similar to what Reaper and Cheyenne did for their wedding."

"That sounds like a perfect plan to me. It's the end of January. What do you say to an April wedding, if not sooner? I know it'll take time to get a dress and maybe find someone to cater it."

"April is doable. I'll get together with Cheyenne and see what we can do."

"Good, now let's get back to other things."

"Like what?" I asked, trying to sound innocent, as if I didn't already know. I could feel his hard cock pressing into my chest. I was laying between his legs facing him now. He smirked at me as he pressed his hips up.

"Oh, you mean this," I said, as I raised up and scooted down far enough I could reach his cock with my mouth. I snaked out my tongue to lick the head. I could smell and taste our combined cum on him. Instead of turning me off, it made me even hornier. He moaned. Taking my cue from him, I grasped the base of his cock and pumped up and down a couple times before I sucked the head into my mouth.

It didn't take me long to be taking him down my throat, making me swallow around him, tightening my throat muscles around him, as I played with his balls and teased his whole long length with my lips and tongue. I was really getting into the groove of it, when he yanked me off him and tugged me up to straddle him.

"Ride me, baby. Ride my cock and make us both come," he grunted.

I placed him at my opening and pressed down slowly on him. I moaned as he filled me. Once he was planted fully inside of me, I started to ride him. Every so often I'd throw in a twist of the hips, or I'd intentionally tighten my Kegel muscles. Every time I did that, he'd groan in pleasure.

I got myself off twice, but he still held on. I doubled my efforts to make him come. It wasn't long into the third cycle that I was racing up on another orgasm. As I tipped over the edge, he flipped me on my back and pounded his cock in and out of me harder and faster. I screamed then screamed more when he shouted then came. I floated for hours it seemed like. When I finally came back to earth, he had to practically carry me to the bathroom to get cleaned up. I think I was asleep before my head hit the pillow.

Today, Ink had taken the day off from the shop to take me to my old apartment. Even though I hadn't been living there for months, due to the Soldiers of Corruption threat, I still had a lot of my stuff there. It was time to let it go. If I was marrying Ink, it made no sense for me to keep it. Hell, I hadn't been here in three weeks. And I wasn't working full time, so it was eating into my savings. I refused to let Ink pay my rent, although he tried.

Looking around the place, I decided to start in the

kitchen. It and the bedroom would be the two big rooms. A lot of the furniture was still in good shape and I decided to give it to the club. They could either use it in the clubhouse or some of the rooms used by prospects. If anyone decided to build their house and needed it, they could use it. One of the storage buildings on the back of the compound was used for things like that.

I went through my kitchen appliances, dishware, glassware and pots and pans, deciding what we needed at the house. Those were boxed up in one set of boxes while the giveaway stuff went in another. Ink and I worked well together and it went smoother than I imagined getting that part done.

I was in the bedroom, going through linens, when I heard a knock at the door. Who in the world could that be? I came out to see, but Ink beat me to the door. I should've known. He was still hypervigilant any time we left the compound, especially if I was with him. I stood there mystified when I saw my landlord standing there. How did he know I was here?

Ink and I had planned to go see him after we were done packing and it had been hauled away, so I could terminate my lease officially, pay any fees and hand over the keys. His beady eyes stared at Ink, looking both terrified and sneering. His eyes landed on me and he started to go off.

"What do you think you're doing?"

I glanced at the boxes, as if to say, *duh, what does it look like I'm doing, asshole.* I bit my tongue not to say it out loud. I was hoping I might get at least some of my deposit back.

"Mr. Brown, hello, I didn't expect to see you until later. We're just packing the rest of my stuff up and moving it to our house. We should have it all done by tomorrow at the latest. As soon as we are, I'll stop by the office to hand in the keys and go over things."

"I need to be notified when you move out. I need to oversee the packing and moving."

"Oversee? Why would you need to do that?"

"To ensure that tenants don't take things that don't belong to them."

His comeback pissed me off. What the hell could I steal? Other than appliances and the blinds off the windows and the damn doors off their hinges, there was nothing to worry about. Besides, he would do a final walk through to ensure I'd cleaned it and not trashed the place. If he did that, he'd see if I took anything I shouldn't. I opened my mouth to make a smart remark, deposit refund be damned, when Ink popped into the conversation.

"What exactly is she going to steal? If you're worried about the appliances, as you can see, they're here. I have much better ones at home. Viking is the only way to go. The washer and dryer are here. Again, I have much better ones at home. All of our windows have window coverings that have been custom made for the windows, so your blinds are safe. I think we're done with the oversight. We'll see you when we're done."

I watched as he slammed the door in Mr. Brown's stunned face. I couldn't hold in the laughter. He came over to me as I laughed and grinned as he wrapped his arms around me.

"You liked that, did you, Whirlwind?"

"I did. He didn't know what hit him. He is such a pompous, asshole. I won't miss him. Every time I had to contact him for something that needed fixed in the apartment, he acted like it was a major inconvenience and he took his good old time to have it fixed, if he fixed it at all. He's been here forever, I hear and thinks he can do no wrong."

"Well, he can take his shitty customer service and shove it up his ass."

Putting Mr. Brown out of our minds, we finished packing. It took us until early evening to get done. By then, I was tired, hungry and all I wanted to do was go home and put my feet up.

"Baby, we'll give Brown the keys tomorrow. The guys will be here to load it up and take it to the compound early. I told them to make it nine o'clock. It should take us a couple of hours."

"Are you going to be able to take another day off? Honey, if you need to work, I can handle this with Dillon and Dante's help. There's no need for you to come again." I hated to have him miss work because of me.

"I can take the time to help move my woman to our house. The rest of the week is booked and we had no problem moving people around to give me the time. My days of being a slave to the shop is over. I need to spend time with my woman."

His pledge made me weak in the knees. The love he felt for me, was evident in his eyes. I couldn't resist giving him a kiss. We kissed until he called it quits, so we could leave.

Since we were both tired, we grabbed takeout from our favorite Chinese place, the Peking Palace. I called Chey to see if her and Reaper had already eaten or if she had fixed dinner. She told me no, that she was too tired to cook, so we got enough for the four of us and we took it to their house.

I made Cheyenne rest while I got out the plates and silverware and opened the various boxes we'd gotten. All of us loved this place, so the whole island was covered in food. Leftovers wouldn't go to waste. We had Kung Pao chicken, Sweet and Sour chicken, Chinese dumplings, chow mein noodles and fried rice, Sichuan pork, wonton soup, scallion pancakes, bao buns, and spring rolls.

When we finished, I was stuffed and felt like I would explode. I was sitting on the couch, talking to Chey when Reaper turned to me.

"Alisse, Ink said you'll be having the prospects pick up your stuff at nine tomorrow morning. Do you mind if I steal him for about an hour? I want to go over something at Punisher's Lager. I promise I'll bring him back in time to do some of the work and I'll even help."

"Reaper, you don't have to ask me. If you need him for club business, then take him. I'll do fine with Dante and Dillon. They're great workers."

"Thanks, honey." He told me with a wink.

"You're welcome, honey," I teased him back. He laughed. I wouldn't do that in front of the whole club, but when it's just the four of us were together.

We didn't stay for too long, because Cheyenne needed to get her rest. Besides, I was feeling like I needed my bed. Tomorrow would be here before we knew it.

Ink: Chapter 11

The ringing of my cell phone woke me. I grabbed it off my nightstand and looked at the time. It was three in the morning. I saw that it was Reaper calling.

"Reaper, what's up?" It had to be something serious, for him to be calling at this time. My heart jumped, wondering if something was wrong with Cheyenne and the baby. I prayed there wasn't. It would kill Reaper if anything happened to his old lady and unborn baby.

"Ink, I need you to get your ass to the clubhouse. We're rolling out in a few minutes. Got a call from Chief Carlton. He said the fire department was called to Alisse's apartment. It's on fire."

"What the fuck? Are you kidding me? Okay, I'll be there in five. I got to get dressed." He hung up. My brain had trouble comprehending what he said for a second.

My raised voice roused Alisse. She rubbed her eyes and sat.

"What's wrong, honey?"

I didn't want to tell her, but I knew I couldn't keep it from her. "Babe, that was Reaper. He got a call from the police chief. The fire department was called and your apartment is on fire. We're going to go check it out."

She stumbled out of bed. "What?! I'm going." She rushed to the dresser.

I was grabbing my clothes and putting them on as fast I could. I knew it would do me no good to tell her to wait here and to go back to sleep. She'd only worry herself to death, even if I could force her to stay. It took us less than five minutes to be out to the garage and on my bike headed toward the clubhouse.

Reaper and most of the guys were already there waiting when we got there. They were on their bikes. "Let's go." He gave me a concerned look as he noted Alisse with me. All I could do was shrug. He had an old lady. He knew what it was like. Alisse hung onto me. I prayed that the fire wasn't a serious one and they had gotten it out before it got too out of control. The thought of all her stuff going up in smoke would be a blow to her.

When we pulled into the parking lot of the complex, I saw two fire trucks, a couple of police cruisers and a crowd of people standing around watching. They parted when me and the club rode our bikes right up to the police tape line. I hopped off after helping Alisse get off my bike and headed straight toward Chief Carlton. She held onto my back pocket. Reaper was with me. The rest of the guys fell in behind us. I could see there were still flames and fire fighters were battling them furiously.

"Carlton, what the hell happened?" Reaper growled, as he shook the chief's hand. I shook it too. He was alright for a cop. He tended to leave our club alone. He might suspect we weren't always on the side of the law, but he knew we wouldn't hurt innocent people and we kept the less savory people out of our territory. It made his job easier.

The chief shook his head and shrugged. "Hell if I know, Reaper. The call came in and when we got here, the place was in full flame mode. The fire chief will have to do his inspection after they get it out and it has a chance to cool in order to tell us what caused it. When I heard the name of the occupant, I knew it was Ink's woman's place. I've seen him with her around town a couple of times and I know she's your wife's best friend. Lucky as hell she wasn't here. Was all her stuff in there? I heard she's been living at the compound for the last few months." Seems like he was very well informed about us. I wasn't sure if I liked anyone outside the club knowing our business.

"Fuck, her clothes and some other stuff are at our house, but all her furniture, linens and kitchen shit were boxed up and we were going to haul it over to the compound later this morning."

I felt Alisse hide her face in the back of my cut. I wondered if she was crying and hiding it or just blocking out the sight in front of her. Even though a lot of it was going to be donated, it was still her stuff. It had to hurt to see it destroyed. Luckily, we'd already moved her important papers and photos to the house.

I turned to take her in my arms. I kissed the top of her head. "Baby, I'm so damn sorry."

Tears filled her eyes as she raised her head to look

up at me. "It's not your fault. Do you think it burned everything?"

I looked at the flames and the burned outer walls. I hated to say it but I told her the truth. "I doubt anything can be saved, baby. Don't stress it. We'll go shopping to replace the kitchen stuff and linens. The club will be fine without the furniture."

"I hate that all of it just went to waste. It was just stuff, but it was mine. I worked hard for everything in there. Makes me feel like I don't have anything to show for the years I've worked." I hugged her tighter, trying to convey my strength to her. There was nothing I could say to make this feel better.

We stood there and watched the men work. After several minutes, we walked away and the guys surrounded us. Making sure no one was close enough to hear us, Reaper glanced at me then at Alisse. I saw the concern and speculation on his face. "Alisse, honey, I'm so damn sorry for this. I know this fucking sucks. I hate to bring this up right now, but I think I have to. It's likely this wasn't an accident. The question is, did the Soldiers do this? I can't think of anyone else who would do it. Can you?"

"No, but couldn't it have been due to faulty electrical wiring or something like that?" I heard a hint of hope in her voice, but mainly it was fear after hearing the Soldiers brought to mind.

"It's possible, but I think it's too much of a coincidence that it happened to only your apartment and with us being on alert for the Soldiers to pull something after we took out Serpent and his guys. However, with that in mind, why would they bother to burn down an apartment that you're not even living in?" I asked, looking frustrated and angry.

"It doesn't make any sense. They wouldn't waste their time doing something that is more annoying than hurtful. They would go for blood. It would make sense if Alisse had been here," Reaper added. The thought of her being here and trapped, possibly killed by the fire made me sick to my stomach and angry. The guys were all mumbling about who did it. Most were thinking it had to be the Soldiers if it wasn't an accident. Alisse appeared to be only half listening as she continued to watch the firemen put out the flames.

Suddenly, her knees gave out. If it hadn't been for my arms around her, she would have fallen to the ground.

"What the fuck?! Babe, are you alright?" I asked, as I hugged her even tighter and held her up.

"I-I don't know. All of a sudden, my head felt funny and my legs went weak. I'm so tired," she whispered to me. She looked pale and drawn.

"I need to take her home and put her to bed. This is too much. She worked her ass off all day packing and now this." I told Reaper. He nodded in agreement. "Come on, baby, let's go."

She weakly waved at the others as they told her to go get some rest. I half carried her to my bike. "Are you going to be able to hold on?" Maybe I should call one of the prospects to bring a cage for her.

"I can hold on. I won't fall off," she assured me. I held onto her arm even as I swung my leg over the bike then helped her to get seated behind me. After she got her arms around me, she laid her head on my back. I fired it up and took off.

I rode slower than I usually would. I was still afraid she might fall off. The ride home seemed to take forever. When we pulled into the garage, she was sagging even more. I got off the bike without knocking her off, then I maneuvered her off it and up into my arms. I carried her inside and went straight to our bedroom. I gently laid her down on the bed and tugged off her shoes and socks after I got her coat off.

"Can I get you anything? Are you feeling any better?" I asked. I couldn't keep the worry out of my voice. She looked worse to me.

"I'm still dizzy. All I want to do is sleep."

"Let me get you undressed the rest of the way then you can, babe." I quickly undressed her and slid her under the covers. She closed her eyes, while I got ready for bed. After taking care of things in the bathroom, I laid down and took her in my arms. She laid her head on my chest. She was out in less than thirty seconds. It took me longer to fall asleep, as I thought about what happened and tried to figure out if it was the Soldiers or not. I knew Spawn would be searching for any cameras in the area that might have recorded something. I went to sleep hoping he'd have something for us by the time we got up.

I was up and pacing the house by seven. I tried to sleep longer, but I was too wound up to do it. I was ready for some action. Alisse was still asleep. She never moved when I got out of bed, which wasn't like her. Usually, she'd wake up or at least wiggled around when I got out of bed. It was because she was more times than not half asleep on top of me. What could I say, I was a cuddler. I loved having her draped over me while we slept. Something I hadn't known until now. Hoping that I wouldn't wake up Cheyenne, I called Reaper. He answered immediately.

"I haven't heard anything yet. The fire chief still has to do his investigation. That takes time. The shit has to cool down," he told me right off the bat. I heard his frustration and tiredness. I wondered if he'd slept at all. He took being president of this club seriously. Anything or anyone endangering it, made him livid. Alisse was mine and his old lady's best friend, she was a part of the club.

"I figured that. I was calling to see if Spawn found anything by any chance," I asked hopefully, although it was unlikely. Otherwise, Reaper would've called me. Unless he wanted to let us sleep.

"Nope. Seems like there aren't any cameras in that damn complex. The fucking landlord should be shot. He doesn't give a shit about the safety of his tenants. Any cameras at the surrounding businesses don't face that way or are blocked by other buildings. Spawn searched all of them and got nothing. Some cars were in and out of the complex, but that wouldn't be unusual. People come and go all the time, even at that time of night. I told him to check them out anyway. He could get license plates on most of them."

"Goddamn it, Reaper, I don't believe it was faulty wiring. It was intentional. It has to be those damn Soldiers of Corruption. Any word on how Undertaker is doing on his mission to that Ohio chapter they infiltrated?"

"According to Sean, he's made contact. Sloan is working with him, so he has backup this time. He's not happy about it. He wanted her to stay where it's safe. They have no idea how long it'll take him to get those assholes to trust him and then find out the dirt, so they can take them down."

"Shit! Well, I can't say that I'm surprised. I can't imagine having to do what he's doing." It would take nerves of steel and more patience than I had to do undercover work like that.

"Me either, but that's Mark. How's Alisse doing? She looked wasted last night. Thought she was going to faint on us."

"She's still asleep. She was even worse when we got home. I had to carry her in the house and undress her."

A note of curiosity came through on his next question. "Is it just because she's tired and then the fire hit her hard or is it something else?"

"What else could it be? Unless she's coming down with something. "

"Maybe it's something that'll last about nine months then go away." I heard him chuckle as he said it.

It took my brain a couple of seconds to realize what he was implying.

"Nah, she's not pregnant. She's on birth control. Although she's going to stop it in a week or so. Her shot is due then and we decided not to renew it."

"Have you been wrapping it up?" Came his response.

"Why the hell would I do that? She's my old lady and she's on birth control."

"Man, that doesn't always work. Shit, look at how many of the Warriors have kids. I know for a fact some of them were on birth control when they got pregnant. More than a few."

Now he had me wondering. I didn't want to get my hopes up. The likelihood of her being pregnant, after only being together a few weeks, was next to none. Or was it? Now he had me wondering if it could be the reason.

"You know what, I'll call you later. Let me know if you hear anything. I need to go check on Alisse."

All he did was laugh then hang up. Bastard. He knew he had my head going in circles, wondering if she might be. Damn, I had to ask her. I ran upstairs and burst into our bedroom. She wasn't in bed. I was about to call out to her, thinking she was in the bathroom, when I heard her moan. I hurried into the bathroom and found her lying on the floor near the toilet. She was moaning and weakly moving. Like she was trying to crawl to the toilet.

I rushed over to her and dropped to my knees as I

eased her over onto her back. She was looking pale and had dark circles under her eyes. She was sweating.

"Whirlwind, what's wrong? Did you fall?"

"No, I just couldn't walk and I need to use the toilet. God, how humiliating. Please help me onto the toilet," she pleaded, looking so pathetic, it tore out my heart.

I gave her a quick kiss. "Of course. You should have yelled for me or called my cell. I'd have carried you." I chastised her as I got her up off the floor and into my arms then carried her to the toilet. I had to pull down her underwear and lower her down on the toilet seat. She was so weak and out of it. She swayed, so I held onto her.

As she sat there, I asked her the question burning through me. "Baby, is there any chance you're pregnant and that's why you're feeling this way?"

Her head snapped up and she stared at me in shock. She didn't say a word. I could see the thought racing through her head on her expressive face. She was wondering if she might be.

"When was your last period?" She hadn't had one since we started sleeping together. That was three weeks.

She furrowed her brow and was in deep thought for a minute or so then she groaned. "It's been five weeks. I should've started a week ago. But Austin, there's no way I'm pregnant. I'm still on the shot."

"You know nothing is foolproof. Birth control fails all the time." I repeated what Reaper had said to me.

She moaned and hunched over. "God, I feel like shit. If I am pregnant, this better only be for a short time, or I'm going to kill you. Chey didn't say anything about this shit happening with her pregnancy." She grumbled half under her breath.

"Come on, finish up then I'll help you lie down and we'll figure this out. It could be you picked up something at work. Has anyone been there with symptoms like this." I wasn't letting myself get my hopes up even more. Just because she was late didn't mean anything.

She shook her head and gestured to me, like she wanted to stand up. I helped her to her feet. It was awkward for her, but she took the toilet paper away from me that I'd wadded up and wiped herself with a frown. I guess that's going too far for her. Hell, what did it matter. It wasn't like I didn't touch and taste her pussy every day. Wiping was nothing. She staggered to the sink, I steadied her, as she washed and dried her hands. Not wanting to chance her falling, I swept her up in my arms and carried her to bed. She sighed when her body touched the mattress. I laid down beside her.

"I can't recall anyone coming into the office with these symptoms. There is a respiratory virus going around, but I don't have any of those symptoms. That's been all congestion, coughing and sinus issues with a fever," she explained.

"It might be something else, but with you being late, I think we should check to be sure you're not pregnant."

"Okay, I don't have anything. You'll have to go get

one of those tests at the pharmacy in town. I doubt Cheyenne has any."

"I'll check to be sure. If she doesn't, I'll send one of the prospects, that's what they're for."

She groaned. "God, I bet that'll thrill them. *Hey, go get a pregnancy test for my old lady. I think I might have knocked her up.* I can only imagine the look on their faces."

I laughed at the image she brought to mind. I took out my cell phone and shot off a quick text to Reaper. I didn't want to disturb Cheyenne if she was asleep.

Me: Does Chey have any pregnancy tests left at the house?

Reaper: I already checked and no she doesn't. Already sent Dillon to fetch a few. He should be back soon. Told him to bring them to you.

Me: Damn, always a step or ten ahead, Pres.

Reaper: I have to be with this bunch.

Me: Thanks, I appreciate it.

All I got in return was a thumbs-up emoji. Alisse had patiently watched me. When I got done typing, she asked, "Well, does she?"

"No, but Reaper said he already sent Dillon out to get some. He'll be here soon."

"How did Reaper know I might need one?" She asked in puzzlement.

"I was talking to him, finding out if we knew

anything yet about the fire, when he asked how you were doing. I told him how wasted you were when we got home last night. He was the one to suggest you might be pregnant, even if you're still on birth control."

"Austin. I swear, I never for a second thought that. Which is stupid, being a medical person like I am. I know you can still get knocked up even if you are using birth control. If I am, we know not to go without shots and condoms, when we're not trying to have another baby."

"Hmm, yeah, that might work. Or we could just keep you barefoot and pregnant all the time," I teased her.

She tried to shove me off the bed. At least she appeared to be feeling a little better. "Don't even suggest it. I want more than one kid, but not a whole damn football team. You need to find yourself a new woman if that's what you want."

I growled, as I rolled her underneath me and I hovered over top of her. "You're the only woman I want or need. I love you and I don't plan on giving you up for any damn reason. A few kids work for me. When we're ready to stop, I'll get clipped."

I kissed her. It meant it to be a kiss that showed her how much she meant to me. It quickly turned into more. I grew hard and she moaned. Knowing we didn't have time for this right now and that she wasn't feeling her best, I eased away from her. She pouted.

"Baby, don't look at me like that. Dillon will be here any minute and you're not feeling well. I want to, God

196

knows I want to, but I want you to be better."

"Fine, but you owe me. When I'm feeling better, you owe me at least a dozen orgasms, mister."

"I'll give you those and more if you let me." The flush across her cheeks told me she liked that idea a lot.

We were interrupted from saying anything more, by the ringing of our doorbell. I hopped up to get it. Downstairs, I opened the door to an unhappy looking Dillon. He shoved the bag in my hands. Before he took off, he said, "if we're going to keep having women around here popping up pregnant, we need to get Lash to stock these in his damn medical room. The looks from the ladies at the pharmacy made me feel like I was a pervert or something. I swear one woman saw me and ran."

"Jesus, that's all it takes to make you squirm?"

"In this case, yes. In others, no. I'd rather be tortured than do that again," he confessed.

I laughed as he rushed to the cage he was driving. I wondered for a second why he wasn't on his bike, then I forgot about the prospect and got back to the issue at hand. Finding out if my woman was carrying my baby or not.

When I came back into the bedroom, Alisse was sitting up on the side of the bed. I took the bag to her. She removed four pregnancy test kits from it.

"What next? Do you just pee on them then wait?"

"Yeah, basically, but since I just peed, I'll need to

wait until I have some pee to give. Also, it's usually preferred if you do this during your first bathroom visit of the day. That allows more of the hormone to build up and show, if it's there and you're not that far along. They can detect it as of the first day of your missed period, so if I am, it should show it."

I didn't want to wait a second longer than we had too, so I got up and went down to the kitchen to get several bottles of water out of the fridge and brought them to her. She rolled her eyes but didn't say anything as I opened the first one and handed it to her. To kill time, I turned on the television and found a movie I figured we both could enjoy. Honestly, I barely paid any attention to it. I was too busy handing her more water as soon as she finished a bottle. Finally, after almost an hour and three bottles of water, she nodded.

"I'm ready. I think I can definitely pee now. God, my bladder feels like it's going to explode."

I picked her up and carried her to the toilet. She had grabbed two of the tests as I picked her up. As she got them unpackaged, I paced. She fumbled a little as she stuck them between her legs and peed. After she was done, she capped them and set them on the counter.

"Three minutes," she told me. I set the timer on my watch. She finished up and then stood to wash her hands. I was glad to see she was steadier, even though I stood next to her with a hand on her. She turned to me.

"Austin, don't be surprised or disappointed if it's negative. This is a longshot. I know we're both anxious to start our family, but this isn't likely the start of that. I wish it was. I think I'm just coming down with something or maybe I was just overly tired after yesterday." She caressed my cheek as she told me.

I removed her hand from my face and kissed the palm of it. "Whirlwind, I know it's a longshot like you said. If it's negative, we'll stick to our plans to stop your shots in a week and go from there. I have no doubt we'll have a family. However, if it's positive, I can't tell you how fucking thrilled I am that it is. I can't wait to see and hold our baby. If it's a girl, I want her to look just like her momma."

She smiled as she raised up on her toes to kiss me. It was a kiss full of love and passion. When she lifted her mouth, I wanted to protest. The beeping of my timer alerted us that it was time. We both took deep breaths before she picked up the first one. We looked at it and my heart jumped. It showed two pink lines. They were clear to see. She laid it down and picked up the other. That one said *pregnant* on it. Our eyes met. I could see she was stunned like me. Grabbing her, I swung her around, whooping out my happiness as she laughed. Finally, I remembered she was carrying precious cargo and I sat her down. I ran my hands over her belly.

"Did I hurt you?" I asked her anxiously.

"You can't hurt me or the baby doing that. He or she is very well protected in there. God, Austin, we're going to be parents. I don't know what to do. Yes, I do. We need to call Dr. Simpson and get me an appointment for a blood test. I'm not saying these are wrong, but I'd feel better if I had a blood test backing them up."

"Do it. Call her right now."

"It's barely after eight. The office doesn't start seeing patients until nine."

"So, you have her number, call her. I bet she'll squeeze you in. After all, you do work for her, baby. There has to be some perks to that."

I didn't have to prod her much. I followed her back to the bed, where she got her phone and within seconds was calling.

"Hi Dr. Simpson, it's Alisse. I hate to disturb you before work, but I wondered if you had time for me to come into the office and have my blood drawn today. I just had two positive pregnancy tests but I want to be sure and the blood test is the way to go," she explained. I couldn't hear what the doctor said but for the smile on Alisse's face, it must be good.

"Thank you, I'll see you soon." She told her before hanging up. "She said to come in any time and she'll have them draw my blood and tell us. If I am, we'll have to call Dr. Hoover's office and set up an appointment. He's Cheyenne's OB/GYN. I want to use the same one as she does. He's nice and she likes him."

I wasn't thrilled at the idea of another man seeing my woman's private parts, even though I knew it was for medical reasons. Some of my thoughts must have shown on my face, because she laughed at me.

"Austin, are you seriously thinking about me not having a male doctor because he'll have to see my pussy?"

I nodded. "Yeah, I don't like it. I don't want anyone but me looking or touching you like that. I'm surprised Reaper is okay with it."

"I can't believe you. Dr. Hoover is like sixty years old."

"So. Doesn't mean he's not sexually active and not checking out all the women who come through his clinic."

"Sweet baby Jesus, save me from a caveman. Okay, you come with me and you'll see, he's perfectly professional."

Damn right I was going. No way she'd be going to any of those appointments without me if I could help it. Not only because of him being a male doctor, but also because I didn't want to miss anything with this baby.

Alisse: Chapter 12

After talking to Dr. Simpson and having a laugh over Ink's reaction to the baby doctor being a man, he didn't waste time in having me get ready to go to town. I barely had time to comb my hair, brush my teeth, wash my face, and put on my clothes before he was ushering me out to the car. He waved at Dante as he stood by the gate.

I thought I would have to remind him not to speed, but he surprised me by sticking to the speed limit. He kept one hand pressed to my stomach the whole way there. It was sweet as hell.

Luckily, I didn't have to go through the usual rigmarole that others went through at the doctor's office. I was waved to the back as soon as the receptionist saw me. She was smiling as she led me to a room. "Someone will be in to see you in a minute, Alisse."

"Thank you, Vivian."

I sat down on the paper covered table. Ink stood beside me, holding my hand.

"Are you nervous?" I asked him.

"A little. I can't help but worry what if the tests were wrong," he confessed.

"Me too. Well, we'll know one way or the other soon." I squeezed his hand to convey comfort and to get some for myself.

A swift knock at the door alerted us. The door came open and in walked one of the nurses Cheyenne and I worked with all the time, Remi. She was smiling at me. She was the nicest one here.

"Hi Alisse, you love this place so much, you can't stand to stay away even on your day off? Better watch it, we might put you to work," she joked as she came over to me carrying her phlebotomist tray. "Hi Ink, how're you doing?" She asked him. All the staff here had met him before.

"Hi Remi, I'm doing good. Hopefully, if this test is positive, I'll be doing great. How're you?"

See, my biker could be civil when he wanted to. He had manners to go with those sharp edges of his.

"I'm actually pretty good myself. I heard from the doc that you want us to run a blood pregnancy test. Let's see if I can make your man happy. Which arm?"

I presented her with my left one. She was quick and efficient at tying the tourniquet and finding a vein. I barely felt the needle pierce me, as she drew up the vial she needed. Once she was done and I had a Band-Aid on my puncture spot, she hustled out of the room promising to be back as soon as she could.

Now, all we had to do was wait. Luckily, our office had a machine in house that could run the test and get the results rather quickly. I figured we might have to wait an hour, maybe more if more pressing labs were ahead of me. Another knock had Dr. Simpson coming in.

"Hey, you guys, just wanted to pop in and say hi. I wanted to let you know, we'll call as soon as we get the results. There's one test being done before yours. Why don't you go ahead and head out and I'll call as soon as we know? There's no need to hang here unless you want to. If it is positive, congratulations. It seems I can't keep my staff from falling in more ways for you bikers. Lord, protect us all. Tell your brothers, Ink, that none of them better get any ideas about the rest of my staff," she teased him. I knew Doc liked the Punishers. She had surprised us all with the knowledge she'd been around bikers in the past.

"Doc, I can't make any promises. And it might not be them that my brother goes after. You might want to worry about yourself," he told her with a wink. Although she was in her forties and older than any of the Punishers, Dr. Simpson was a beautiful, attractive, and single woman. They'd do worse than to go after her. She laughed and shook her head.

"Sorry, Ink, I don't see that happening. Go on, get. Alisse, I see you and Cheyenne on Friday."

"Yes, you will. Thanks for working me in."

She gave me a hug and patted Ink on the arm. "Not a problem, I'm glad to do it and can't wait to see the results." She waved as she exited the room. Not wanting to sit here and wait, I jumped down from the table. Ink frowned at me. Oh God, it was about to start. The over-the-top protective caveman stuff that Cheyenne had to put up with from Reaper. He'd always been protective of her, but it doubled when he found out she was pregnant. It looked like my man was going to be the same.

"Don't do that. You might fall or hurt the baby."

"It won't hurt the baby, if there is one and I'm fine. I don't feel weak like I did earlier. How does breakfast sound? I'm starving."

I knew I could distract him with food. He nodded his head. As we got in the car, I knew exactly where he would take us. For something like this, Annie's Diner was the place. It was no more than five minutes away. Pulling into the parking lot, I saw it wasn't packed. However, it was between the morning and noon rush. Ten o'clock on a weekday seemed to be a good time to come.

We were seated and given our menus quickly, as our waitress walked off to get our drinks. I was perusing the menu, trying to see what tripped my trigger when I heard Annie's voice coming up on us. I looked up and smiled at her.

"Well look what the cat dragged in. I haven't seen you two in a while. What have you been up to? Tell Reaper, I'm coming to the damn compound, since he's not brought Cheyenne to see me lately. I need to see how my niece or nephew is growing."

Ink stood up to hug her. I waited for him to get done to do the same. She sat down at the booth with us.

"It's good to see you, Annie. I'll tell Reaper, so he can

hide. You know he's scared of you," Ink joked with her.

"I wish. Nothing scares that man other than something happening to Cheyenne, their baby or his club. What brings you into town this morning?"

"I had to see Dr. Simpson. Then I was starved and we came to get breakfast. We're not too late, are we?" I asked, knowing I was hungry for breakfast not lunch.

"Honey, you tell me what you want and it's yours. I hope everything is alright. Seeing Dr. Simpson on your day off isn't something I'd expect out of you." I could see the worry on her face as she checked me out. I glanced at Ink. Should we tell her what we suspected, or should we wait until the test results came in? He gave me a tiny nod.

"Promise you won't say anything. We don't know for sure."

"I promise. What's wrong?"

"Nothing is wrong. We're hoping it's right. I took two pregnancy tests this morning and they were positive. I wanted a blood test to confirm the results."

She crowed with excitement and I had to shush her as I was laughing. People turned around to stare at her. I saw several raised eyebrows. People around here gossiped about everything. If they heard us, it would be all over town by nightfall. She fought to quiet down. She squeezed my hand.

"Oh honey, that's wonderful. I'll keep my fingers crossed that it's positive. Were you planning this?"

"We were going to start trying soon, but it looks like mother nature might have got the jump on us." Ink told her, as he grinned at her reaction.

"Oh, I can't wait. Another niece or nephew. I'll keep my mouth shut until you tell me I don't have to. What do you want to eat?" She asked, as her waitress brought our drinks. We gave her our order and Annie rushed off to the kitchen. She had a cook, but she did a lot of it herself too.

When the food came out, she'd piled them high with more food than I could possibly eat. When she came over to check everything was to our liking, I told her that. She waved me off with the excuse I was eating for two now.

By the time we were done, paid, told her goodbye and got more hugs and got in the car, I was exhausted. And I was anxious for the results. It had been over an hour.

Ink looked over at me. "Anywhere else you want to go before we head home?"

I was about to tell him no, when my phone rang. I was holding it in my hand. I glanced at the screen and saw it was the office. I answered it and put it on speaker phone as I did it.

"Alisse speaking."

"Hello Alisse, I wanted to call with your results. Congratulations, you're pregnant." Dr. Simpson told me gleefully. I gave Ink a huge smile of happiness. My heart was pounding. He looked excited.

"Thank you so much. That's what we wanted to hear."

"I know and I'm so happy for you and Ink. Don't forget to make your appointment with Dr. Hoover. You need to start taking prenatal vitamins as soon as possible. If you can't get into him within a week, let me know and I'll call in a prescription for you. Hell, never mind, I'll go ahead and do it now. No need for you to wait. I'll see you in two days. Go tell the crew."

"I will and appreciate you calling that in for me."

She told me it was nothing and hung up. As soon as she did, Ink had his seatbelt off and was over the seat grabbing me. His kiss curled my toes and made my panties get damp and my heart raced for a whole other reason.

"Thank you, baby. Thank you for giving me my own family," he whispered in my ear.

"Thank you for giving me one too. How about we go home and when everyone gets home from work tonight, we'll tell them the news? I'll have to tell Cheyenne first though. She'll kill me if I don't. How soon do you need to be at the shop?" He'd called in this morning after the tests and had them reschedule his appointment for this morning, so he could take me to the doctor.

"I have to be there by one o'clock. That gives us just enough time to get to the house, go over and tell Reaper and Cheyenne our news then I'll have to head back to town. I like the idea of telling the guys tonight."

Giving me one last kiss, he got back in his seatbelt and started the car. We made it back to the compound and over to Reaper and Chey's house in no time. Reaper was the one to answer the door. He was checking me out closely.

"Come on in. Alisse, you look better than you did last night and better than Ink described you this morning. Cheyenne's in the living room." He led us there. My best friend was relaxing on the couch with her feet up. She went to get up, but Ink told her to stay still. He gave her a hug then I did before I sat down next to her. He sat in one of the chairs and Reaper sat on the arm of the couch with his hand on Cheyenne's arm. He had to be constantly touching her.

"So, did you take those tests that Dillon got you?" Reaper asked.

"What tests?" Chey chimed in. Apparently, he hadn't told her. Good, I wanted to surprise her.

"I wasn't feeling well, so Reaper suggested to Ink that I take a pregnancy test. We didn't think it was possible, but we did it anyway. After all, I'm on birth control. I took two and they both were positive." Cheyenne began to squeal. I held up a hand to stop her. "I wanted to be sure, so I had Doc take blood and run the test for us. She called about fifteen minutes ago to say it was," I paused before saying, "It's positive."

This time there was no holding Chey back. She squealed loud and long as she wrapped her arms around my neck and held me to her. Damn she was strong. As we laughed and giggled, the guys were doing that man hug thing where they half hug and pound on each other's backs. Once Cheyenne let go of me, Reaper gave me a hug and a kiss on the cheek.

"Congratulations. Any idea how far along you are? When are you going to tell the others?" Reaper was the one to ask.

"I can't be more than six weeks, according to the way they count the date from your last period. I'll know for sure once I see Dr. Hoover. I have to set up an appointment with him. As for telling people, we want to tell the guys tonight. Annie already knows we had the two positives. I'll call her unless Ink wants to. She promised to not say a word."

"Annie? Where the hell did you see her?" Reaper asked.

"We went to her place for breakfast after we left the office." Ink told him, as they went to the kitchen to grab drinks out of the fridge.

Ink wasn't able to spend long and enjoy our friends' company, but at least we did get to tell them together. Reaper sent out a text telling the guys they needed to have their asses at the clubhouse tonight at seven o'clock. He didn't tell them why. Ink reluctantly kissed me and said goodbye as he headed out to get his bike and go to work. He left the car for me to drive home after ordering me not to drive if I didn't feel good. Reaper promised he'd make sure I got home alright. Sheesh, it was only down the road from Reaper's. I stayed to spend more time with Cheyenne while Reaper took himself off to work in his office.

Hours later after taking a nap, fixing dinner, that Ink scolded me for doing, we headed to the clubhouse. Besides telling everyone about the baby, I was anxious to find out if Reaper or anyone had any news about the fire in my apartment. In all the excitement, I'd forgotten about it until late afternoon. I'd texted Ink to ask if he had while he was at work, but he'd responded saying no.

Ink held my hand as we entered. The guys all called out to us as we came into the common room. I saw Cheyenne was seated at a table with Reaper. I blew kisses to the guys as I headed for the table. Ink pulled out my chair and scooted me close to it.

"Baby, what can I get you to drink?"

"I'll take whatever flavored water or tea they have." The guys made sure to stock those for us ladies along with the alcohol and sodas.

"Cheyenne, Reaper, anything I can get you?"

"Nope, we're good," Reaper answered him. As he went to get our drinks. Chey leaned over to ask me.

"How excited was Annie when you called her?"

"She was thrilled. She's already talking about having another niece or nephew. Although, Reaper, she told us this morning, since you won't bring Cheyenne and her niece or nephew to her, she's going to invade the compound soon."

He groaned. "God, she just saw her last week. I swear she'd only be happy if she could see her every damn day. She needs a hobby."

"Or a man," Cheyenne suggested.

Reaper looked horrified. "A man! Hell, no. That's all we need. Can you imagine the kind of man it would take to handle her crazy ass? Nope. Don't put that out in the universe," he warned her.

I couldn't hold in the giggle he produced with his look of horror. By this time, Ink had returned and heard what we were talking about. He looked almost as horrified as Reaper and was shaking his head no.

Lash and Ratchet came over to join us. They sat down. "What're you four talking about over here?" Lash asked.

"Annie. We think she needs a man," Cheyenne happily told him. Lash spit out the drink of beer he'd just taken and looked at her aghast.

"Are you kidding me? Please, say you're joking. No way does she need a man."

He said it so loud it brought the others over to us.

Maniac asked, "Who needs a man?"

"Annie does," Cheyenne explained.

I almost fell out of my chair laughing at their looks and exclamations of horror. I knew the real reason for it. None of them thought there was a man good enough for Annie. She was like a big sister to all of them. She was a mother hen to the whole club.

After they started to settle down, Reaper nudged Ink. I knew it was showtime. Ink got up to face his brothers. They all got quiet.

"I asked Reaper to call you all here tonight. We have some news."

"News? Did you find out something about the apartment?" Tinker asked.

"No, it's not that. Although I was hoping Reaper or maybe Spawn might have some news about that for us. No, it's actually good news." He took my hand and smiled down at me for a moment. "Alisse and I had a little scare this morning and we had to have some tests done to check out a suspicion. Luckily, we did, thanks to Reaper and Dillon. Alisse and I will be joining Reaper and Chey as parents. She's pregnant," he told them proudly.

No one seemed to be that shocked at the news. All of them were smiling, congratulating us and some were teasing us about taking so long to get that way. I was kissed and hugged by all of them, even the prospects. When Dillon hugged me, I whispered in his ear thank you for going to get the tests for me. He blushed and shook his head like it was fine, but I knew he had been embarrassed. Ink had told me what he said.

When they all settled down, Reaper cleared his throat. "I do have some news about the fire. I hate to bring that up, but Ink did ask and I know he's going to ask again in a minute. Carlton called right before I came over here. The fire chief and his arson investigator were able this afternoon to go through Alisse's apartment. They determined that it wasn't an electrical wiring issue. I'm sorry to say Alisse, it was intentional. They found evidence of accelerant being poured in the living room and your bedroom. Now, we have to figure out who did it. The only likely culprits are the Soldiers of Corruption. I asked Spawn earlier today to search the cameras around town for any sign of men on bikes. I know they wouldn't be bold enough to wear their colors, but any group of riders could be them."

My heart sank, hearing this news. I had hoped it was an accident, even though deep down I had my doubts. I couldn't think of anyone other than the Soldiers who would do something like this.

"What did they hope to accomplish by burning down an empty apartment? It makes no sense," I told them.

"It doesn't make sense to me either, honey, but since when do they do anything we expect? You know what this means. The ladies have to still go nowhere without an escort. I suggest as much as possible none of us go anywhere without at least one other member or a prospect with us. No use giving them an easy target. Ladies, I can't let you go back to work more days than you already do. I'm sorry. It's for everyone's protection. Besides, now that you're both pregnant, you need to get your rest. Growing babies is hard work."

"It is. Luckily, I do have something to keep me busy on my off days." I told them.

"What's that?" Crusher asked.

I glanced at Ink. He didn't even know this. I'd done it today while I waited for him to get home from work.

"I'm going to be working on some of my nursing classes. I called the college and spoke to them. There's a lot of them I can take online, the theory courses anyway. Later, I can do the clinicals. I can start as early as in two weeks. As soon as they get me enrolled and set up with financial aid and stuff."

"Oh, Alisse, I'm so happy for you! I know how much you've wanted to do that." Cheyenne told me.

"Babe, I'm thrilled you can start. Just make sure you don't push yourself too much and take too many classes at once. You still need to rest. As for financial aid, I can pay for the classes. There's no need for you to have them do that." Ink said, after he gave me a kiss.

"I won't push too much. And no, you won't pay. I can do it. Most people take out loans and then repay them. I won't have to worry about doing that until after I finish. I'm also applying for a few grants and scholarships they told me about." I saw he was about to argue with me. However, he didn't get the chance. Instead, Reaper interrupted us.

"Alisse, I have a proposal for you. Seeing how Lash is our medic, he's not always available and sometimes, more than one of us gets hurt and needs attention. I think it would be a good idea if the club had a backup medically trained person to call. With you becoming an RN, you could be that person. Cheyenne knows enough to help as a medical assistant, but she's told me there's a lot she doesn't know. How about the club pay for your schooling? You can repay us by providing medical care to us, and hell the kids when they start coming and getting into things. I know Lash would love the help sometimes. It would leave him more time to help at our other businesses."

I stared at Reaper, not knowing what to say. I couldn't deny I was tempted by the offer. But could I really do enough even over the next forty years to cover the cost? It wasn't like they got hurt all the time or that it was major when they did, that I'd seen so far. Mainly it was Tinker and whoever helped him at their home restoration business, Iron's Rehab. They got cuts and stuff on a regular basis, but most only needed to be cleaned and bandaged.

"That sounds like a good idea to me. Alisse, I could use the help and I've wanted to be able to help Tinker out more on the restoration projects. I stick around here in case someone needs me. And I can teach you stuff too, so when you get to your time to learn it in school, you already have a jump on it. Stitching up wounds comes to mind," Lash said, tempting me to say yes.

The rest of the guys were all chiming in, putting in their two cents worth on how much they liked the idea. I gazed at Reaper. Finally, I said the only thing I could. "Doesn't this have to be voted on by everyone in church?" I knew enough from Ink to know that things like large money expenditures, they usually decided and voted on as a club.

"Yeah, we usually do," he agreed. He looked around the table at everyone standing there. "Everyone in favor of the club paying for Alisse's RN degree, raise your hands." I saw hands pop up without hesitation. I laughed to see Cheyenne raising hers even though she didn't have a say. "Anyone not in favor, raise your hands." All of them dropped. Not a single one was in the air.

"It's unanimous. The club is paying for your classes. Don't argue, because you won't win. If you do, I'm going to have Ink take you home, tie you to the bed and wear you out until you say yes," Reaper said, with a wink and a smirk.

As hard as I tried, I couldn't stop the blush that covered my cheeks. The guys all made catcalls as Ink growled in my ear how much he wanted me to argue. I wisely decided not to. Not that I didn't want Ink to tie me up and fuck me until I couldn't say no. In fact, that sounded amazing to me. I just didn't feel like arguing. I was touched that they wanted to do this for me.

"Thank you everyone, I'll gladly accept your gift."

We hung out for a while longer before Ink called it a night and we headed home. I saw that Reaper was hustling Cheyenne out of the clubhouse. It was time for the single guys to have some fun. Even if it was in the middle of the week, I knew some women from town or the bunnies would come in soon. I didn't need that sight. JoJo had avoided me since our confrontation, but I knew someday we'd be face-to-face again. I hoped she'd keep her mouth shut and her hands off Ink. Pregnant or not, I'd beat her ass.

Ink: Chapter 13

It was Saturday, and I came into the shop to do the tattoo I'd rescheduled from Wednesday, when I took Alisse to get her blood test. I'd been floating on air since we found out we were going to have a baby. I couldn't wait until her visit with Dr. Hoover next week to find out when she was due.

I was getting my wish. A baby by the end of the year. The Punishers were starting out right, two babies within a year. We had some catching up to do in order to try and compete with our friends, the Archangel's Warriors. Luckily, we had the Pagan Souls down in Cherokee doing the same. Maybe we should have a bet with them on which of our chapters would have the most old ladies and babies by the end of next year. That could be fun. Bikers loved to bet on shit, it didn't matter what it was. Regardless of the other clubs, me and Reaper's kids would grow up with each other. I was hoping they'd be best friends if they were both boys or girls. If not, then hopefully whichever one of us had a son, he'd watch over the other's daughter.

I'd told everyone at Punisher's Mark our good news. They were excited and happy for us. I'd finished up my tattoo and a very satisfied customer had just left, when I heard the front door chime announcing someone had entered. Whoever it was, the others could handle them.

I was going home to Alisse. I had plans for us today. In fact, I had Dante picking her up at home and bringing her to the shop, so we could leave from here. I made sure to drive a cage this morning rather than my bike for this reason.

I'd finished wiping down my workstation when Greta's head popped around the doorway.

"Ink, hate to disturb you. I know you're headed out with Alisse when she gets here, but there's a woman at the front desk, who is insisting she has to talk to you. I have no idea who she is. She refused to give me a name. I've never seen her before," she whispered to me, as if she was afraid the unknown woman could hear her.

Rolling my eyes, I gestured for Greta to go before me. This wouldn't be the first time someone insisted on seeing one of us, despite not having an appointment. I'd send whoever this woman was on her way. If she was expecting me to tattoo her today. I wasn't going to do it. If she pissed me off enough, I might decline her business altogether. Coming to my place and insisting on speaking to me and refusing to give a name, didn't endear her to me.

I followed Greta back to the front desk. As we rounded the corner, I saw a blonde with her back to me. I started talking to her, even as I was gazing out the window to see if Dante had arrived yet with Alisse. "I understand you wanted to talk to me. I'm not doing tats today. If you want one, you'll have to make an appointment or see if one of the other artists can do it."

"Austin, I'm not here to get a tattoo. I'm here to talk

to you." An overly sweet voice answered back. I knew that voice. I swung around to glare at Amber.

"What the hell are you doing here, Amber? And I've told you, my name is Ink, don't forget it. I thought you and I had our last discussion at the bar the other night. I have nothing to say to you now or in the future. You need to leave."

"I think we do. I have something I need to tell you."

At that moment, the door chimed again and I held in my groan of despair, as I saw Alisse entering with Dante. Just my shitty luck. Why couldn't it have been five minutes later? I didn't want Alisse to have to see her cousin. It would only upset her and that was the last thing she needed. The smile of welcome on her face fell away to be replaced with one of annoyance when she spotted her cousin standing there.

I saw the smirk Amber gave her. If I hit women, I'd knock that look off her face. Bitch. I went around her to get to Alisse. I tugged her into my arms and kissed her. I made damn sure it was a kiss that showed nothing but love and possession. She was flushed when I stopped and her pupils were dilated with passion.

I turned to face Amber with an arm still around Alisse. I knew seeing her cousin was hard for Alisse. At least Amber wasn't smirking anymore. She was glaring at Alisse with what looked like hatred in her eyes.

"Like I said, we have nothing to talk about. Now, I'm out of there. Me and my fiancée have a date." I told her. As we turned to leave, Amber spoke again.

"I need to tell you about your son."

I felt Alisse go rigid. Panic washed over her face. She kept her back to Amber. She started to shake and her pallor went pale. I saw the shock on Greta's face. I needed to get this out of the front of the shop. No one needed to hear this shit, especially any customers who might walk in.

"Greta, show Amber to my room. I'll be there in a minute." As Greta took Amber back to my workspace, I checked on my woman. She wasn't looking any better. "Baby, I want you to sit here and try to relax. I'll go talk to her then get rid of her as fast as I can. We both know, she's full of shit. She's just wanting to cause trouble. It's what Amber does best." I reminded her.

"Austin, I can't sit here and do that. As much as it hurts, I have to hear what she says. If you have a son, then we both need to know, so we can decide what to do."

As much as it hurt and angered me to do it, I knew she was right. She deserved to hear what her cousin had to say. Sitting here and worrying would do more harm in the long run, I was sure.

"Okay, but let me do the talking. You sit and listen. Let's go find out what game she's playing." At her nod, I led her back to my room. When Greta saw us enter, she left. I guess she didn't trust Amber to be alone in my room. She gave me and Alisse a worried look. I saw her squeeze Alisse's hand as she passed us.

I shut the door. Amber scowled. "What is she doing

in here? I need to talk to you alone."

"You don't tell me what to do, Amber. I want Alisse to hear what you have to say, so there are no misunderstandings later. I'm not a patient man, so get on with it. Tell me what bullshit story you have come up with then get the fuck out."

"It's not bullshit. I thought it was time to tell you that you have a son. He's ten years old. His name is Christopher," she told me in a rush.

"Amber, you might have a kid, but there's no way he's mine. I don't know what kind of game you're playing."

"It's not a game and he's yours. I never told you, because I knew you were pissed at me and wouldn't want to believe he was yours. However, I've come to realize that's not fair to you and he deserves to know his father. I made a mistake all those years ago. I still love you and I want you back. I want us to be the family we should've been all along."

I saw the look of horror that came over Alisse's face. Then she looked sick, like she might puke. I went to her and stood in front of her, so Amber couldn't see her. Her pain wasn't for Amber's enjoyment. I reached back to grasp her hand behind my back as I turned back to Amber. Her fingers were cold. I gave them a gentle, reassuring squeeze.

"Let's get something straight. You and I will never be together as a family. I'm marrying Alisse. We're going to have a family. As for the boy, if he even exists, I doubt very much he's mine. If I recall, you and I hadn't had sex for over a month before I found out about your boy toys. I doubt they were the only ones you were screwing behind my back. Also, I used a condom every time we did have sex. Why don't you tell the guys who might be his actual dad that he exists?"

She came to her feet and rushed over with her phone in her hand. She held it up. There was a picture of a boy. I estimated him to be about ten years old. He had dark hair like me, but other than that, I couldn't see a resemblance. His eyes were blue like hers and his skin was much paler than my olive skin. My friends she'd slept with had dark hair too. This didn't prove anything.

"Nice looking kid, but that doesn't prove he's mine. When was he born?"

"November twenty-fifth, two thousand and two."

We'd broken up in April of that year. I made a production of taking out my phones and bringing up the calendar for that year. I did a quick count. I knew that was more than forty weeks after we had sex for the last time. It was forty-two weeks or more. I knew from Alisse that pregnancies were calculated in four-week months making it ten months to be at full term to have a baby. To be mine, he'd have to have been conceived at the beginning of February. His birthdate meant he was conceived at the end of February.

"Try again. In order for him to be mine, he'd have to have been born a few weeks earlier than that, Amber." I happily shot down her date.

"I was overdue. It's common with first babies. I was forty-two weeks pregnant when he was born."

My patience was at an end. I didn't have time for this bullshit. She gave me a pleading look. I could see her face trying to look sincere, but her eyes told me she was lying her ass off. Something I'd never noticed when we were together. If I had, I could've saved myself a lot of shit back then.

"If he's Ink's then you won't care if he has a paternity test done. That'll prove once and for all if you're telling the truth, Amber. We can arrange for it to be done at a doctor's office or even a clinic. They're done all the time. It only takes a couple of weeks to get the results." Alisse told her. I looked back at her. I saw the agony there, but her voice sounded steady. I knew the only way we'd ever be free of Amber was to prove she was a lying cunt. I glanced back at Amber in time to see the anger that flashed in her eyes before her face got a pretend look of hurt on it.

"Why would I lie? I explained why I never told Austin about his son. I made a stupid mistake. I was young. I've grown up. I think our son deserves to know his father and to have his family be together in one house. He'll be growing into a young man soon and he'll need his father to guide him."

"It would be best for the boy if he did have both parents." I said, seeing hope on her face at my words. "However, if he's mine, he'll have both parents and a stepmother. There's no way in hell, you and I will ever be together again, Amber. I love Alisse. She's the only woman I have ever loved or will ever love. We're having our own baby soon. If Christopher is mine by some miracle, then he'll be a big brother. He'll like it when he spends time with us. I'll make sure he knows how to treat women and kids and all the other things it takes to be a real man. When do you want to do the test? I want it done sooner rather than later."

"I-I-I don't know," she stuttered. I could tell this wasn't going like she hoped. Good. Lying bitch set my teeth on edge. "I'll have to check my schedule. But he's so anxious to meet his dad. Can't you come see him and then we can work on getting the test done?" She batted her lashes at me. Honestly, was she not catching a clue? Nothing she could do or say would get her easy with me.

"Nope. I don't want to get his hopes up and then dash them when he finds out you lied. We'll do a formal meet once I know for sure he's mine. Give me your number. I'll call when we get the test setup."

She didn't give it to me at first, but after seeing I wasn't going to back down, she reluctantly rattled off her phone number. I saved it in my phone. She was staring holes through me, trying to see Alisse. Having that out of the way, I brought this farce to an end.

"Well, I'd like to say it's been nice, but it hasn't. I need you to leave and don't ever come to my place of work again. I'll call you when I have a date and time. Alisse and I have somewhere to be." I ushered her to the door. Alisse stayed behind as I showed Amber to the front and out the door.

As I watched her walk away, talking animatedly on her phone, I told Greta, "She isn't allowed back here. If she returns, call the cops on her ass."

"Okay, I can do that. Ink, what in the world was she

CIARA ST JAMES

spouting off about?"

"Nothing that's true. Forget it. I need to get Alisse out of here."

I hurried back to my room. I found her slumped over in her chair. Her head was hanging down. I dropped my knees, so I could see her face. The tears on her cheeks gutted me. All this pain due to me being a dumbass when I was young and sleeping with the wrong fucking woman. I had to make this right. I wouldn't lose her over this. I couldn't. If I did, I'd never be happy and would live a miserable existence. Alisse and our children were as important as breathing to me.

"Why is she doing this, Austin? Why? Does she hate us so much, she wants to try and destroy us? Why did she come back now? What if she's not lying? God, I can't imagine having to co-parent with her. We'll never be free of her."

Her sobs were making her shake. All I could do was gather her in my arms and rock her as I tried to calm her down. It took a while to accomplish. By the time she was calmer, I could tell she was exhausted. Our plans for the day would have to wait.

Taking her hand, I helped her to her feet and we walked out of my room. She didn't even say goodbye to Greta as we passed, that's how upset she was. I could see the sympathy on Greta's face as she saw the state Alisse was in. I didn't waste time getting her tucked into the car and headed home. She stared unseeingly out the car window the whole way there.

Once we got home, She went straight to our room

and curled up on the bed. "I just want to sleep for a while. Will you hold me?" She asked softly.

"Of course, I'll hold you, baby." I kicked off my boots, took off my cut then got on the bed with her and held her against me. It took a little while for her to fall asleep. As soon as she did and I knew she was fully out, I eased out of bed and went downstairs to make my call. He answered on my second ring.

"Hey brother, what's up?"

"Spawn, I need to know if you ever got a chance to check into that Amber woman I told you about. The one who we heard at the bar supposedly was pregnant when we broke up?"

"The one that's Alisse's cousin. Shit, no I got caught up in some stuff for Reaper then the fire at Alisse's place. Damn, I'll get right on it. Sorry, man. Anything I should know?"

"Yeah, the bitch came into the shop today while Alisse was there. She wanted to talk. Said a bunch of shit about me having a ten-year-old son named Christopher. She claims he was born on November twenty-fifth of two thousand and two. I broke up with her mid-April of that year. In order for him to be mine, he'd have to have been born ten and a half months after our last time having sex, which was in earlier February of that year. I want to know everything you can find out. If you can find any medical records that show how far along she was when she gave birth, that would be great. I've told her that I want us to do a paternity test as soon as possible."

"Fuck, that's messed up. What did she say to the paternity test?"

"She wasn't thrilled by it. She wants to introduce me to him then we can do the test later. I have no idea what game she's playing, but I want it to stop. She has Alisse bawling. I need proof that I'm not the kid's father. I don't want Alisse to have a single doubt about it. Plus, I want to keep that cunt out of our lives. If by some miracle he is mine, I'll do everything in my power to make sure he never sees his mother again. I can only imagine what his life has been like, living with her narcissistic ass."

"I'll get right on it. Let me know if you need anything else. You worry about taking care of your woman. This stress isn't good for her and the baby. Damn, this shit on top of her apartment. She can't catch a break. Later, brother."

"Later."

After hanging up, I wandered the house, while I let her sleep. I was thinking about what I could do to get Amber out of our lives and to remove the threat to my woman from the Soldiers of Corruption. I'd do anything to make those things happen.

Alisse ended up sleeping for two hours. When she got up, I noticed she seemed to be lethargic and not interested in doing anything, not even talking or watching television. Later, when it got closer to evening time, I made her rest in the living room where I could keep an eye on her, while I fixed dinner. She picked at her food, even though I offered to make her something else. She said she wasn't hungry.

We made it an early night. She and I tried to watch a movie in bed, but I noticed she wasn't paying attention. It wasn't too late when she slipped off to sleep again. I finished the movie then turned out the lights. My gut was churning with worry over how this was affecting her. If she didn't snap out of it by tomorrow, I'd have to take steps to have someone else talk to her. Maybe she'd open up to Cheyenne. I knew one thing, she wasn't going to stop eating. Her and our baby needed that nutrition. I'd make sure they were both healthy.

The next couple of days passed with no news from Spawn. I was trying to be patient, but it was hard. Alisse was still acting despondent. Her eating wasn't a whole lot better, although she was trying. I got Cheyenne to talk to her the day after the whole disastrous meeting with Amber. I don't know what was said, but Cheyenne afterward told me that she would keep working on Alisse. I could see she was worried for her friend.

It was Tuesday and I was at the shop again. I had an almost full day of appointments. I was working hard to concentrate on the tattoos I was doing. I didn't want to fuck them up and have someone leave my place upset and dissatisfied. Start having that happen and our reputation would be ruined.

I heard the front door chime. A few seconds later, I heard raised voices coming from the front desk. I hurried out to see what was going on. While Greta could handle herself in most situations, I didn't want her to run the risk of getting hurt. I saw Chuck rushing up the hall behind me. He was headed to protect his wife. I beat him there. When I saw who was arguing with Greta, I had to clench my fists to keep from punching something. Or better yet, someone.

Standing there with her hands on her hips, giving Greta attitude and glaring was Amber. Only she wasn't alone. Next to her, looking scared was her son. I recognized him from his photo. He was trying to cower behind her. When she caught sight of me, she gave me one of her insincere pleading looks.

"Austin, I mean Ink, tell this woman that I'm allowed to see you. She's trying to tell me I have to leave or she'll call the police. You wouldn't let her do that, would you?"

"Amber, I not only would let her do it in a heartbeat, but I'm also the one who told her to do it, if you ever showed your face here again. What are you doing here? I told you to never come back." I was careful not to swear. I might be a biker, but I even tried to clean my language up around young kids.

A scowl came over her face. On the surface, she appeared to be a beautiful woman. Many men would be fooled by her. Hell, I had been. However, once you knew the real her, it was easy to see beneath the outer beauty to the ugliness inside. That made her an ugly bitch in my eyes.

"Why would you tell her that? Ink, I wanted to introduce you to your son, without Alisse here to muck things up. I can tell she doesn't want you to have anything to do with your son. He's been anxious to meet you. Haven't you, Christopher?" She didn't even bother to look at him when she spoke to him.

Christopher met my eyes for a second then looked back down at the floor. I could tell he was uncomfortable and scared. Wanting to get him out of the danger zone, I looked at Greta. Chuck was standing with her, his arm around her, glaring at Amber. She was too stupid to run. Chuck was an intimidating bastard who made grown men shake in their shoes.

"Greta, would you mind taking Christopher in the back and getting him something to drink? I think we still have some of those cookies and the cake that Cheyenne sent over. Close the door so it's quieter. He can watch television there."

"Certainly, Ink." She went over to the boy and crouched down. She smiled at him. "Hi, Christopher, I'm Greta. Why don't we go see what goodies we can find and watch a show? Do you like cartoons?"

He didn't answer her, but he did give her a shy nod. She held out her hand, which he took. She quickly took him down the hallway. Chuck went with her. I glared at Amber when I knew they were out of sight. I stormed closer to her, but not close enough she could touch me.

"That was a dirty, fucked-up thing to do, Amber. What's your goddamn problem? I told you that I didn't want to meet him unless we had the paternity test done and it shows he's my son. Why would you do that to him?"

"Au- Ink, he wanted to meet you. I told him you're his father. I don't need the test to tell me that. He acts just like you. His hair is like yours. Yes, he's paler than you and has my blue eyes, but he's your son."

"The hair doesn't mean shit and neither does his mannerisms. I'm not going to let you do this shit. You're not foisting someone else's kid off on me. You're not breaking up me and Alisse. What brought you to town? All these years and you just happen to show up and want to talk to me, after I meet and fall in love with your cousin. I don't buy it's a coincidence, Amber. Who told you I was seeing her?"

She shifted her eyes to the left for a second, which told me she was about to lie to me.

"I didn't know you and my cousin were together. I told you, he's getting older and asking about his dad. He needs a male presence in his life. I realized how cruel it was to keep us apart. I can't help if Alisse is threatened by me being the mother of your son. Honestly, I don't see how the two of you got together to begin with. You've never had trouble getting women. Why would you settle for her?"

Her implied insult that her cousin didn't have anything to attract me, pissed me off. I sneered at her as I answered her question.

"What does she have? Let me see. She's honest, kind, giving, beautiful, sexy, smart and the best woman I've ever met to name a few reasons. I'm the lucky one to have her be with me. She's the only quality woman I've ever been with. I know she wouldn't lie to me. She wouldn't do things like cheat, try to say a kid was mine when he wasn't and she's beyond loyal. She's the perfect package and I love her like she loves me. We're going to be married soon. And our first baby is on the way. Life is looking pretty damn good for me right now. I'm not letting a bitch like you mess with us."

She took a step back at the venom in my voice. She could tell I was pissed. I had my hands clenched at my sides, so I didn't give into the urge to wrap them around her throat and choke the life out of her. I saw her swallow nervously.

"I-I just wanted you to meet him," she whispered. Her self-assurance from earlier seemed to be gone. Good.

"I'm going to go talk to the boy. I'll explain the best I can that we don't know if I'm his dad or not. You go stand outside and wait on us to get done. I don't want you in here causing trouble with my employees or customers."

"I won't leave him alone. He's a child."

"Then take him and go."

Seeing that I was serious and not going to back down, she huffed then said bitchily. "Fine, go get him and we'll go. But I'm warning you, I'm not going to give up, just because my little cousin is with you. She's not going to get the life I should've had."

This woman was nuts. That's all there was to it. I think she honestly thought I'd leave Alisse for her. Even if Christopher was my son, that would never happen. I laughed.

"Amber, even if he is my son, there's no way in hell

you'll ever be my old lady. That spot belongs to Alisse and it always will. Nothing you can say or do will change that. However, I'm warning you, if he is mine, then I'll do everything in my power to make sure he's living with us, not you. He's had enough of your shit. I can't imagine how big of a shitty mother you are. I know you're one, because you only care about yourself."

Her gasp of outrage followed me down the hall. I found him watching television, happily munching on cookies. He looked up when I came in. I went over to him. I hunkered down by his knee. He looked apprehensive.

"Christopher, your mom is waiting for you. It's time to go."

He hesitated then stood up to take the hand I held out to him. "Are you really my dad?" He asked in a whisper. I hated to see him looking almost hopeful. I told him the truth, or at least as much as a ten-year-old should know.

"Honestly, I don't know. There's a slight chance I am. I've asked your mom to have a test done so we can find out. I want you to know, if you are, I'll be in your life. There's no way I'll walk away from you if you are. However, it won't ever be me living with you and your mom. I have a wife. Her name is Alisse. You'd like her."

His shoulders dropped in disappointment. I gave him a hug as we got to the front to find she'd listened to me and was outside on the sidewalk. I walked him out to her. She didn't say a word to him. She glared at me as she grabbed his hand and jerked him to her, as she took off down the street. He gazed back at me with a pitiful look as she practically dragged him. I wanted so badly to go after him and take him home with me. Even if he wasn't my son, he didn't deserve to be treated like she treated him. I could only imagine what it was like at home for the boy.

Back inside, Greta was back at the desk. She frowned. "That poor kid. What an awful woman. To tell him that you're his dad, when you don't know if it's true is dirty."

"It is. If she comes back again, don't even engage her, just pick up the phone and call the cops. If he's with her, maybe he'll get lucky and they'll take him away from her. Thanks for taking care of him. He didn't need to hear that crap. Hey, let me know when my next appointment gets here. As soon as he's done, I'm going home." I needed to be face-to-face with Alisse when I told her what happened. As much as I didn't want to stress her more, she needed to know.

"I was going to tell you that he called and canceled, but I got sidetracked by her walking in the door. You're free to go."

"Excellent. I'll see you and the rest of the gang tomorrow. Good night."

She told me good night. I went to find Chuck and tell him the same. At the moment, the others were busy with clients or off for the day. That was why no one else had come out to see what was going on. I hated the idea of any of the customers hearing what was said, but it couldn't be helped. I could only hope they didn't think I was denying a son's existence and think I was a deadbeat dad.

Alisse: Chapter 14

The past couple of days had been hell for me. I couldn't get over Amber and what she said at the tattoo shop. I was scared to death that her son might be Ink's. If he was, she'd never leave us alone. Thoughts of putting up with her for years, made me sick and killed my appetite. That had Ink worrying about me and the baby. I wanted to reassure him I was fine, but I couldn't lie.

When Ink walked in early from work, I knew something was wrong. Not only in the fact he hadn't texted to say he would be home early, but by the look on his face. He looked super pissed off. I lowered my legs to the floor. I had them up on the couch. I leaned forward as he came into the living room. He'd taken off his cut and boots. I knew he would've left them by the door.

"What's wrong? What happened?" I asked him anxiously.

He came over and sat down beside me. Without saying a word, he gripped me behind my neck and dragged me forward to claim my mouth. His kiss was one full of passion. His tongue teased inside my mouth and his teeth nipped at my lips. I returned his kiss. When he was finally done, he sank back in the cushions, taking me with him. He arms snuggly around me. I was almost sitting on his lap.

"I missed you."

"I missed you too, Austin. What happened? I can tell you're upset."

He sighed and closed his eyes for a moment before opening them to stare into my eyes. His hand rubbed gently along my cheek.

"I had visitors at the shop today."

"Who?" I wondered what kind of visitors would put this look on his face.

"It was Amber and her son. She thought she could do better I guess, if she waylaid me there and without you around. She was trying to guilt me into seeing the boy."

"Oh my God, how could she do that to him? He had to have been so scared. She told him then that you're his dad?"

He nodded. "Yeah, she did. She was arguing with Greta out front and I heard them. I had Greta take him in the back so I could talk to the bitch. She's unbelievable. I think she thinks I'm going to be dumb enough to believe her without the test and that I'll leave you for her and him. I told her that's never happening and that you're going to be my wife and we're having a baby soon. She wasn't happy when I made her leave."

"Did you talk to him?"

"I did. I told him that we didn't know if he was mine or not, but if he is, he'll be in our lives. Also, I told him that it would never be with me living with them. I told him about you. It was so damn hard to see her drag him off like he was a piece of meat. That poor kid having to live with her. It makes me sick to think about it. Even if he isn't mine, I wanted to snatch him away from her and bring him home to you. You're a real mother, baby," he growled.

"Honey, I can only imagine how much it must have taken for you not to lay hands on her. Did she say anything else about why she's here now, telling you about him?"

"She claims it was just time. I don't believe it. Someone told her about us. I know it. She can't stand to think you got something she had and lost. She's a jealous narcissist. I need to call Spawn and see if his search has come up with anything. It's been a few days. He should know something by now." He'd told me about asking Spawn to look into Amber's claim. Well at least we knew the boy was real and her son. The rest was still to be determined. I prayed he might have good news for us.

He took his phone out of his pocket and pulled up Spawn's number. As he sat it on his knee, I saw it was on speaker. When Spawn answered it after a couple rings, Ink was quick to tell him he was on speaker with me.

"Hey, Alisse, how're you feeling, babe? The little one giving you fits yet? Are you puking up your guts?" Spawn asked, in a teasing tone. I couldn't help but smile.

"I'm doing okay. No fits yet and luckily, no puking. I have been nauseated a couple of times though. Thanks for asking."

"Hey, any time. I bet I know what you're calling about. You want to know what I've found out about Amber. I was going to call you tonight once I heard back from a source. However, since you called, here goes. She does have a kid and it is a son named Christopher. He was born on the date she told you. I'm waiting to get access into her medical files. I was hoping my contact could get that for us. The birth certificate has the father listed as unknown. She's lived with him in various places all over the DC and Virginia areas. There's been several men in and out of her life since you kicked her ass to the curb. None of them have lasted more than a year. Back when she was with you, Ink, I found some really old emails she deleted that showed she was communicating and likely screwing at least three guys in addition to you. That's all I have right now. I wish it was more." The regret that he didn't have more, was evident in his voice.

"That's more than we had, brother. Thank you. I know the son is real. She brought him into the shop today, trying to ambush me, I think. She's telling him I am his father."

Spawn swore, "Sonofabitch! What's her malfunction?"

"She's an uncaring bitch. I sent them on their way after telling him we don't know if I am his dad or not. Shit, I need you to see if there has been any Child Protective Services calls made on her," Ink told him.

"You think she's abusive?" Spawn asked. I could hear him typing in the background.

"I think if she's not, she's at least neglectful."

"I'll get right on it. I hate the idea of any kid having to live with a woman like that. Nothing in her emails and social media accounts make me think she's mom material. It all revolves around her. Hell, there's no mention of him or pictures. It's like he's a dirty secret. Does the rest of the family know about him, Alisse?"

"I don't know if her parents do. If they do, they never mentioned him to me or my mom. No one has ever said anything about it."

"Are you close enough to her mom and dad to ask?" Spawn asked.

"I mean, they're my aunt and uncle. I wouldn't say we're close, but I could ask. I'd like to ask around and see if anyone else in the family knows about him. And I have the perfect way to do that all in one day, as a matter of fact," I told them happily.

Ink gave me a quizzical look. "How?"

"I just got an email invite. It looks like the family is all getting together this weekend here in Bristol. It's over at a cousin's house. They were asking for as many family members to come as possible. It's been a while since they've all gotten together. I was kind of shocked that they invited me. I didn't think I'm their favorite person. You know how they treated me growing up, Ink. I was never good enough because of my mixed race."

"What the fuck? That's bullshit, Alisse. Someone needs to kick their asses," Spawn snarled.

"I'm with you on that, brother. I wish she was kidding. Babe, I think this is perfect. However, I don't want to chance her staying away if she knows we're coming. Don't tell them we're coming and we'll surprise them."

"You want to come with me?"

"Hell yeah, you can't think I'll let you go alone to face those assholes. I'll be there to make sure they keep a civil tongue in their heads. We can hit up as many as possible all in one day."

I couldn't help but kiss him. While I did, Spawn rambled in the background.

"You two go do that then let me know what you find out. I'll keep working on my contact to get in those medical files. Also, I'll check into CPS. Is there anything else I can do?"

I had to let him up for air, to respond. "No, that's it. Thanks," Ink said hoarsely.

Spawn chuckled. "I'll let you two go. It sounds like you have better things to do. Later." He hung up fast.

"I think he's thinking we're doing more than kissing," I told Ink with a laugh.

He chuckled. "I bet he does. Which I think is an excellent idea. We have time until dinner. Wanna go up and get naked with me?"

"I always want to get naked with you, Austin." I wiggled out of his arms then stood up. I glanced down at him and grinned. "I'll race you."

I took off running for the stairs. He yelled at me. "Slow down, you might fall."

I did slow down a tad, but that was more so I could strip off my clothes and leave them in a trail to our bedroom. He came charging after me like a hungry bull. I shivered in anticipation of what my man would do to me. Whatever it was, I knew that I'd love it. I let thoughts of Amber melt away.

He caught me in the hall on the way to our bedroom. He scooped me up in his strong arms and carried me the rest of the way. Inside it, he took me to the bed and laid me down on it like I was precious and easily broken. I knew he didn't want to do anything to hurt me or the baby, but I'd already told him that he wouldn't.

He watched me as he stripped off the rest of my clothes then his. My mouth watered and my hands itched to touch him. I wanted to taste his cock in my mouth. To taste the tang of his cum on my tongue. I wanted to lick, kiss, and feel his whole body. He was so damn different from me and I loved those differences. He was hard where I was soft. No one could ever accuse me of being a gym rat. I hated to exercise, even if I knew it was good for me. That was one reason why I'd never have a skinny ass or thighs with a gap between them. Although, looking at the desire on his face, I didn't think that bothered my man a bit. He seemed to love my curves and softness. In fact, he told me he did all the time.

Before he could get started on his exploration, which would mean mine never got started, I held up a hand to halt him. He gave me a concerned look. "You change your mind, baby?"

"No, I didn't change my mind. I want to explore you first. I know if I don't, I'll never get the chance. You'll drive me insane and wring me out dry. All I'll be able to do after you're done is take a nap."

"Are you complaining?"

"Never. Love how you make me feel. I want to give you as much as you give me, that's all."

He eased down on the bed next to me. "Baby, you give me as much, if not more than I give you. Your surrender makes me so damn happy. But if you want to play, I'm all yours." He laid back on his back and tucked his hands underneath his head. He wiggled his eyebrows suggestively at me, which made me laugh.

I got up on my knees and straddled him. I knew if I rubbed my pussy on him, he would feel how wet he already had me. It only took a look or hearing his voice to have me wet and ready. I'd never had a man make me feel or react like he did.

I gave him a deep kiss filled with lots of tongue before I broke away from his all too tempting lips to move further down. I nibbled and licked down the column of his neck, pausing to suck on his beating pulse. It jumped in my mouth. While my mouth was busy, my hands weren't idle. I was caressing all over the hard muscles of his chest and arms. He was like a living breathing sculpture.

After I was done with his pounding pulse, I made

my way slowly down to his nipples. They were tight nubs, which only beckoned me to suck and tease them like he did mine. I was rewarded with a groan. I inched my hips further down his body. This caused my pussy to run across his hard cock. He lifted his hips off the bed, to press it into me. I was the one to moan in delight this time. Before I could forget my intentions, I slid onto his thighs.

From there, I was able to reach his ribs and flat, ripped stomach. I traced his tattoos with the tip of my tongue then sucked and scraped my nails along his abs. They contracted. This broke him. His hands landed on my shoulders. He pressed me further south. I laughed, knowing what he wanted. I took my time in giving it to him.

Eventually, I took pity on him and got to the place he was dying to have my mouth. I took him in my hand and pumped up and down his hard length, smearing the precum on the head of his cock on the shaft. I looked up at him. His eyes were burning with desire and he was watching my every move.

"Suck it or I'll take over, baby. Either I get your mouth on me or that pussy. Which is it?" He growled.

I tsked him. "Patience, honey. Wouldn't you rather have both?" I stuck out my tongue and swiped it across the head of his cock. I lapped up the rest of the precum smeared there. His hips pushed upward, pushing his cock into my mouth. Taking pity on him, because I knew if I didn't, he'd take over like he threatened, I sucked him deeper into my mouth.

As I worked him inside, I made sure to lick and suck while fisting the base and stroking up and down on the part of him I couldn't get into my mouth. I worked hard to take as much of him as I could. When he hit the back of my throat, I fought the gag reflex, so I could take him deeper and have him cut off my air.

He was moaning and thrusting up. Knowing he had to be getting close, because I could taste even more of his essence, I hummed. This made him swear. Before I could do more, he grabbed me underneath my arms and jerked me up and off of him. He flung me over onto my back and he came up over top of me. His face looked almost feral.

"My turn," he growled.

He started at my mouth and worked his way down my body, mimicking what I had done to him. By the time he made it to my pussy, I was almost in tears, I was so ready to come. That first swipe of his tongue made me explode. While I orgasmed, he didn't stop teasing me. His lips, teeth, tongue, and fingers worked me, so that I went from one orgasm to the next without hardly a break in between. It wasn't until he'd wrung three of them out of me, that he wiped his face on my thighs and sat up.

His face was tight with arousal as he gripped my hips then flipped me over on my stomach. "I want you on your hands and knees, Alisse. I need to go hard and deep," he ordered me gruffly. I scrambled to get my ass in the air with my knees under me and my chest bent to the mattress. His hands grabbed onto my hips then I felt the head of his cock probe my entrance once, before he slammed his cock into me in one long, fast thrust. I cried out at how good it felt.

He stretched me, making me take all of him. My inner swollen muscles resisted him, but it was futile. He buried his cock to the hilt inside of me. I barely had time to take a breath, before he was pulling back and the pounding began. I lost count of how long he fucked me. All I knew was he made me come more than once or twice and I was about to lose my mind.

Just as I thought I couldn't take any more or come again, he proved me wrong. He slid a wet finger in my ass as he increased his speed. I came screaming and shaking. Wetness gushed from me, soaking the bed. He thrust a couple more times then held himself deep and came. I could feel his warm cum filling me as his cock jerked inside. It seemed to take him forever to stop coming and me to regain my senses.

I saw the reluctance on his face when he had to remove his softening cock from me. I rolled onto my side and he laid down behind me, so he could spoon me. His lips grazed my back and shoulder. "I love you, Alisse."

"I love you too, Austin. Give me a little bit and I'll go clean up."

"Don't bother cleaning up. I'm just going to get you dirty again. Why don't you take a nap? I'll wake you up when it's time."

I didn't argue. Nothing would make me happier than to have him make love to me again. My eyes drooped and I did what he suggested. I took a nap.

By the time Saturday rolled around and we were on our way to my cousin's house for the family get together, we had more information on Amber. It seemed that she had CPS called on her twice. Once for accusations of neglect and the other time due to her son going to school with bruises on him. Both times, the cases were dismissed as being investigated and that they were unsubstantiated. I was willing to bet she'd used her charms on whomever investigated her. It was men who investigated her in both cases. She had a way with men.

In addition to that, Spawn had gotten into her medical records. I didn't want to ask how he did it or what kind of people he knew to help him do it. I was just glad he was on our side. According to the records, she was forty-one weeks when he was born. It didn't absolutely absolve Ink as the father. He promised that he'd make her take the paternity test, so we would know for sure. A part of me almost wished he was his son, so we could take him away from her. She was the last woman who should be a mother.

I was nervous as we drove into the driveway of my cousin's house. It was actually my mom's cousin's house, my second cousin. This was where they often had family parties when I was younger. They had the space for a lot of people.

I made sure I had my property cut on. I wasn't going to hide the fact I was claimed by a biker. As if they could have any doubt looking at him. His cut and everything about him declared loud and clear he was one. He looked dangerous, sexy and delicious. It was all I could do to keep my hands off him.

He smirked at me as he helped me out of the car. He knew what I was thinking, as evidenced by him leaning down to whisper in my ear, "Later, baby. I'll take care of you as soon as we can blow this place."

"Promise?" I whispered back as I smiled at him.

"Promise. Now, let's go face the lions and show them who's boss. I brought a fucking whip if we need it." I couldn't help the laugh that came pouring out of me. I was still laughing when the door was answered and I saw my second cousin. She looked shocked to see me. She recovered quickly and pasted on a fake ass smile.

"O-oh Alisse, I didn't know you were coming. Welcome," she said, as she stepped back and let us in the door. I sailed in like I owned the place. My days of feeling inferior to them was over. Ink had shown me that I was worth more than all of them.

"Hello, Cousin Cora. I'm sorry, my reply must've gotten lost. You know how social media is. I hope we're not going to make the numbers off."

She didn't answer me at first. She was too busy eye fucking my man. He was looking bored. Cora was in her sixties, but she wasn't dead. I saw the appreciation and desire in her eyes as she gazed at Ink. I even saw her lick her lips. I fought not to laugh or call her out on her behavior.

Shaking off her trance, she finally answered me. "Of course you won't. Who is this with you? Have we met?" I could tell she was trying to remember where they might have met. Ink didn't look that different other than the facial hair and the hair cut was different. He had a few more lines on his face and more tattoos.

"Oh, this is Ink. He's my fiancé. Ink, this is my mom's cousin, Cora."

He didn't hold out his hand, but he did give her a tiny smile and chin lift. "Hello, I'm excited to meet more of Alisse's family on this side of her family. She's told me so much about all of you. This invitation came at the right time."

I could tell by the look on Cora's face, she didn't know how to take his words. While he sounded calm and polite, she knew that they hadn't been all that nice to me growing up. She was wondering if I left that tidbit out or not.

"Well, it's a pleasure to meet you, Ink. What an unusual name." She was leading us further into the house, where we could hear voices coming from. We entered the large kitchen living room combo she had, to find a sea of people standing and sitting in there. They were talking, drinking and some were snacking on foods she had sitting out. One thing I could say for her, Cora knew how to be a hostess. No one left her house hungry or thirsty.

Everyone grew quiet and stood there staring at me and Ink. He was giving them a steely eyed look as he scanned the crowd. I saw more than one guy look away.

The women were staring at him like he was on the menu. I wanted to slap every damn one of them and tell them hands off, he's mine.

"Everyone, look who decided to come, Alisse. And she brought her fiancé with her, Ink." Cora told all of them.

They murmured greetings or just gave us nods. Cora turned back to us. "So, you were going to tell me how you got your unusual name. Can I get you a drink?"

"I'll take a soda," I replied.

"I'll have a beer if you have any. Nothing light, that's for pussies," Ink told her.

She scrambled to get our drinks out of the nearest cooler. After she handed them to us, and Ink opened mine for me, he answered her question.

"Ink is my road name. I'm a member of the Iron Punishers MC here in Bristol." He turned so she could see the back of his cut for a moment. "They call me Ink because I'm an ink slinger."

"Ink slinger?" Cora asked with a frown. It was obvious that she wasn't familiar with that term.

"Yeah, I'm a tattoo artist. I run Punisher's Mark in town."

"Really. How did you and Alisse meet? The last I heard she was working in a doctor's office as some kind of assistant."

"I work for Dr. Simpson as a medical assistant."

"But she's going back to school to get her RN. We met because her and her best friend took care of one of my club brothers. However, it wasn't until later that I found out we'd met years ago, when we were younger."

"You did? When?"

Others had eased their way over and were listening to the conversation. "Hell, I bet we've met before. You look familiar to me. I used to date Amber when I was younger." He dropped the bomb on them. I saw several of them look around as if looking for her. They had a queasy look on their faces. Ah-ha, she was here. I scanned the room for her.

"You dated Amber?" Cora said in surprise.

"Yeah, when I was young and dumb. Thank God I found out what kind of woman she was and we broke up. That was the best decision of my life. It allowed me to find this wonderful woman." He hugged me close. The look he gave me was full of love.

"In fact, I love her so damn much we're getting married soon and are expecting our first baby. It looks like we'll be adding a little color to the family. Looks like it's needed." This remark had the others scowling. My family looked like a meeting of the white supremacists. They were mainly pale with light hair and light eyes. Someone like me stood out. Ink did as well with his dark swarthy olive complexion. I wasn't naïve enough to think all of them were racists, but history had shown me a lot of them were not very tolerant.

Cora gave a nervous laugh, like she thought he was

joking.

Another cousin, his name was Johnny, came up to us.

"Alisse, you do know that Amber is here, don't you?"

"I figured she might be, but what does that matter?"

"Do you think it's a good idea to come here with her ex-boyfriend, who cheated on her? Are you trying to rub it in her face?"

"Cheated on her? I didn't cheat on her. We broke up because she cheated on me. I found out she was sleeping with a couple of buddies of mine. Alisse told me what Amber told all of you. I shouldn't be surprised that she'd lie about it." Ink said with a tone of reprimand in his voice.

Murmurs broke out as others began to talk about this revelation. I was about to say something when I saw Amber enter the room. She caught sight of Ink and I saw her go pale. She turned like she was going to run, but I didn't let her.

"Amber, why don't you join us? Ink was just telling everyone how he knows you."

She glared at me as she reluctantly headed over to us. With so many eyes on her, she couldn't leave without raising more questions in the minds of our family. Some were giving her funny looks.

She stood there looking very uncomfortable, which was making me feel good. Everyone had eyes on her and us. They were waiting to see what happened next.

I knew what I wanted to happen. I wanted to punch her in the mouth and pull all her hair out for messing with our lives. Her move with her son the other day was a slimy one. Thinking of that, I asked all innocently, "Where's Christopher?"

If possible, she got paler. I saw my aunt and uncle, her parents, come in through the glass slider. They were frowning at all the family members standing around.

"Who's Christopher? I didn't know you were dating anyone, Amber," Johnny asked.

"Oh, he's not her boyfriend. He's her ten-year-old son. Haven't you met him?" I asked, spitefully. I was enjoying the hell out of this. I could see she was squirming like a worm on a hook. The death glares she was giving me would have worried a lesser person. I wasn't worried. I could take anything this bitch wanted to dish out.

"Her son? She doesn't have a son," I heard someone exclaim.

"Oh, yes she does. I've met him. He's ten," Ink told them.

Her parents made it to her side. I looked at them. "Why didn't you ever mention that you had a grandson? I would've thought you'd want to show him off to the family. Did any of you know about him?" I scanned the room. By the looks on their faces, none of them had. They were frowning and looking pissed off.

"Alisse, I don't think this is the place to be having this discussion," my aunt Margaret said with a frown.

"Why not? She came to my work and in front of my employees tried to say her son is mine. She didn't give a shit who heard it, even if it was my customers. Who in the hell waits ten years to tell someone they're a father, if it's true? In her case, I highly doubt it is. She's lucky if she can figure out which guy is his father with how many she was sleeping with when she was with me." Ink added.

"That's enough! You need to leave," my uncle Leon said, puffing out his chest. He stood several inches shorter than Ink and he had a huge pot belly. Ink gave him a bored look.

"Leon, you didn't scare me when I dated Amber and you sure as hell don't scare me now. I got what I wanted. Proof that she didn't even tell her family she had a kid. So where is he while you're here, Amber? Home alone? You've had CPS called once for neglect and once for bruises. I can promise you one thing, if by some chance he is my son, I'll make sure he comes to live with me and Alisse. Where he can have a real mother and family. Not one where he's hidden away like a dirty secret."

Uncle Leon bellowed in anger and took a swing at Ink. I didn't know what the hell he was thinking. Ink easily grabbed his fist and squeezed it, making Leon whimper in pain. Once he saw he had been subdued, he let go of him. He turned to me.

"Let's go, babe. I've seen and heard enough."

I proudly took his hand and walked out. The chatter behind us was loud. I caught some of what was being said. Most were shocked and upset that they didn't know about Christopher. Deep down, I hoped this would clue some of them in on the fact she was not the perfect angel they all thought she was. I rode with Ink to town so we could do some shopping with a smile on my face.

"The only reason you want that other set is the price. I know you like this one more. You can't keep your eyes or hands off it. We're getting this. I can afford it and it'll stand up to being used for multiple babies, not just this one."

She tried to deny it, but I didn't listen. She was still dragging her feet when we went to checkout. When the cashier gave me the total, I took out my wallet.

"Can you split that total across two cards?" Alisse asked, as she got in her purse.

"No, she can't. I'm paying for it. You paid for the stuff at the other store, it's my turn."

"Ink, this is way more expensive than the stuff at that store. I want to pay for my share," she objected.

I handed over my card. The cashier wisely ran it. Alisse fumed. I knew I'd hear more about this once we were alone. After confirming the delivery address and date, we left. I was right. As soon as we were alone in the car, she jumped me about it.

"Austin, why didn't you let me help pay for that. I'm not penniless."

"I know you're not. However, you're mine and I take care of my family. This is for our first child. It might seem chauvinistic and old fashioned to you, but I intend to be the provider for our family. That doesn't mean you can't work. I know you want that and I'm all for it. However, your money will be for you to use on other things, the fun stuff, if you want. If you want to save it all, then we can do that. I make more than enough with the club to cover all of our expenses. Baby, don't get mad. It's what I need to do to make me happy. Can you let me have this?"

She scanned my face then I heard her sigh. "Okay, I guess I can give you that, but don't think this means you're going to get your way every time, Austin Kavanagh. I love you, but I'm not going to let you walk all over me and boss me around."

I leaned over to nibble on her earlobe and to whisper, "Unless it's in the bedroom. In that case, you'll let me do the bossing, won't you?" She flushed a pretty pink color and smiled.

I held her hand all the way home. The club was going to have a cookout tonight. She and Cheyenne had made several things yesterday for it. We knew we weren't going to be at her family gathering for a long time today. In addition to what they made, Annie was providing some other food as well. She insisted she was coming to the compound to see both her future nieces and nephews.

I saw everyone was there, by the look of the bikes when we came through the gate. I even saw Annie's car.

"Baby, do you need to go to the house first, or are you ready to stop here?"

"We can stop here. I told Chey to have Dante or Dillon to get the food I made from the fridge while we were gone. Unless you need something from the house."

"No, I don't. Do you need to take a nap? We've been busy today."

"I'm fine. If I get tired, I'll tell you and go lie down. Right now, I feel good. Park the car and let's go see what these nuts are up too. You know if they go too long without supervision, they get out of hand."

I couldn't help but laugh because it was true. They did get out of hand sometimes. I parked then helped her out of the car. It was a sunny day, although the temperatures weren't out of the forties. I heard voices coming from inside the clubhouse, so that's where we went.

Inside, the noise was louder. Everyone seemed to be in good spirits. We barely made it inside, before Cheyenne and Annie whisked Alisse away and over to a table in the corner. I let them go. I went up to the bar to get her a drink and myself one. Reaper came over to me.

"How did the family thing go?"

"It went over like a lead balloon. We didn't get a chance to ask them who knew, but it worked out. We told them about her cheating on me and then how she has a son. You could tell by the looks on their faces, they had no idea he existed, except for her parents. Her dad, Leon, tried to hit me, but I stopped that shit. I also let them know that she'd had CPS called on her ass twice already. We left her with a lot of explaining to do. They didn't look like happy people. It was fantastic," I chuckled. Reaper was laughing.

Dante handed me Alisse's drink. "I'll be right back, Reaper." I walked over to give it to her.

She smiled and said, "Thank you, baby."

"You're welcome. Do you need anything else?" She shook her head no. "Okay, if you do or if you need me, I'll be at the bar with some of the guys." I gave her a kiss which had Annie saying aww.

Back at the bar, Reaper and I got to discussing more about our day. Some of my other brothers came and went. Overall, it was just a nice way for us all to de-stress and catch up with each other. Throughout the afternoon, I checked in with her numerous times. I was happy to see her looking relaxed and smiling. The shit with Amber and her apartment had been weighing on her.

Annie, Chey and her were having a good time. I had no idea what all they were talking about, but whatever it was, they were laughing more than anything. As it got closer to evening, the food was heated up then brought out to be served buffet style on long tables we'd set up for this very reason. I went to get Alisse and took her with me to the line.

I elbowed Shadow in line. "Hey, try to leave some of that for us. I know you love fried chicken, but damn you have a whole plate."

"Don't worry, there's plenty. Annie told me she brought a whole extra pan, just for me. It's still in the back. This is just my first run through."

"Shadow, how in the world can you and the rest of the guys eat like you do and not be as big as a house? It really pisses me off, I have to tell you. Guys have all the luck. I look at food and five pounds automatically go to my ass," Alisse told him in disgust.

"Baby, don't you worry about that ass. I love that ass and if you want to give me more to love, I'll take it." I growled as I looked at her ass and squeezed one cheek with my hand.

"I know you do. There's something seriously wrong with you," she shot back at me with a grin.

"I hate to risk being killed by my brother, but I have to agree, Alisse. Your ass is spectacular. You don't have anything to worry about, babe," Crusher popped in to say. He grinned at her and winked.

I bared my teeth and growled. He busted out laughing and held up his hands, as if in surrender. Alisse smacked me on the arm. "Down, Cujo, he's only messing with you. It does a woman good to hear men appreciate their ass. You have to say it, because you're mine. He doesn't. Although, now I might be creeped out worrying about Crusher ogling my ass."

This made him laugh and wiggle his eyebrows at her. I couldn't hold onto my glower. I laughed along with him and the others standing close to us. From there, they all got into telling me what they liked about my old lady. By the time we made it through the food line, I was ready to kill and bury all of them. I couldn't wait until the rest of them found old ladies. I'd gladly give them payback.

I made sure she ate enough. I was glad to see her appetite seemed to be better today. I wanted to hear what Dr. Hoover had to say about her weight when we saw him this week. We were supposed to do it last week, then it got canceled because he got called out for an emergency at the hospital. I was hoping that wouldn't happen again.

After the eating was over with, Reaper and the others got out their instruments to play for us. I didn't play, but I did sing. I sang for Alisse once. I was feeling like tonight would be another singing night for me. The urge to tell her through songs how much she meant to me was burning inside of me.

Even though I told her every day I loved her and I did it more than once a day and I tried to do things for her to show that love, I wanted to do more. I never wanted her to doubt for a second that I loved her more than anyone else in the world and that she was the center of my universe, just like our children would be. Yeah, I loved my club and I always would. I'd have my brothers' backs like they would have mine, but I lived for her.

The three ladies were front and center when the music started. The three bunnies had joined us, since it was late and the single guys would soon be looking for company. Tonight, there were no hang around from town. The bunnies stuck closer to the back of the room. I think they knew not to sit with our women. I didn't want JoJo opening her mouth tonight. She'd laid low ever since Alisse had faced off with her, but I still didn't trust her. I knew if she ran her mouth, Annie would put her in her place and maybe on her ass.

We ran through a selection of heavy metal, classic rock, and new country songs. We were at it for over an hour and everyone was still begging us for more. Finally, after two hours, we called it quits. I went to the bar to grab something to sooth my parched throat. Singing took a lot out of you. I picked up the bottle of beer Dillon had handed me. As I turned to go join Alisse, JoJo popped up in my face. I held in my groan of annoyance.

"Excuse me," I told her. I tried to move around her, but she shifted.

"JoJo, get the hell out of the way. I want to go sit down."

"Ahh, come on Ink. Surely, your old lady isn't so insecure you can't even speak to another woman. What's she going to do about all those women who come into the shop to have you do their tattoos? They bare their asses, breasts, and even more to you. Is she going to tell you that you can't ink any women?" She asked, with a sneer on her face.

"No, I'm not. I know that Ink is nothing but a professional. I only take objection to it when bitches like you, won't take no for an answer. I think he told you to get out of his way. I suggest you move that skinny ass of yours," came the reply.

I glanced over my shoulder at Alisse. She was staring at JoJo. I gave her a smile. She winked at me.

"You're not the boss around here, Alisse. Just because you're Ink's old lady for now, doesn't mean you can tell everyone else what to do. All I'm doing is talking to him. Why don't you chill? Afraid I'll get him in bed again? After all, I do know what he likes." She smirked and licked her lips suggestively.

Alisse laughed. "Yeah, you know what he likes but I know what he loves. I think he'll be in my bed for the rest of his life. He knows quality over whatever you were, convenience, maybe just an available hole to stick his cock in. Whatever it was, he's done with that and you. In your case, I don't like you, so don't talk to him. Baby, are you ready to join the others and chat more before leaving? Or would you rather we go home and do those things you love?" She was the one to smirk then lick her lips this time. She reached out to take my arm. I couldn't wipe the grin off my face.

JoJo gave a shriek of outrage. She lunged at Alisse. I went to get between them. No way was I going to let her hurt my pregnant woman. Only I was too slow. Alisse struck like a snake. Her leg came up and straight out in front of her. She snapped off a front kick that was full of power. It took JoJo in the gut and had her flying back several feet, before she doubled over, holding her stomach and crying out in pain.

"You bitch!"

"You slut. Stay the hell away from Ink and me. I won't tell you again, JoJo." This time she wasn't smiling. She had a deadly look in her eyes.

Ignoring a swearing and crying JoJo, we went back to the table where the other ladies were sitting with some of my brothers. Mayhem whistled.

"Damn, remind me not to piss you off, Alisse. That was a wicked front kick. Where did you learn that and what else can you do?" I heard the admiration in his tone. As our enforcer, he loved anything to do with fighting. MMA being a favorite one of his.

"I took a lot of classes growing up and my dad taught me a lot. I used to back home workout with an amateur MMA fighter. She and I would spar as well as a few of the guys she worked with. It was fun."

"Shit, don't let her and Capone's Mackenzie get together," Ratchet said.

"Who are they?"

"Capone is one of the Archangel's Warriors down in Dublin Falls, Tennessee. His old lady, Mackenzie, was an amateur MMA fighter who was set to go pro until they met," I explained.

"Are you talking about Mackenzie Mathews by any chance?" Alisse asked excitedly.

"Yeah, that was her name. Why? Do you know her?"

"I don't know, know her, but I sure know of her. She's a great fighter. I loved to watch her matches. In fact, I went to several just to see her fight in person. I can't believe she's married to one of your friends."

"Well shit, we need to get them to come here or us go down there so you can meet her. She's nice as hell. She gives Capone a run for his money for sure. Should've seen him trying to tame her," Tinker chuckled.

"Giving you guys a hard time is what you need. Otherwise, your heads get too big. I can't wait to see who brings you guys to your knees and tames your asses," Cheyenne chimed in with Annie cheering her on.

"Oh no, you're not cursing me with that fate. I'm

going to stay single for the rest of my life," Tinker told her.

"Keep thinking that. It'll happen and I can't wait," Annie told him.

Out of the corner of my eye, I watched JoJo leave the clubhouse all hunched over and holding onto her stomach. She glared over at our group. I'd be keeping an eye on her. She might be the kind to try and get revenge. If she laid a hand on Alisse, I'd end the bitch. We spent another half hour talking to the gang, before I decided it was time to go home. I'd seen Alisse stifle two yawns.

I stood up. "Baby, it's time for us to head home. You're tired. It's been a long day. I think we need to relax before we go to sleep."

She didn't object. We said our goodbyes then headed to the house. I hadn't lied. It was time to rest and she was tired. And I had the perfect thing to make her relax and sleep like a baby. I found after a few orgasms, she went out like a light. I wanted a taste of my Whirlwind.

When we got to our bedroom, I suggested to her. "Why don't you go and have a nice soak in the tub. It'll help you relax."

"Will you join me?"

"Not tonight. I think you should be alone. If I get in with you, I won't be able to keep my hands off you."

"I don't mind."

"I have other plans for you. After you get out of the tub. Only don't rush. You need to soak for at least fifteen minutes."

"What are you up to Austin?"

"You'll see." I told her as I winked. I helped her undress and ran the tub for her. I held onto her hand as she stepped into it. She had a bath bomb in there and I didn't want her to fall. Once she was seated and I gave her a kiss, I went back to the guest bathroom. I took the world's fastest shower then hurried to get the room ready. I was in the mood to play tonight. I took out one of the toys we'd been playing with for the past few weeks. Tonight was the night to take it to the final step, if she was willing to go there.

I laid back to wait. When I heard her pull the drain on the tub, I went to help her out of the tub. I dried her off then rinsed the tub, so it wouldn't be slick the next time. Gathering her in my arms, I carried her to our bed. I laid her down in the middle. She spread her legs, to let me see the treasure between them. I had to moan at the sight of her pretty pink pussy. It was already starting to get wet and I hadn't even touched her yet.

She ran a finger up her slit then circled her clit. I saw the mischief and desire in her gaze. "See something you like?" She asked me.

"Oh yeah, I see something I love. Why don't you play with that pussy and get it nice and wet? I want to see how you get yourself off, baby." I sat down on the edge of the bed and palmed my cock. It was hard and standing at attention.

She watched me as I leisurely stroked my cock. I watched her as she teased her clit and sank her fingers into her pussy. While the one hand was busy down below, the other was working her breasts. She was tugging hard on her nipples, making them hard pebbles. It was hot as hell to watch her masturbating. Surprisingly, I'd never asked a woman to do it. I knew that this would be something I'd have her do again.

Her fingers were soaked with her cream. I leaned toward her. "Give me a taste." I opened my mouth. She lifted her hand then stuck her wet fingers in my mouth. I sucked and licked them clean and groaned as I did it. She tasted so good, so sweet.

"God, you taste so good, baby. Give me more." For the next several minutes, she took turns pleasuring herself and feeding me her cream. By the time I called a halt to it, I was ready to erupt. If I wanted to get to the main event soon, I couldn't do that. However, there was nothing that said she couldn't get off.

I crawled onto the bed, reaching under my pillow to take out my surprise. She gasped when she saw what it was. We'd been working slowly up in size on her butt plugs. I had been preparing her for us eventually having anal sex. She'd told me she wanted to try it.

This one was the largest we had and we hadn't ever used it. I lubed it up with the lube from the bottle I had. After it was covered, I eased my fingers into her ass to get her ready for it. When I felt I had prepared her enough, I pressed the plug to her puckered hole and pressed it steadily, but slowly inside her tight ass.

She couldn't hold back the moans and cries of pleasure as I worked it into her ass. After I had it fully seated, I laid down between her parted thighs. I raised her ass off the bed and buried my face between those luscious thighs. She moaned as I feasted on her. As I feasted on her, I would periodically stroke the plug in and out of her. It didn't take me long to have her crying out with her first orgasm. I didn't stop there. I pushed her into another one. After the second one, I knew that I couldn't hold out any longer. I had to be inside her.

I got up on my knees and held her off the bed, I pushed inside of her pussy. I moaned as I eased inside. She was so damn wet and tight. Her pussy felt like it was on fire, it was so damn hot. I stroked in and out, over and over, until she was thrown into a third orgasm. I rode it out, gritting my teeth, so I wouldn't come.

As soon as she came down from that high, I withdrew my cock. "I want you on your hands and knees," I told her.

She scrambled to do as I asked. She was breathing heavily. When her ass was in the air and her chest was on the bed, I took the plug out of her ass and threw it aside. I looked at her gaping hole and swore. "Fuck, you look so hot, babe."

"Hurry, Austin, I need you. Put that big cock in my ass and fuck me," she ordered raspily.

She didn't have to tell me twice. Holding her cheeks apart, I placed the head of my cock to her hole and pressed inward. The popping sensation of me passing beyond her sphincter rings made me shudder. She was moaning.

"Are you alright? Is it too much?"

"No, keep going. It burns but it feels good too. Don't stop."

Taking her at her word, I kept working my cock into her ass. It was the tightest thing I'd ever been in. I was fighting not to spill my load right there. Soon I was buried to the hilt, I gave her a few moments to adjust then I drew back before thrusting back. Her body shook and she clamped down on me.

In no time, I was riding her ass harder and faster. I pressed deep as I could go every time I stroked inward. I was close, so damn close. Reaching around, I tweaked her clit. She stiffened then tightened down on my cock and screamed as she came. Her cream gushed from her to soak us both. I thrust a few more times then held myself still as I came in her ass. I swear I saw stars as her tight ass milked my cock for every drop of cum it could get.

After we both were done coming and could think, I slowly withdrew then laid down on the bed, pulling her into my arms. She turned her head so she could look over her shoulder. She gave me a kiss. When we broke apart, she smiled.

"You can do that again, anytime you want. I might be walking funny tomorrow, but it was so worth it. Damn, that was hot."

"Tell me about it. I thought I was going to lose my load as soon as I got in your ass, babe. I see we have something else to put on our do again list."

She laughed and nodded. Once we'd rested some, I

got her up and took her to the shower, so we could clean ourselves off, then it was back to bed. She snuggled into me. I held her as she drifted off to sleep after we said we loved each other. I planned to let her get a couple of hours of sleep before I woke her up to have her again. Once was never enough with her.

Alisse: Chapter 16

After the confrontation at Cousin Cora's house last weekend, I figured no one in the family would ever contact me again. I was wrong. Over the last few days, I'd gotten multiple text and DM messages on social media from family members expressing their outrage that Amber had hidden her son from us all.

I knew some of them wanted to find out if Ink was really Christopher's dad or not. Others I thought might actually be honestly concerned. They kept asking how I was doing. One cousin told me how the family had torn Amber a new one for hiding him. They were inclined to believe now that Ink had been the injured party when they broke up, not Amber.

I kept my answers brief without giving them too much more information. They hadn't been that supportive my whole life, so why start now. I wasn't convinced that it was because they suddenly saw the error of their ways. Ink was fine to follow my lead when it came to them. He said we didn't need them, we had a family with the Iron Punishers and by extension, their friends in the other clubs. Some I'd met at Reaper and Cheyenne's wedding, although not all of them.

I was putting all thoughts of my messed-up family and Amber out of my mind today. We were seeing Dr.

Hoover and would find out when I was due. I was excited. I knew that we wouldn't see much on the sonogram, but we should be able to hear a heartbeat at least. I had my fingers crossed.

Sitting on the table in the exam room, I tried not to fidget as we waited. When we checked into the waiting room, I had the pleasure of women staring at my man like he was a steak and they were carnivores looking for their next meal. A few didn't, but those were the ones who seemed to be scared to death of him because of his cut.

I'd been weighed, my vital signs taken and a few questions asked by the medical assistant who checked us in then she left us alone. She stared at Ink as well. To his credit, he appeared to be blind to their interest. Or maybe he was just that good at pretending not to notice.

A brisk knock on the door was followed by it opening and admitting Dr. Hoover. I'd come with Cheyenne to one of her appointments, so I had already met him. I knew as soon as Ink saw him, he wasn't thrilled. Even though I had told him that Dr. Hoover was in his sixties, I had to admit he didn't look his age. He was physically fit and was what a lot of women referred to as a silver fox.

"Hello Alisse, I'm Dr. Hoover." He held out his hand. I shook it. He gave me a quizzical look. "Have we met before?"

"Yes, we have. I came in with my best friend, Cheyenne Grier."

"Oh, yes, now I remember. Well, it's nice to see you

again. And I assume this is dad. Hello." He held out his hand to Ink. I watched as Ink took it and gave it a shake. I could tell he was trying not to break his hand too much. I rolled my eyes.

"This is Ink. He's my fiancé."

"Ink, ah, you're in the same club as Cheyenne's husband. Reaper, right?"

I nodded.

"He was a very intense guy. I see you're going to be the same. So, before we get started, let me cover a few things that might make you feel better. I'm a heterosexual male who has been happily married for thirty-five years. I have five kids and three grandkids. Yes, I look at women's privates all day long, but I can honestly say, I don't see them in a sexual way. If I did, my wife would have killed me long ago. She's a very jealous woman. I will treat Alisse with nothing but respect. Does that cover everything?"

I couldn't help but laugh at the stunned look on Ink's face. After a few moments of silence, Ink answered him.

"Yeah, I think that covers it. You can't blame a guy for worrying when he has a woman as beautiful as Alisse. Anyone who does make a move on her, won't like what I do to them."

Dr. Hoover nodded and smiled. With that out of the way. He got down to business.

"I see here your date of your last period and how far along you think you might be. I got your lab result and visit note from Dr. Simpson. I see she started you on your prenatals which is good. Have you had any issues or concerns?"

"No, I've been tired, but no vomiting. I have been nauseated a few times, but that's all."

"Her appetite hasn't been the best. I'm worried about her losing weight or not getting enough nutrition for her and the baby," Ink interjected.

"Hmm, according to what you put down as your usual weight, it does look like you're a few pounds down. We'll keep an eye on it and if it continues, we'll have to do something about it. Anything else?"

When he saw us both shake our heads, he continued. "Good. So, I'll see you once a month until you get to eight months then we'll go to bi-monthly visits. At the nine-month mark it'll increase to weekly. I expect you're wanting to see if we can hear a heartbeat and figure out your due date. I'll get my tech in here and we'll get you on the sonogram machine."

He stopped out. It wasn't long before a tech came in. This one was a man. I watched Ink give him the eye. In no time, my stomach was covered in gel and he was moving the wand around and clicking away. When he was done, he excused himself to get the doctor. Dr. Hoover came back to do the same check. When he was done, he smiled at me as he turned on the sound of the machine. We could hear the swooshing sound and the heartbeat. I gripped Ink's hand.

"It looks like according to your measurements that you're six and a half weeks along. I only see one sac, so we're not looking at a multiple pregnancy. Based on this and the first day of your last period, I estimate you to be due around November eighth. You'll have a new family member in time for Thanksgiving and Christmas."

Ink held out his hand to him. Dr. Hover shook it. He wiped off my stomach. Ink pulled down my top after he rolled up the waist of my yoga pants.

"I have a packet of things for you at the front desk. They'll give that to you when you make your next appointment. Read it and let me know if you have any questions. My number is in there in case you need to get a hold of me after hours. If you have any issues, please call me. It was a pleasure meeting you and I can't wait to see what this little one will be. Have a great day."

We thanked him. Out in the waiting room, we got the packet then made my next couple of appointments. It would help Ink not to schedule appointments at the shop on the days of mine. He wanted to come to every one of them.

We had one of the last appointments of the day, so Ink was able to do some ink slinging before we went. It was close to dinner time now, so he insisted we go out to eat rather than me or him having to cook at home. He was good about splitting the cooking and other chores with me. To be honest, for such an alpha man, he was rather cool with it.

"Where do you want to go for dinner?"

"Can we go to Annie's? I feel in the mood for her chicken pot pie and chocolate cream pie."

"Babe, we can go anywhere you want. If it'll get you to eat, I'm happy. And you know I love Annie's food, so I'll never say no to her."

"Would you be okay if we saw if anyone else wants to join us? They have to be getting off work and I know your brothers will be starving."

"Great idea. Let me send a text."

I waited as he sent out a text. We sat in the parking lot of the doctor's office for about ten minutes. By then, all of his brothers had responded. To my delight everyone said they could come. We'd even invited the prospects. I felt sorry for them and how many times they missed out on fun. They all agreed to meet at five thirty. Seeing it was still a little away, we took the meandering way through town to get there. When we did, I saw some of the bikes were already here.

Walking in the door, I caught sight of Maniac, Mayhem, Ratchet, Crusher and Tinker in the back. They had several tables placed end to end, so we all could sit together. Annie was talking to them. We didn't waste time joining them and giving our drink orders. Over the next ten minutes or so, the rest of the club trickled in. I hugged Cheyenne when she came in with Reaper. We sat down. Annie was back to visit again.

"So, what did Dr. Hoover say? When are you due? Is there more than one in there?" Chey asked me excitedly. Everyone got quiet to listen to my answers.

"There's only one in there, thank God. According to the measurements, he said the baby should be here around November eighth. I'm six and a half weeks along."

"Dang, we were hoping the baby might hit on our birthday, that would be wild," Dante said.

"When is your birthday?" I asked.

"October twenty-first," Dillon answered.

"I mean it could still happen. Some babies do come early, you know."

"We'll have to place our bets on your due date and what the baby is going to be like we did for Cheyenne," Ratchet chimed in with his usual infectious grin. I rolled my eyes. I swear, they'd bet on anything. This got them all talking about what their bets were. Tinker, as the club treasurer, was the one who kept track of everyone's bets. He opened up something on his phone and jotted down notes.

I exchanged head shakes with Cheyenne and Annie. It was a loud group that placed their orders and chatted about their day. I soaked in the family feel of it all. Ink was right, this way our family and we didn't need any other.

"How is your first class going?" Annie asked me. I started my nursing coursework last week. I decided to start out easy and just do one class to see how much work it was. If it was doable, next time, I'd do more than one at a time.

"It seems to be okay. It's a microbiology course, so there's a lot of terms and stuff, but I took that in high school and I can remember some of it from that. The assignments don't seem to be outrageous, so I think I should be fine."

"You're going to make a wonderful nurse. I know you've wanted to be one since you were a kid."

Anne had known me most of my life. My mom and I came in here a lot when we'd visit family. "Thanks, Annie, I hope so."

Anne got back to work and I got back to enjoying the food and company.

Ink:

As I watched my family laugh around me in the diner, I thought back to last night when we held church.

All of us had gathered around to see if there were any updates, outside of the usual ones on how the businesses were performing. Any difficulties were discussed as a group and solutions were found. That is if the managing member hadn't already taken care of it. This time, I was more interested in finding out if anything had been found on the cameras Spawn was monitoring all over town.

I impatiently drummed my fingers on my thigh. I'd have done it on the table, but Reaper might have killed me. One time someone did that and he almost broke his fingers. Same for clicking a pen over and over. It drove him mad. The last one reported off on their business, now it was time for the other updates.

"I know we have Ink chomping at the bit to find out if we've figured anything out about Alisse's apartment and who set it on fire. So far, the police have no idea. They found nothing at the scene to identify who did it and like Spawn found out, there are no cameras within the complex. Spawn, you tell us what you've been doing." Reaper handed it off to him.

"Okay, you already know that the cars that I saw coming and going turned out to belong to tenants. So there

was nothing there. We suspected it was the Soldiers of Corruption behind it. Even with most of them taken out in the sting operation that Undertaker led, we can't be sure they got everyone and there are still those other cubs who might have members who were really Soldiers. They're working through them to be sure they've got them all. Based on that, I've been watching for groups of bikers riding around town. Anyone that showed more than one biker together or if they were sighted near one of our businesses, I ran their plates to see who they were. So far, it's been a bust. The bikes I've seen and checked out all belong to residents or people just riding through. There have been no groups of riders that I haven't been able to identify."

My gut fell in disappointment. How the hell could we stop worrying, if we couldn't figure out who did it and why? There was no way the Soldiers were going to stay away if there were any of them left. Not when we took out four of their members. They had to suspect we were the cause of it. Yeah, Serpent had been a drugged-out junkie, but that still didn't mean anything. Or it wouldn't have been in our club. Maybe they were dumber than we were. Unless they had decided to hold off doing any more of those until the heat died down. If there were members out there, it would be in their best interest not to come after us. They couldn't have that many of them left. Which reminded me, I wanted to ask Reaper something.

"Shit. Okay, thanks brother. I know you're doing your best. Hey Reaper, is there any news on how Mark is doing?"

His face showed how sad he was. He shook his head. "Nope. He's still in a coma. They say he could wake up any day. Everyone is worried to death. I took Cheyenne up there to see him and to meet Sloan yesterday. Damn woman won't leave his side. He's got a good one there. It's been three weeks. The longer he's in a coma the less likely it is he'll wake up. His ass needs to wake up. I found out while we were there that he's going to be a daddy. Sloan is due just over a week before you and Alisse."

"Man, I wish there was better news, but he's tough. Watch, he'll just open his eyes one of these days and boom, he'll be asking what the hell happened," I tried to reassure him.

"I hope so. Speaking of them, our two friends in the prison, Slither and Ogre. It seems that they're on borrowed time. They're soon going to be the victims of some unfortunate attacks. I wish I could be there to see that but I'll just have to be content with knowing they'll never be able to send anyone after Cheyenne again."

The evil look on Reaper's face made me think of how he got his name. He was the reaper of souls. He'd gotten in contact with some guys we had on the inside, who owed us favors. They were going to get rid of our problem. We might be mainly legit now, but we did have all kinds of contacts.

"Well good fucking riddance, I say. It couldn't happen to two more deserving assholes," Maniac muttered.

"Okay, let's for a minute assume that all of the Soldiers have been rounded up and there's none of them out there. Who else could have a hard-on for Alisse or the club?" Crusher asked. As our sergeant-at-arms, it was his job to assess risk to the club and figure out ways to eliminate it.

"That's the problem. I can't think of anyone the club has had a problem within the last year or more that would be looking for ways to get back at us. And even if there was someone, why would they pick Alisse? Why not go after one of us while we're out riding or one of our businesses? I don't think it has anything to do with the club," Mayhem suggested.

"So, you think it's personal against Alisse. Okay, you heard her, she doesn't know of anyone who would be that mad at her to want to harm her." I reminded him.

"What about her bitch of a cousin, Amber? There doesn't seem to be any love lost between them," Lash suggested.

"Really? You think she did it? I mean she's a bitch and I can see her holding a grudge, but I can't imagine her getting her hands dirty to do something like this," I told them.

"She could've hired someone to do it for her. I say we see if Spawn can find any large expenditures in her banking accounts. It's worth a try. Think about it. She said that shit in the bar to that other biker. It was a couple of nights later that Alisse's apartment burned." Reaper was the one to make this suggestion.

As much as I doubt she did it, I couldn't just not have it checked into. I had to be sure. Luckily, there hadn't been any other incidents, which made me wonder if it was someone just being arsonists and it had nothing to do with Alisse or the club. It was purely a coincidence.

"You're right. I can't discount it as a possibility, no matter how slim of a one it might be. Spawn, will you check into that for us?" I asked him.

He was already typing away on his laptop. He nodded. "I'm on it. It shouldn't take me more than a day or two to get into her accounts and see if she made any large withdrawals. I've been through her texts and emails already and if she hired someone, she spoke to them directly. I could pull her phone records and see if anyone suspicious shows up."

"Do it. The sooner we know the better. If we don't find anything, I want to suggest we ease up the restriction a little. I don't mean we let the ladies go wild on their own, but they don't have to go everywhere with a guard. What do you think?" Reaper asked. He was looking at me when he did it. We were the ones who had the most to lose if someone was out there gunning for us.

"If we don't find anything and nothing new happens within a week, then I'm okay to ease up a little. I know we can't do this indefinitely and it's been months as it is." My gut wasn't liking the idea, but the idea had merit. If I had my way, she'd be wrapped in cotton wool and under guard twenty-four seven.

With nothing new to add, it wasn't long before Reaper called the meeting to an end. I stayed long enough afterward to have one beer with the guys. Alisse had stayed at home to work on her class. She'd told me that I should hang with them for a little bit after church. I assumed that was, so she got enough time to finish up whatever she was working on. She hadn't gotten to work on it today, since this was one of her days at the doctor's office.

Ratchet pounding on the table as he laughed at something, brought me back to the present. Seeing that everyone was done eating, including dessert, I told the others we were going to head home. They all agreed and got up. Reaper settled the bill using the bank card that was attached to the joint club account.

I led a very full and happy Alisse out to the car. I tucked her in and fastened her seatbelt, before I got in and got myself belted in and set out for home. We were only a couple of miles from home when her cell phone rang. I saw her take it out and look at it. She had a confused look on her face.

"Who is it, babe?"

"I don't know. It's not anyone's number I know. It says it's a Virginia prefix. Let me see."

"Hello," she said. A few seconds later I saw her face tighten. Her hand was gripping the phone like she wanted to crush it.

"Who is it?"

She pressed a button then I heard the voice on the other end.

"I mean it, you and Austin had no right to tell anyone anything about Christopher. You're such a jealous bitch, Alisse. You're trying everything you can to make sure you keep me and Austin apart, but it's not going to work. I had him first. He's mine. Why don't you go find someone that's more your type? You know, a loser mongrel."

Amber's hate filled voice was loud in the car. My blood pressure instantly went through the roof, hearing what she was saying to my woman. How dare she call and say shit? I didn't even hesitate.

"Listen you cunt, there is no you and me. There will

never be a you and me. You might have had me first, but that was the biggest mistake of my life. Your goddamn family needed to know what kind of lying whore they have in the family. This way they know not to trust your ass. Don't you ever and I mean ever call my woman and say shit to her, do you understand? Don't call, text, message, hell, don't even send a carrier pigeon. And don't have anyone else in the family do it for you. You don't want me to make you stop this shit, Amber. And since you called, I'll expect you to have Christopher here by the end of the week to have his paternity test done. You have the address and phone number of the place I want to do it. They're the best in the area. One other thing, for the last fucking time, my name is Ink. You have no right to call me Austin," I snarled at her.

There were a couple of heartbeats of silence before she started to whine and plead.

"Ink, I'm sorry. She just made me so upset. The whole family is angry with me. I can't handle that. I don't know why she's trying to turn everyone against me. All I want is what is best for our son. You and I are what's best, you have to see that. It's not good for boys to be from broken homes. Those are the ones who grow up to be criminals."

"If he grows up to be a criminal, it'll be because of you being a shitty mom. Keeping that boy a dirty secret all these years is what's going to make him be a criminal and possibly a serial killer, not the fact that he didn't have a dad in his life."

"That's not fair. I did the best I could. I was on my own raising him."

"Because you fucked up. If you'd been honest from the beginning, your son might have had a father. Admit it, you lied because it suited you and now it doesn't and you're trying to manipulate me into being his father Well, I'm done. We're going to take the damn test and find out the truth."

"I'm busy this week at work. I can't take time off to bring him there for the test. We'll have to find another week to do it. I need at least a month's notice so I can ask for time off."

"You'll be here by Friday or I'll come get him myself and bring him here for the test. Why don't you get our parents to bring him? After all, they've known this whole time you've been hiding him. They're as bad as you are. Goodbye and don't blow me off," I warned her before I nodded to Alisse and she disconnected the call.

I grabbed her hand. "Babe, I want you to block her damn number in your phone. You don't need to hear anything from her again. I'm not sure she'll stop, so this will make sure of it."

"I think she truly thinks she's the wounded party here, Austin. I'm beginning to think she has a mental illness. When I answered, she started the conversation by calling me a whore and asked why I don't just die."

Seething, I got out my phone and called Spawn's number. He answered right away.

"Miss me already?"

"No, but I need you already. Alisse just got an angry call from Amber. She asked her why she didn't just die. I think what we talked about last night might be the right track after all."

"Goddamn bitch. Okay, I'm working on it. I'll let you know as soon as I find something. You take little momma home and get her to relax."

"I will. Thanks."

"No problem. Night."

"Night."

After he hung up, I glanced at her. She was still looking upset. She was frowning. "What did you mean about what you talked about last night being the right track?"

I hadn't told her what we'd talked about in church, other than to share that Undertaker was still in a coma and he was going to be a daddy.

"Can you wait until we get home? I'll tell you there, but I want to do it where you can relax while I explain."

"Okay, I can do that."

I sped up to get us there, so I could tell her what we talked about in regard to Amber. Once that was out of the way, I planned to get her to relax.

Alisse: Chapter 17

I sat on the couch at home waiting for Ink to tell me what was discussed in church last night. Normally, I'd never ask, but in this case it directly involved me and had something to do with Amber. I needed to know what they said.

Her call had upset me, not so much that she called me names. It was her insistence that Ink was hers. What had triggered her after all these years to come back and try to claim him? I knew it was more than the fact her son was getting older and needed a male role model.

Finally, Ink sat down after getting us both a bottle of water. I could tell his mind was preoccupied with Amber. "Tell me what you guys talked about. Just spit it out. I'm tired and I want to go to bed, but I won't be able to do that, until I know what Spawn was referring to."

"Okay, last night in church we pretty much eliminated the Soldiers of Corruption as the ones behind the arson at your apartment. There may be a few stragglers out there, but they'll be busy trying to save their own asses. They won't have time to fuck with us. So that left us with who else either has a grudge against the club or you. Amber's name came up."

"What is Spawn doing?"

"He's checking into her phone records and bank accounts looking for either unusual phone numbers called or large money withdrawals. If she's behind it, I don't see her getting her hands dirty. However, I can see her hiring someone to do the dirty work for her. With her making the reference on the call to you dying, it only reinforced that we might be on the right track in thinking she's behind this."

I didn't know what to say. It was kind of unbelievable that she would want Ink back so badly that she'd go that far. But if she was that upset about us being together, I could see her paying someone. She was never shy about using her parents' wealth to get her what she wanted or to get her out of trouble.

After several uneasy minutes of silence as I mulled the idea over, I responded to Ink's disclosure.

"I could see her paying someone, if she was mad enough. I don't know why you didn't just tell me this last night. If Spawn hadn't said something, would you have told me?"

"Eventually, but right now I think you have enough stress on you. You have this whole fire issue, starting school, working on our wedding, and your newly pregnant. I didn't want to add any more to it. If we'd found out that she was involved, then I would've told you."

I got up to pace. He watched me like a hawk. Anger was building in me. Not so much at Ink or the club for not telling me their suspicions, but about Amber. How dare she come back and try to pick up where they left off? How damn self-centered could you be? She thought the world revolved around her. I cringed thinking what kind of life her son had been living these past ten years. I never saw her as motherly. I was surprised she didn't have an abortion.

"Why do you think she had her son?"

"What do you mean?"

"I mean, she never had any interest in kids. In fact, she would run the other way if any were round. She said they were annoying pests and she was never having any. She doesn't have a single motherly bone in her body. Why have the baby when she got pregnant? Why not get an abortion?"

"I don't have a clue why she didn't."

"Did Spawn by any chance identify the other men she was likely sleeping with when you caught her cheating?"

"I think he did, why?"

"I wonder if there is something about one of them that made her keep him. You know, as a way to use him as leverage later. Maybe she tried that and it didn't work, so she decided to try it with you, hoping you'd let her get out of taking the paternity test."

"Christ, I never thought of that. Let me call Spawn."

He placed the call to Spawn and like last time he put it on speaker.

"Yo, Ink, what's up?"

"I told Alisse what we talked about regarding Amber in church last night. She had a thought. Amber never liked or wanted kids, so why didn't she have an abortion? Alisse wants to know who the other men that you found were likely sleeping with her when I was with her. Is one of them someone she might want to use a kid as leverage against them one day? I know it sounds nuts, but anything is possible. She also thinks that Amber might have tried to extort this other guy and she failed, so she moved on to me."

"Damn, Alisse, babe, I love how your mind works. I do have the names. I didn't dig into them. I was waiting to see whether the paternity test was done and what the results were. I'll add that to my list to look into along with the other stuff. Good idea. I can look into their accounts too. Maybe she's doing this to all the potential baby daddies. From what I saw, she seems to live a lavish lifestyle."

"Oh, she does. Her parents have a lot of money and she's always used it as if it was hers. She's an only child and they spoil her rotten. How many sixteen-year-olds get a Jaguar for their birthday and first car? She rubbed it into all the cousins' faces."

"The more I find out about her, the more I hate the bitch. How in the world can a family produce someone like you and her? It boggles the mind. Okay, I'm going to get back to work. Ink, get her ass to bed and make her rest. You're cooking my nephew or niece in there. You need to be as stress free as possible. I'll talk to you tomorrow."

"Thanks Spawn, I'll try to rest, I promise."

After Spawn hung up, I glanced at Ink. "Is there anything else we need to discuss tonight?"

He shook his head. As I stood up to head to our bedroom, he swooped in and picked me up. He held me bridal style.

"Austin, I can walk."

"I know, but why do it when I can carry you? You're exhausted. I'm putting you in the bath and then afterward, you're going to lay down and let me massage you."

The thought of a massage sounded heavenly. "I can do that. Thank you for taking such good care of me."

"Baby, it's my privilege and right to take care of you and our baby. It always will be. When it comes to your health and safety, I'll always do what will protect you the most." I laid my head on his chest and let him carry me off. I was tired and I needed my bed.

Despite the drama with Amber, I woke up this morning feeling refreshed. I'd slept like the dead after Ink had me soak in the tub and then he gave me a fabulous massage. The man had talented hands in more than one way. When I told him that, he laughed.

I was trying to focus on my schoolwork and the wedding. It was fast approaching and I didn't even have a dress yet. Ink had wanted us to have it by April, which was next month. Luckily, Annie and Chey had helped me with getting decorations and things like that squared away. The cake was being done by a local bakery. The catering was going to be done by Annie. Since my dad was dead, I didn't know who to ask to walk me down the aisle. Ink had suggested Reaper; however, several of the brothers had volunteered, so I put their names in a hat and drew one out. Mayhem was the lucky man. He had appeared to be excited when I asked him. Chey was going to be a matron of honor. Reaper was Ink's best man.

I wished we had a guy like Bull in the Warriors. Apparently, he walked all the old ladies down the aisle who didn't have a dad. I thought that was so cool. Another member, Bear, officiated the weddings. He had been the one to do Cheyenne and Reaper's wedding, so Ink asked if he'd do ours. He and his family would be here for the wedding anyway. He'd kindly agreed. The colors I chose were the blue and purple that you see in a lot of hydrangea flowers. They were bright and striking. They would be paired with cream and a small amount of gold. Cheyenne's dress was an ombre effect of those two colors.

I was perusing wedding gowns locally when I saw someone had put up a wedding dress she was selling. It was on social media. The pictures of it were gorgeous and it happened to be my size. Crossing my fingers, I gave her a call. I lucked out. No one had bought it yet. She lived just a little over an hour away in Asheville, North Carolina and was willing to let me come check it out. I told her I'd get back to her with a date and time.

As soon as I hung up with her, I texted Ink.

Me: I might have found my dress for the wedding. Can we go to Asheville, NC to see it on Friday? The lady is willing to hold it for me until then.

Ink: How did you find it? And yes, we can do that.

Me: She posted online about it. It looks in great shape, my size and the design I like.

Ink: Tell her we'll be there. You pick a time and I'll make sure it happens. Love you.

Me: Love you too.

I called her back and made the appointment for ten o'clock on Friday. She gave me her address. After arranging that, I was too excited to work on more wedding or school stuff. I'd spent hours on it anyway. I decided that I had been cooped up in the house for too long. I needed some fresh air.

Slipping on my tennis shoes, I took my phone and went outside. Since it was only me and Cheyenne as old ladies, and it was a work week, we were the only ones on the compound other than Dante and Dillon. Reaper usually would be, but earlier Chey had told me he was going to be at the microbrewery today.

I headed over to see if Cheyenne would walk with me. She was happy to do it and we were off in no time. We decided we'd walk the main road that ran through the compound. It started at the main gate and ran through the property to the small, hidden back gate. We wanted to check out the storage buildings that the club had on the back of the compound. It would give us a good walk.

It was sunny and in the mid-fifties, so a light jacket was all that we needed to stay warm. After walking for a little while, I started to sweat, so I took it off. I was updating her on the wedding dress I found.

"Do you want to come with me to see the dress on Friday? Ink won't care. I'm going to make him stay outside anyway, because I don't want him to see the dress before the wedding."

"I'd love to. What do you think? Should we ask Annie to go too? She's been doing so much and I know she'd love to see it, if that's the one you end up getting."

"Great idea, I'll call her when we get back and ask."

"Alisse, did you ever think we'd be married or almost married and expecting babies five months ago when we met Reaper and Ratchet?"

"God, no! If you'd told me that, I would've said you were nuts."

"Neither would I. I certainly wouldn't have believed I'd be married to a biker and be the old lady to the president of the MC."

"And I never expected to end up with my teenage crush who is also a biker and my cousin's ex-boyfriend. God, we sound like one of those TV shows where people come on and they say things like my cousin is my daddy and my brother."

We both burst out laughing at that thought. We were at the part of the compound where there were no houses and the storage buildings were off in the distance. I looked around.

"I doubt they'll ever have enough houses to build all the way back here. It seems like such a waste of space. Has Reaper said anything about how they plan to use it?"

"No, but he might have ideas. I haven't asked. They've talked about putting in a pool near the clubhouse and a playground, similar to what they have in Dublin Falls and Hunters Creek."

"I'd love to see how they have their compounds setup. They sound amazing. Maybe we'll get to go see them soon and then we can check them out and come back with suggestions. This will need to be a family and kid friendlier place."

We walked closer to the fence line, because there was a thick patch of daffodils growing there. They were one of the first plants to bloom when spring comes. I pointed them out to Cheyenne and we went over to look at them.

As we're admiring them and debating whether to take any of them home to make a bouquet, the chain-link fence caught my eye. I got closer to it and then froze. It had been cut and then someone had put it back in place. I pushed on it and it was large enough for a person to get through. Who in the hell had done this? I didn't see any of the Punishers allowing this to remain here. They would've had it fixed immediately.

I gazed around us uneasily. I didn't see anyone, but that didn't mean anything.

"Chey, we need to head back. We need to get someone out here to fix this and the compound needs to be searched. Someone has been on the property and they could still be here."

"Oh my God, I hope not. Come on, I'll call Reaper if you call Ink. They'll know what to do."

We turned around and began to walk briskly back. My hands shook as I took out my phone and called Ink. He answered on the third ring.

"Hey, baby, how's your day going?"

"Ink, please listen. Chey and I took a walk on the compound. We headed to the back part of the property. I found a section of fence that's been snipped open. They put it back, so it's hard to see, but I pushed around on it and it's big enough for a person to get through."

"Where are Dante and Dillon?"

"Well, I don't know. We didn't take them with us, since we weren't leaving the compound."

"Goddammit, I want you to call them and tell them where you are so they can come get you. Get your asses to Reaper and Chey's house and have both of them stay there with the two of you. You don't go anywhere. Have them secure all the doors and windows. I'll be there and me and the guys will check out the property. You can tell me when I get there, exactly where this snipped fencing is. Hurry and be careful."

"I will."

I didn't get a chance to say more before he hung up.

He was so rattled he didn't even tell me he loved me.

Chey finished talking to Reaper about the time I was done with Ink.

"He's pissed. We're to go to my house and have the prospects stay with us."

"Sounds like what Ink said. He also said we need to call them and tell them where we are so they can come get us."

"I'll do it," Chey volunteered.

I didn't have long to wait before she got a hold of Dante. She explained what was going on and what we'd been told to do by our old men. I could hear his swearing even though the phone wasn't on speaker. When she hung up, she gave me a rueful look.

"They'll be here as fast as they can. He's getting Dillon. He wants us to continue to head toward the clubhouse."

Both of us were both looking all around us. The back of my neck was itching. Goosebumps erupted all over my arms. There were trees all over on both sides of us. They were great hiding places for men. I strained to see if I could see movement or shadows.

By the time I saw and heard the prospects coming in one of the club's SUVs, I was a bundle of nerves. Every shadow had looked like a man hiding. When they stopped, they didn't waste time jumping out to get us and help us into the car. They had their guns out. I wanted to kick myself for not bringing mine. I had to realize that as secure as the compound is, it's not impenetrable. They raced to Reaper's house. Dante stayed in the car with us, while Dillon cleared the house.

He came out on the porch and signaled to Dante all clear. We were hustled into the house and the door locked. Cheyenne and I sank down on the couch in their living room. I felt shaky. She looked pale and was rubbing her stomach. She was far enough along that you could finally see her tiny stomach.

"Are you feeling okay, Chey?"

"Yeah, I'm just nervous. How about you?"

"Same. We need to remember to take our guns with us whenever we take a walk even inside the fence. Wonder how long it'll take the guys to get back?"

As I said this, I heard the first bike come through the gate. We could look out the window and see the clubhouse. It was Maniac who pulled in. Over the next ten minutes or so, we watched as the rest of the club filtered into the compound. They all went inside the clubhouse. I assumed they'd be having a quick meeting when everyone got here, to discuss what they were going to do.

Dante and Dillon stayed busy texting someone. I resisted texting Ink. I didn't want to distract him. I'd seen him as one of the first ones back. He'd stared hard at the house like he wanted to come over. Waiting for them to come talk to us was driving me batty.

"I'm going to go to the bathroom. I'll be back," I told them. Dante stood up.

"I don't need an escort to the bathroom for God's

sake, Dante."

"Ink and Reaper said we're not to let you out of our sight. If someone were to break in here, I need to be close to you so I can protect you, Alisse. Don't make me disobey an order. Ink will kill me if I do. I'd like to live and get my patch."

Sighing, I gave up and let him follow me to the hall bathroom. I snickered when he checked it out before letting me in. It was a tiny room, there was no place to hide. Closing the door, I got down to business. A few minutes later, I was finished and walking back to the living room to rejoin Chey.

However, instead of joining her on the couch, I went into the kitchen and opened the fridge. It was late afternoon and I had missed lunch. So had Chey. I didn't know about the guys. "Who's hungry?" I asked.

All three of them said they were. Cheyenne joined me and we pulled out the bowl of fruit salad, meats and cheeses to make sandwiches. She had a large salad she'd made at some point. It came out. On top of this, she had a large container of leftover chicken soup she had made. She warmed up the soup while I got the bowls, plates and silverware out.

Dillon and Dante joined us at the island and made their sandwiches. We were all eating when there was a pounding on the door. The guys both got up and went to answer it with their guns drawn. They peeked out the small window in the door then unlocked and opened it. In came Reaper and Ink.

They came straight to us and we were engulfed in

their strong arms. Ink kissed me as if he hadn't seen me in months. I wasn't complaining. I loved when he did that. He let me up for air.

"You gave me a heart attack with that call. No more going anywhere by yourself, even here."

"I understand. Did you find anyone? Do you need me to show you where the fence was cut?"

"The guys are checking. Reaper and I are going to join them. We just wanted to check on you first. We're going to walk the entire fence. There could be more than one place cut. After we get done, we'll come back and get you. Stay here in the house with the prospects. Do what they tell you."

I could see he was on edge and any objections or push back from me would not be tolerated at the moment, so I nodded and let his bossy attitude go.

"Do you have time to eat?"

"We had lunch before you called. We're good. You finish up then put up your feet. You don't need to be up and stressed."

Again, I nodded and let him ramble on. I knew it was only his concern for me and the baby talking. They left a few minutes later to join the others. All we could do now is wait. I hated waiting.

Ink:

As I walked my section of the fence, I seethed. I was so pissed that someone had been able to cut and get into the compound without us knowing it. Admittedly, with a chain-link fence, that was always a risk, but I thought the cameras we had up covered them enough so that we could see every inch of it. I knew realistically, there was no way for Spawn to monitor the cameras twenty-four seven.

Maybe it was time we do what the Warriors did and have the chain-link fence changed out to an actual stone or cement block fence. It would cost a fortune to do it, but the safety of our family would be worth it. I was going to bring it up in church.

It took us several hours to search the entire fence line as well as the clubhouse, the other houses, and the storage buildings. I was exhausted from the tension running through me. We stopped back to speak to the women again to reassure them we'd found the opening. In fact, we found two of them. We'd work on fixing those right away. First, we needed to have church.

I could see this was hard on the women. They both looked tired and were pale. I ordered Alisse to lie down with her feet up. We didn't want them fixing dinner. Reaper gave Chey the same order. By the time we all filed into church, I was ready for the day to end. I was too tired to even open my beer.

"Well, we all know why the hell we're here. Two damn cuts in the fencing. Someone has been on the compound. At both spots there's evidence of footprints. No more than two or three it looks like. The question is, when did they do it and what for? Is someone here to spy on us or to do harm?" Reaper summarized.

"The cuts hadn't had time to rust over, so they're recent, probably in the last few days. If whoever it is wanted to do harm or take someone, why didn't they? Both women have been here alone in their houses. They'd have been easy targets," Crusher said.

"Exactly, why not take them or do harm? Are we off base and this has nothing to do with the threat to Alisse and it's someone totally unrelated, who's looking to steal from us? Maybe they were merely casing the place before they hit us," Tinker suggested.

"It could be. There's no way to know. Spawn has been checking the camera footage on the fence. It may take a while to look at all that footage," Reaper.

"It won't take as long as you think. I've gotten the fence designated in sectors. I programmed the computer to focus on the recordings of those two sectors only. It'll speed things up. Now, it may be a few hours, since we have to go back possibly for more than a few days," Spawn explained.

His abilities on a computer amazed me. He could whip out a computer program off the top of his head and have it doing what he wants in no time.

"So we're stuck doing nothing until you find something. Goddamn, this sucks. How was it only the prospects were here with the ladies?" I asked. I knew that usually Reaper and Spawn were here. Why not today?

"I had to be at the microbrewery. It was shit that I couldn't do remotely," Reaper answered.

"I had to do some work at the storage units, so I worked from there today," Spawn explained.

"Sorry, I'm not saying you should've been here. I guess we've gotten used to thinking that as long as the prospects are here, it's safe because they're behind the fence. Now, we know that's not true. This might not be the time for this, but I'm going to bring it up, so we can all think about it and discuss it in the near future. I think we need to change out the fence to something like they have down in Dublin Falls. It can't be cut. Yes, it can be blown up, but that would attract attention," I recommended.

Murmurs broke out around the table as the guys talked about what I suggested.

"I agree it's worth looking into. The cost is going to be crazy, but if we want to ensure this compound is as secure as it possibly can be, then we have to bite the bullet and pay," Reaper said.

"If we do some of the labor, we could cut costs a little that way," Ratchet suggested.

"I could see if Warriors' construction company could do it and what they'd charge. I'd rather give the business to someone we know than a stranger," Maniac said.

"Let's table this for now. Spawn, let us know if you need help watching any of those recordings. Until we get this done, the women are not to be left alone, not even in their houses. At least one person must be with them. Keep your places locked. Watch for any sign someone has been in the compound. That's it for now. I need to go home and see my pregnant wife. She's worried out of her mind, just like Alisse. Dismissed!" Reaper yelled.

As Reaper stood, he gestured for me to join him.

"I don't know about you, but I'm ready for something to eat and to hold my woman. Let's go to the house. We can bring in takeout."

"Sounds like a plan to me. Lead on."

The walk thankfully was a short one. I was aching to hold Alisse in my arms and make sure her and the baby were alright. I couldn't stop worrying about stress harming them.

Ink: Chapter 18

I anxiously made it to Spawn's house. He was working from there today. He'd been working nonstop since yesterday on those camera feeds to see if he could see anyone. I was about to find out what he found. It was barely dawn, but he'd texted and I came running. I left Alisse asleep with Dante guarding her. He was in the living room. I left her a note, so she'd know where I went and not to come out naked. I'd have to kill Dante if he saw what was mine. I was hoping I'd make it back before she even woke up.

Spawn met me at the door. I saw Reaper behind him in his foyer. I didn't waste time entering.

"Morning." I grunted. I hadn't had my coffee yet.

Reaper walked over and handed me a hot cup. He was holding one too. He knew me.

"Morning. Sorry, I know it's early, but I knew you'd both want to see what I found. Come on," he led us down the hall to his office. I swear every time I saw it, I was amazed at the computers and tech he had in it. It was a duplicate of the one at the clubhouse. He'd set it up that everything could be accessed and saved from either place. Something about a bidirectional feed, yadda yadda, he'd explained one time. I had no idea what the hell he was talking about. All I cared about was that it let the man do what he did best. And that always benefited the club. Luckily, the club had just finished his house. He only had this room, his bedroom and the living room furnished.

He had one of the monitors turned outward toward two chairs in front of his desk. We took a seat there. He sat behind it and clicked on a couple of keys. Suddenly, the screen was filled with video. It was of the fence. Hunkered down was a dark figure. By the size, I assumed it was a man. He was dressed all in black. He even had a mask over his face. All you could see was his intense dark eyes. He was quickly snipping the fence, making one of those openings we'd found. Once it was big enough for him to fit through, he crawled through with a bag and put it back together.

When he stood up and walked off, he was trying to stay low to the ground. He wandered out of the frame. I glanced up at Spawn.

"Is that it? Do we know where he went or when this was?"

"Unfortunately, we don't know where he went. The cameras we have, have all been ones to watch the outer perimeter of the compound, not inside. Before you say anything, I plan to rectify that mistake. This was yesterday morning, around six a.m. Now, look at this."

Another video came up on the screen. This time it was at the second opening. I recognized the tree close to it. The same man in black was exiting the compound. Why he decided to cut another hole, I had no idea, but it explained why we found two of them.

"That was an hour later. Whatever he was here for, it didn't take him long to do it. What I can't understand is why he didn't take Alisse? She would've been home alone. All he had to do was wait for you to leave and walk in. He could've knocked her out or incapacitated her and took her out the fence like he left. This doesn't make any sense. Or if he wanted her dead, he could've done that too."

The thought of her being taken or killed filled me with rage. I wanted to destroy something. I gave Spawn a narrow-eyed glare.

"Hey, don't look at me like that. You know I'm right. I don't want her to get hurt, you know that. It just doesn't fit. Now, we have to try and figure out what he did for that hour. Was he setting up cameras or doing something else? We looked at the whole perimeter of the fence yesterday for cuts. Today we need to check inside the compound for cameras. I suggest we start first with any of the buildings then branch out from there. Keep in mind, wherever he put them, even if they're in trees, he has to be relatively close to get the signal and they have to be in places which would allow him to see people and what's going on."

"I'm gonna get the rest of the guys up. We need to get this done ASAP. Meet you at the clubhouse in half an hour. Know you'll need to check on her. Do that then join us. Thanks Spawn, good job," Reaper told him, before he left the room. I got up and gave Spawn a fist bump.

"Yeah, good job and thanks, brother."

"Anytime. I'll see you at the clubhouse."

I hurried to my bike and headed back to my house. It wasn't a terrible walk, but speed was of the essence for me. When I walked in, Dante jumped to his feet. "Everything okay, Ink?"

"Yeah, I hope so. Hey, I'm going to need you to stay here. We're going to be searching the compound and I don't want her to be alone. If she wants to go outside, you stick by her. I'm not sure how long it'll take. Is she still asleep?"

"I think so. If not, she hasn't come down. I'll go hang outside until you're ready to leave." He didn't wait to go out the door.

I took the steps two at a time so I could get to her faster. Opening the bedroom door, I drank in the sight of her curled up in our bed. She looked so relaxed and beautiful. I got hard just looking at her. How I wish I had time to wake her up the way I had planned. With my mouth on her pussy then my cock in her. It would just have to wait until later.

I sat down on the edge of the bed and ran a hand up her bare leg to her hip. I kneaded her ass. She hummed in pleasure as she slowly opened her eyes. She gave me that sexy smile of hers that I loved.

"Morning, baby," she mumbled.

"Morning, Whirlwind," I leaned down and gave her a kiss. It wasn't a peck on the lips. It was deep, long and filled with tongue. When I got my taste, I sat back up. She whimpered and tried to pull me back down to her.

"I'm sorry, babe. I can't stay. I wanted to come check on you and tell you that I'll be working with the guys. We're going to search the compound for cameras. Spawn found footage of a man breaking in and then leaving. We have no idea what he did while he was here, but he left after an hour. I want you to stick with Dante. He'll be downstairs. If you need to go outside, take him with you. You're not going anywhere alone, do you understand?"

"I understand. Can I help?"

"No, I want you here. Rest, work on some of your schoolwork, or read. Whatever. Hopefully, this won't take long. I figure Reaper will have Dillon stay with Chey. If you want, go visit with her."

"I might do that. We can talk more about the wedding. Okay, I'm going to get my shower then get the day started. Be careful."

"There's nothing to worry about. I love you. Be back soon."

"I love you too," she said as she gave me a kiss this time. It was hard to tear myself away, but I did. I had to get out of there before she got in the shower or I wouldn't be able to leave without having her. She tempted me more than any other women ever had. I was obsessed with her. And I loved every second of it.

On my way out, I signaled for Dante to go back inside. He gave me a chin lift and did it. I decided to walk over to the clubhouse rather than take my bike. Inside, the place was buzzing with voices. Some of the guys looked rough, like they had only gotten a couple of hours of sleep or maybe none. Several were on their phones. From what I overheard, they were making arrangements to cover them at work. All of us had to work at least part of the day. Mine was this afternoon.

Eventually, they all got off their phones and got quiet as Reaper waited. Seeing that he had all their attention, he filled them in on what we were going to do and why. No one objected. Spawn laid out a map of the compound. He indicated the sectors he had the compound divided into. I assume those were correlated to the camera sectors. Assignments were given out. There were eleven of us without the prospects and twenty-four sectors. We started with those overlooking and closest to the buildings which were one through fifteen and twenty-one through twenty-two.

We'd taken down most of the trees around the houses and buildings. So that left only a few of those in each location to check. We'd left enough to provide shade on hot days. We also were checking the outside of the houses and buildings to see if he had mounted cameras in the eaves. They could be easily hidden if you knew what you were doing and what kind of use.

As I searched, I couldn't help but think of us doing this again soon, when Spawn put up the cameras inside the compound. Knew he wouldn't delay on that. He hated when something wasn't done that he felt he should've thought of. He was kind of a perfectionist that way.

Time crept by as we searched our sectors. So far no one had found anything. I was about to despair of finding anything. I was back checking out one of the storage buildings on the back part of the compound, when I heard a couple of bikes come racing down the road. I ran out to see what they'd found. That was the only reason they'd be riding like that.

Reaper and Mayhem came to a screeching halt. Their faces were tense and I could see worry on them. They shut off their bikes so we could talk.

"What did you find?" I asked, as I went to get on my bike. I'd follow them back to wherever the camera was.

"Ink, I'm going to need you to stay calm," Reaper stated.

"Calm! Why the fuck are you saying that? What happened?"

"We need you to come with us back to your house," Mayhem said.

"My house? Goddammit, tell me what you found! I checked my house. There weren't any cameras on it." My heart was starting to race and fear snaked its way through me. "Did something happen to Alisse?"

"She's okay for now, but we need to get back," Reaper told me.

"Tell me what the fuck happened!" I screamed at them. Right now, the fact I was yelling at two officers of the club and one of them was the president, didn't matter to me. All that mattered was Alisse.

"Shit, okay, she went out to go over to my house to see Cheyenne. She decided she wanted to walk. Dante was with her. She told him she had to get in her car to get her sunglasses. When she got in, she sat in the driver's seat to check the center console. They heard a loud click. Dante told her not to move and he started to search around her seat. Fuck, Ink, there's a trigger device underneath the seat. That must have been what that guy was doing here yesterday. He put a bomb in her car," Reaper told me in a rush.

I let out an animalistic roar. They had to jump off their bikes and run over to keep me from roaring off on mine. Both of them squeezed my shoulders hard. They shook me until I was looking and listening to them, although it was hard to do over the loud beating of my heart.

"Listen carefully, we don't want to do anything to set it off. So we're going to ride to Burnout Way and park on the opposite side of Punisher's Way. Then we'll walk up to your house. We don't want to chance the vibrations from the bikes setting it off." Mayhem explained.

Burnout Way is the street before mine as you head to the front gate. We'd named all the street terms that related to motorcycles and riding. I lived on Cruiser Lane. I nodded my head so they would know I understood. I wasn't able to speak at the moment. They made sure I was calm then they got on their bikes. We started them and made our way to Burnout. Stopping and leaving our bikes, we walked to my house. The whole front was swarming with the guys. I could see Alisse through the windshield sitting in the driver's seat. I could see how scared she was from where I was. I ran over to her.

"Don't touch her," Reaper shouted.

I hunkered down in the open door without touching the car or her. It hurt not to be able to touch her. She was pale, sweating and her hands were gripping the steering wheel for dear life. Her eyes showed her terror. She was looking at me.

"Baby, I'm right here. I want you to look at me. Everything will be alright. See, there's Reaper and Crusher working on it." I pointed to the font of the car. The hood was up and both men had their heads underneath it. I knew the two of them had experience with bombs. Reaper had been a Navy SEAL and Crusher had been an explosives expert in a Marine Recon unit. I had confidence they could disarm it. If not, they knew who to call to get help.

My mind went to our ally clubs and who we might be able to call to ask for help. I knew a few in the Dublin Falls could. I wasn't sure if any of the Ruthless Marauders had military experience or not. Shit, why didn't I know this shit? I wanted to growl in frustration, but I didn't want to upset Alisse. She was scared enough as it was.

"Austin, if I don't get out of this, I want you to know how much I love you. I'm sorry I took so long to let you in. We could've had more time, if I hadn't." Her voice wobbled. I saw tears in her eyes. I didn't even care that she'd called me Austin in front of the guys. I couldn't let her tell me goodbye. That's what she was doing.

"Baby, don't say that. This isn't over. The guys will fix this. All I need you to do is to stay calm and don't move. I love you too and there's no way I can live without you. We're going to get through this and find the sonofabitch who did this and the fucker is going to pay. Whoever hired him is going to get what they have coming at them."

"How? We don't know who is after me or why. I swear, I can't recall ever pissing anyone off enough to want me dead. Surely, if it's Amber, she wouldn't go this far. I mean I am family, as messed up as we are."

"I don't know if it's her or not, but if it is, you need to let me take care of it. She won't be left to run around, able to fuck up our lives and be a threat."

"Are you going to kill her?"

I knew that she wasn't crazy about that idea. Right now, I did want to kill her, if she was responsible. I couldn't lie to Alisse.

"I don't know, Whirlwind. I don't know. Let's talk about that later. Tell me what you did this morning while we were busy."

For the next several minutes she told me what she worked on. I kept scanning the area around us. I could see Cheyenne standing far away. She was flanked by Dante and Dillon. She was crying. I hated to see her so stressed. It wasn't good for her or her baby, just like it wasn't good for Alisse and our baby.

"Babe, how are you feeling? Any cramps or pain?" I was terrified this would cause her to miscarry. I knew that stress caused that in some women. I'd been reading a lot on pregnancy. This was one thing that had prayed on my mind ever since I read it.

She gently shook her head no. "No, I feel fine. Although it is starting to feel like I need to pee soon. If they don't get this defused soon, I'll have to clean piss out of this seat." She tried to smile.

"Don't worry, that's what we have prospects for," I teased her. She giggled softly and looked over to the prospects.

Reaper's head came popping out from under the hood. He walked around to the driver's side. I waited to see what he had to say.

"I need you to step away from the car, so I can see underneath her seat."

I moved out of the way. As I did, I asked him, "How's it looking under the hood? Can you get it defused?"

"I've worked on several of the wires. I need to see if he set up some kind of secondary trigger or anything. If the fucker did, it's most likely going to be under the seat. I can't find one on the bomb under the hood. It's not a super complicated bomb, or it appears that it isn't. That makes me a little nervous. He's either not an expert or he's a sneaky bastard."

I didn't keep him talking. I backed up a couple more steps so he could get in position. He had tools in his hands. I stayed where Alisse could see me. I held her gaze and sent her nothing but positive thoughts.

It was a tense half hour or so before Reaper stood up. He gestured for me to come closer.

"I don't see anything else. There was another wire that I just caught the edge of peeking out. I've cut it. Now is the true test. There's nothing else we can do but move her. I need everyone to get far back. I don't know the exact blast radius on this thing. I'm going to grab her arms and on the count of three, I'm going to pull her as hard as I can out and away from the car."

I shook my head. "No, you get back and I'll do it."

"Ink, I've got this," he argued back.

"No, you've got a wife and a kid on the way. You're the damn president of this club. They need you. It needs to be me. If you're wrong and the bomb isn't defused and it goes off, I want to go with Alisse. I'm not going to be able to live without her. It's better if we go together."

He could see the resolve and the sincerity on my face. I was dead serious. I couldn't and wouldn't live without her. I'd fallen soul deep for her.

Finally, he nodded his head. He yelled for everyone to get back and he pushed them further and further until they were where he thought was far enough not to be hit by the explosion and the shrapnel. He was holding a bawling Chey in his arms. I went back to Alisse. She was crying. She'd heard what I said to Reaper. Hell, everyone had heard it.

"Slow and easy. Hold out your arms, baby. Don't shift your bottom, just your arms." She did as I asked. I got close and wrapped my arms tightly under her armpits.

"On the count of three, I want you to push up with

your legs as hard as you can. It's going to feel rough and I'm sorry if it hurts, but I'm going to be moving you fast and hard. Okay?"

"Okay. I'm ready. I love you."

"I love you too."

"One, two, three," At the count of three, I jerked her up as she pushed with her legs, I took a huge step back, dragging her with me. I was holding my breath, waiting for the explosion. I backpedaled as fast as I could. Nothing happened. As soon as we cleared the door, I scooped her up in my arms and ran like the hounds of hell were after me. I headed straight for the others. I skidded to a halt and whipped around to stare at her car. It was sitting there looking all innocent.

My heart was about to pound out of my chest. I heard the others swearing and expressing their relief.

After a couple of minutes of me hugging and kissing her over and over, I had to let Cheyenne hug her. The guys were all patting her and telling her how relieved they were. When they were done, Reaper waved at Crusher. They went back over to her car. We stood here on tender hooks again, as they dismantled the bomb under the hood and the trigger under the seat. They brought it over to us when they were done. In their hands, it looked so unassuming.

"Let's take this into the clubhouse. Spawn, I know you have access to a database that will tell you the signatures of almost any bomb maker around. I need you to see if there are any that use these parts and setup. I'm hoping whoever he was, he's been arrested for doing this before," Reaper explained, as we all walked to the clubhouse. I couldn't let her out of my arms. She protested, but I carried her the whole way.

I'd heard rumors there was such a way to look up bombers like that, but I thought it was just a rumor. I guess not. I didn't ask Reaper how he knew of it or how Spawn had access. It was probably through some of the shit he helped the Dark Patriots do in the past. Spawn had helped and we never got in their business. It wasn't club business as much as it was their personal one. Although, after today, I might be asking him.

Inside, I took her to one of the tables. Before I could sit her down, she whispered that she had to pee. I laughed as I took her down the hall to the bathroom. She insisted I let her walk, which I did, but I still went with her. I couldn't let her out of my sight. She rolled her eyes as I stood in the bathroom while she peed and washed her hands.

Back in the common room, I had her sit at a table while I got her a drink. Reaper was doing the same with Cheyenne. They sat next to each other holding hands. The bomb was in the middle of the table in pieces. I checked it out. I didn't know what I was looking at, but I was curious. Spawn had run to his office and came back with one of his laptops. He was busy tapping away on it, staring intently at his screen. The rest of the guys were talking low and gathered close to us or at the bar. Everyone had a beer in their hands. I even grabbed one. It was a drinking kind of day.

Reaper walked off to the side after he gave Chey her water. He was on his phone and was talking urgently into it. I wondered who he was talking to. I didn't interrupt him. If he wanted us to know, he'd tell us. I picked Alisse up and sat back down with her on my lap. She smiled and gave me a quick peck on the lips. I wanted to do more than that, but it would have to wait.

Several minutes later, after listening to the guys' speculation about who did it, Reaper rejoined us.

"I just spoke to Sean, Griffin and Gabe. I sent them the photos I took of this. They have their people working on it too. Hopefully, that'll get us answers sooner." He must've taken the pictures while I had her in the bathroom.

"What will we do if they don't find anything? There's still no way to ID the guy," I said.

"True, but we're not going to give up. When the car doesn't go off, he's going to wonder why. Did we find it? Did it not work? If it didn't work, why not? I expect the questions will drive him crazy and he'll have to come to investigate. Remember, we didn't find any cameras. Which means he's not watching us. He has no idea we found the bomb. He'll wait and when he breaks, we'll be ready for him. I want those two cut sections in the fence left alone for now. We don't want him to know we found them either. We're going to set a trap and sucker him right in. We'll catch him and then find out who he is and why he's doing this. I still think he's the hired help," Reaper explained.

While I hated the idea of waiting, I thought he had a point. I know if it was me, I'd want to know what went wrong. We spent a couple of hours there in the clubhouse. So far, nothing has been found. Spawn and the Patriots were still working on it. Knowing it could take hours or more, I eventually dragged her away from Chey and back to our house. She needed to rest and eat. This had been too stressful for her. I needed to make sure she got the care she needed.

Alisse: Chapter 19

Although I'd had a terrible night of waking up over and over relieving the bomb scare, I refused to miss work today. It was only a half day and I knew it would be busy. Ink was pissed that I wouldn't call off. Finally, after arguing with him for over an hour, as I got ready, he caved, but only if he could come with me and be inside the office while I worked. I knew that Dr. Simpson would allow him there, so I agreed. I joked to him that we should take my car, that way if the guy was around town watching, he'd see it and wonder why it wasn't blown to pieces. Ink got this look on his face and walked off to make a call while I finished getting ready.

When we left for town, Chey was with us. The car had been thoroughly searched to make sure there weren't any other surprises. Ink and Reaper were riding their bikes as our escort and Dillon was driving my car. He explained that while we were at work, he'd stay out in the parking lot and guard the car. That would prevent the bomber from checking it over there. He'd have no choice but to come onto the compound. I was hoping he'd do it tonight. This waiting was killing me.

Unfortunately, Spawn and the Dark Patriots didn't find anyone who fit that bomb signature. Or I should say, anyone who wasn't in jail or dead. It was still a mystery as to who this guy was. As for how he knew how to build a bomb, he might have been in the military or got the plans off the internet. It was easy enough to find them if you knew where to look, Spawn had told us. He mumbled something about an anarchist handbook, whatever that was.

It was hard to concentrate on work, but I forced myself to do it. The patients and Dr. Simpson deserved me at my best. Luckily, I had Cheyenne there to help me. When we closed the office at one o'clock, it was the best part of the day. We didn't waste time hanging around. We bid everyone to have a good weekend and got out of there.

Dillon was leaning on his bike, sitting next to my car. I'd taken him a couple of bottles of water throughout the day. I didn't want him dying in the sun. It might not be super hot, but it could get to be a bit much after doing it for hours.

Reaper was waiting for us. While Ink stayed at the office with us, Reaper had gone to the brewery to work on some things. Before we took off, the guys all talked us into going and having lunch before going home. I was feeling a little hungry, so I agreed. Cheyenne was starved, so she didn't have any objections. We talked and decided we wanted to go to the deli in town, Stacked. They had a huge selection of hot and cold sandwiches plus soup and salad there.

We hit them just as the lunch time rush was thinning out. They still had a lot of people in there, but we didn't have to wait long and could find a table. We sat by a window that overlooked the parking lot. Since we could clearly see my car, Dillon was told to join us inside, rather than eat in the parking lot. He did, but he never took his eyes off the car. He kept quiet and listened only to the conversations going on around him. Anytime anyone would get near my car, he'd straighten up and become tense, but no one stopped or touched it.

After we finished up, we all headed back home. I sighed in relief when the gate closed behind us. We let Cheyenne out at her house then went to ours. Dillon hopped out and asked if there was anything else he could do for us. Ink told him he was free to go do whatever.

We'd barely gotten inside and the door shut, before Ink had me against to the wall and was kissing the hell outta me.

His hands ran up underneath my shirt and he pulled it up and off in a blink. Next, came my bra. It fell forgotten to the floor. He lowered his head and sucked my taut nipples into his mouth. He laved them with his tongue and gently bit down on them. I shuddered at the sensation. I loved it when he was a little rough with me. I found I liked some pain with my pleasure.

As he sucked on my nipples, his hands were busy undoing my scrub pants and shoving them down, taking my panties with them. He paused long enough to yank them down and off my legs, after I stepped out of my shoes. While he was crouched down, he pushed my legs apart and ran his tongue from my entrance to my clit, where he stopped to suck. I moaned. I was already soaking wet and close to an orgasm, just from him sucking on my breasts.

"Fuck, baby, you taste so damn good. I could feast on your sweet pussy all day. Come on, give me more of your sweet cream. I want to swallow all you have to give," he muttered as he took a break to look up at me. The desire on his face was evident. As if the huge bulge in his jeans didn't already tell me how much he wanted me.

"God Austin, you're making me crazy. I need you naked. I need to see how much you want me. I need to taste you too," I pleaded. I didn't know if he'd let me get my mouth on him or not.

To my delight, he gave me one more intense swipe then he stood up. He quickly took off his boots and stripped off his clothes. His cut went on the hook by the front door, where it usually hung when he wasn't wearing it.

I ran my hands all over his hard, muscular arms, chest and stomach. His cock was standing tall and hard, begging me to touch it. I dropped to my knees and cupped his balls. He grabbed me under the arms and raised me to my feet. I gave him a puzzled look.

"No, you're not going to be kneeling on the hardwood floor and sucking my cock. If you want that, we'll do it in the comfort of our room," he said gruffly, before he picked me up and took me up the stairs and into our bedroom. He let me down when we got to the bed.

I pushed him down on the edge. I sank to my knees on the lush carpet we had in there. I spread his legs so I could get between them. I cupped his balls again and played with them, rolling them between my fingers. He moaned. I could see the precum all over the head of his cock. I leaned forward and licked it off. Tasting his addictive cum, I didn't waste time. I sucked the head of his cock into my mouth. I lashed it with my tongue, flicking the underside where he was so sensitive.

His fingers sank into my hair and he gripped me hard. Using both hands to work his balls and pump the base of his cock, I let him take over and guide my mouth up and down on him. He'd set the speed and depth for what made him feel the best. I loved it when he'd fuck my mouth like this.

He didn't hesitate to push deep, trying to get as deep into my throat as he could. I took deep breaths and relaxed as much as I could so he could. When the head hit the back of my throat, I'd swallow, constricting around him. He'd hiss and moan every time. Tightening his hold on my hair, he used it like a handle to raise and lower my mouth on his erection. I sucked and teased with my tongue as much as I could while teasing his balls and pumping his base faster.

Soon his breathing got louder and I felt his balls constricting. I knew he was close. Ramping up my pace, I sucked even harder and pushed down on him as far as I could take him. I swallowed and hummed. This did it. He shouted out, "Fuck," then he came. His cock kept jerking and filling my mouth with his cum. I eagerly swallowed it down. It wasn't often he came like this. He usually liked to come in my pussy or ass.

As he stopped directing my head, I lifted off him so I could lick all over his cock, cleaning him up. He was lying on his back by now. I gave the head of his cock a kiss then his balls, before standing up and crawling on the bed next to him. I laid down and put my head on his shoulder. I rubbed across his pecs. His arm came up around me.

I glanced up to see his eyes were on me. They were slumberous but still held passion.

"That was fucking amazing, baby. Now, it's my turn."

In a flash, he sat up, flipped me on my back, yanked my thighs apart and buried his face in my pussy. This time, I was the one with their hands in their hair and I was hanging on for dear life as he ate me like a hungry wolf. His mouth licked, bit and sucked all up and down my folds. His attention to my clit drove me wild. His fingers in my pussy and ass made me even crazier. It didn't take long for me to have my first orgasm. He never slowed down. He worked to push me to the next one. By the time he was done, I was boneless and had just had four intense orgasms. I felt like I was ready for a nap, but I knew that wasn't going to happen yet.

While he ate my pussy, he'd gotten hard again. He'd want me to take care of that. I reached down and grasped him, pumping up and down his shaft. He groaned.

"Where do you want this, Austin? Do you want it in my wet pussy or my tight ass, or both?" I whispered.

"I want both," he growled. Letting go of him, I got up and got on my hands and knees, so he could easily enter both holes. I watched as he got a bottle of lube out of his drawer. Laying it on the bed, he gripped both my hips and slowly pushed his cock into my pussy in one long shove. I cried out, the pleasure of it was so intense.

I held onto the comforter as he powered in and out of me like a mad man. He kept going deeper and harder, each time he thrust into me. It took only a minute or two for me to come. I was crying out as he kept pumping to extend the orgasm. As I started to relax, he pulled out of me, slicked up my back hole and his cock then pressed the head against my asshole and pushed inside. He took his time to get all of that monster cock of his in there. Even after having sex a few times like this, it still burned when he'd enter me. It was only after he was in and thrust a few times, did the burning subside and the pleasure start.

In no time, I had forgotten the pain and was calling out to him. "Harder. I need you to fuck me harder, Austin. I want you to come in my ass," I wailed.

"Oh you do, do you? You like it when I fuck this tight ass, don't you?"

"Yes, I love it," I muttered. I could feel another huge orgasm building.

He slammed it in harder. His balls smacked my pussy. His hand came down and around to find my clit. He tweaked it between his fingers and bit my lower back. That was enough to send me over the edge and I came. I screamed long and hard as I milked his cock with my ass. He grunted then roared as he came, filling my ass with his cum, just like I asked. We slowly came down together, collapsing side by side on the bed when we were done. His softening cock was still in my sore ass.

He brought my mouth up for a kiss that was full of tongue. When he was done, he smiled at me. "I love you so damn much baby, it hurts. Thank you for loving me back and giving me you."

"I can't ever see anyone ever meaning more than you do to me, Austin. I love you and I'm so glad we found each other. Thank you for not giving up on me."

"I'll never give up. How does a long soak in the tub then a nap sound? We can have dinner and then spend the night watching movies and doing some more of this." He was grinning at me when he said it.

"I think that sounds like a perfect idea." I got shakily to my feet. My legs still felt weak, He got up and held onto me as we went to the bathroom. I was more than willing to go along with his idea. It would only bring me more pleasure and I could never turn that down.

The ringing of Ink's phone brought me up out of a deep sleep. We'd spent the evening and night doing exactly what he'd said. It was close to two in the morning by the time we finally fell asleep after another round of mind-blowing sex. The man was a God.

My bleary eyes saw the alarm clock said it was four. Since it was dark out, it had to be in the morning. I wondered who was calling him this early. He picked up the phone and grunted, "Yeah."

He sat up quickly as he listened. I watched as he leaped out of bed and started to put on his clothes as he continued to listen. I got up to put on mine. Something was wrong. He didn't stay on the phone long. When he hung up, I had to ask, "What's wrong?"

"Mayhem and Crusher were on guard duty. They caught someone sneaking around your car. They're taking him to the storage. I've got to go."

"I want to go with you."

He shook his head. "No, I don't want you around the bastard. It's probably going to get bloody and I don't want you to see me like that. Please, baby, stay here. One of the prospects is staying to guard you and Cheyenne. I promise, as soon as we get what we need and I'm done with him, I'll come tell you what we find out."

I didn't like waiting, but I could tell he wanted me to stay here. Reluctantly, I nodded. He gave me a kiss then hurried out of the room. Since I was now awake and I knew there was no way I could go back to sleep, I finished dressing and went downstairs to make myself a cup of hot tea.

Ink:

I didn't waste any time getting my ass to the storage building. We had two of them and both of them led to an underground bunker. This had been an old military installation years ago. It was one of the things that had caught Reaper's eye when we were looking for a new place to move our compound.

When I got there, I saw most of the guys were already there. As we waited for the rest to join, because I knew none of them would pass up the opportunity to be in on this questioning, I checked out the man Crusher and Mayhem caught.

He was a big guy. It was obvious he worked out and he had the muscles to show for it. He was one of those guys who was so muscular he had no neck. His head was shaved bald. His eyes were cold.

They had strung him up by the arms from a hook that we had hanging from the ceiling for this very reason. He had to stand on his tiptoes to reach the floor. Having your arms like that and your feet not fully on the ground would have his arms and shoulders screaming in pain in no time at all. None of us were talking to him. We talked to each other. After Ink, Sandman and Shadow joined us, we got started.

I walked up to the guy. He stared at me with an air

of indifference, like he didn't have a care in the world about what we might do to him. I knew that would change. It might take us a while, but we'd get the answers we wanted.

"What's your name?"

He didn't answer.

"All I'm asking for is your name. That's nothing. If you don't answer that and start the pain this early, it's going to really suck, for you. What I'd like to do is get this over with as fast and painlessly as possible. I know this wasn't your idea. You're just the hired help. I want whoever hired you. They're the ones I want to make pay. It would be a shame for you to go through so much pain and suffering for them."

I was hoping he'd talk to make his death as painless and quick as possible. He had to know that he was going to die. A man willing to blow up or burn a woman to death, couldn't be allowed to wander the streets. He'd hire out again. I didn't want that on my conscience.

He just stared at me. After failing to get him to even give a name after a few minutes, the fun began. For this part, I let Mayhem step up to the plate. Don't get me wrong. I had no problem hurting the guy and I'd get my licks in, but this was what Mayhem did as our enforcer. This is what he loved to do for the club. And he was fucking amazing at it.

He started him out with some well-placed punches to places that hurt the most. His face, gut and kidneys. When that didn't loosen his tongue, he broke all his fingers. Although there were grunts and cries of pain, the guy didn't talk. I grudgingly had to respect him for that. Too bad he wasn't someone we could have in our club.

As Mayhem worked on him, I kept up with the questions. What's your name? Who hired you? What was he doing here? I should've recorded it and put it on repeat. It would've saved my voice. After an hour, he had all his fingers broken, a couple of teeth knocked out and bruises everywhere. Still nothing.

I could see that Mayhem was ready to up the ante. He went over to dig in his massive storage cabinet we had in the bunker. It was filled with all kinds of toys as Mayhem called them. When he came back, he had an ice pick and a ball peen hammer.

"If you don't tell my brother here what he wants to know, I'm going to break both your fucking arms and legs then stab you with this pick. I know where to place it so it hurts like a mother fucker but you won't die. My brother, Lash, can patch you up if I get too crazy. He can keep a man going for days with IVs and shit. He's great at that shit," Mayhem told our intruder. He wasn't lying, Lash could do that.

"Fuck you," the guy said, as he spit at us. Well, at least he'd said something. We were getting there.

Mayhem walked up slowly and handed me his ice pick. "Hold that, will ya?" he asked. I nodded.

He went up to the man and circled him, as if he was deciding which thing to hit and break first. After making his decision, he glanced over at Tinker. "Hey Tink, grab that two by four piece over there. I want you to hold it behind his left leg. Then do the same to his other as we go."

"Sure thing, Mayhem," Tinker said with a smile. He was back with the two by four quickly. He held it tight to the back of the guy's left leg and Mayhem drew back the hammer and let it fly. The sound of the impact and the scream from the guy made us all wince. That had to hurt like a bitch.

"What's your name?" I yelled at him. He just shook his head, as tears streamed down his face.

Mayhem instructed Tinker to hold the board behind his other leg. Another deafening slam and scream and the guy was pissing himself.

"What's your name?"

"It's Butch, Butch Delany."

"Well, Butch Delany, I need you to tell me, who hired you? Why are they after my old lady?"

"I don't know why they're after her. All I know is they told me to get rid of her. It's been hard to do. She's never alone."

"Did you set the fire at her apartment?"

"Yeah, I didn't realize she was staying here with you. I thought when I saw her at the apartment that day, that she was staying there. I was new to town and hadn't had time to check shit out."

"Ah, so you fucked up. Okay, we're getting somewhere. However, you didn't tell me who hired you."

He closed his mouth. He didn't say he didn't know. He was holding back. I nod to Mayhem. He and Tinker broke the guy's right arm. He cried out this time, though not as loudly as he did his legs. It wasn't until both arms were as broken as his legs that I asked him again. He was hanging like a rag doll from the hook. His chin was resting on his chest. The pain written all over his face was excruciating. He was sweating and pale.

"The names."

"It was a guy. He was an older guy, maybe in his fifties or sixties. His hair is thin on top with a big bald spot. It's gray. He's shorter than me and has a belly. He wanted your woman out of the way. Something about her standing between his princess and her man. He never gave me a name. He just said to call him L."

I looked at my brothers. We all know who that had to be. The description fit Amber's dad. His name was Leon. He had a daughter who was trying to get me back with her. The timing couldn't be better either. Today she was supposed to bring Christopher to have the paternity test done. If I could arrange it and prove she was involved, I'd have her taken care of when she got to town.

"How did you communicate with him?" I asked him.

"He gave me a number to call. It's in my phone under L. The code is nine-nine-one-two," He didn't even blink at giving us that information.

Spawn had his phone. They'd confiscated it when they caught him. He typed in the code then scrolled through his contacts. He nodded.

"It's here. I'll check it out. If he's smart, he'll be using a burner phone. It looks like you mainly texted."

"Yeah, he didn't like to talk."

"Spawn, you go check that out. As for you, Butch, we know you put a bomb in her car. We found it and disarmed it. What did you plan to do tonight?"

"I was going to see why it didn't go off and fix it so it would. The guy wants this done as soon as possible."

"How did he find you for this job?"

"Through word of mouth, he said. It was a guy I'd done work for in the past."

We spent another fifteen minutes just asking him random things, making sure there wasn't anything else we could use. We found that he didn't. Knowing we had other work to do and we couldn't really turn him over to the police in his condition, we finished it. Mayhem made it quick. He fired a single shot through the center of his forehead.

"Get this cleaned up and we'll meet at the clubhouse to talk about next steps. Will two hours be enough?" Reaper asked Mayhem and Crusher. They both nodded their heads. They were already taking down the body and wrapping him in the plastic they had spread out underneath him. They'd prepped for this outcome.

Reaper came over to me. "Go see your woman then we'll see you at the clubhouse. Tell her what you think she needs to know. Hopefully, by tomorrow this mess will be behind you."

"I hope so. See you in a bit."

I didn't waste my time in getting my ass home to tell Alisse what we found out. I'd thought of Amber but for some reason I never thought of her parents. I was burning to know if she asked them to do it.

At the house, Alisse ran to me, throwing her arms around me as she kissed me. When I broke the kiss, she anxiously asked me what he said. I explained quickly that he was working for Amber's dad and that we'd be meeting in a couple of hours to figure out how to take care of that. She looked stunned. She sat down on the couch.

"I know you had Spawn looking into Amber, but I seriously didn't think she was the one. Now, you're telling me it might be her and my uncle. If Uncle Leon was in on it, Aunt Margaret has to know too. They tell each other everything." She had tears in her eyes and I could hear the sadness in her voice. She was torn up to find it was her own family doing this. They wanted her dead and for such a stupid reason, if what Butch said was true. It made no sense for Amber to be after me after all these years.

I held her close and rocked her. "Babe, I know it's crazy and hard to think."

"After you guys get done with church, will you come tell me what you've decided to do?"

"Yeah, I'll tell you. Alisse, I know they're your family. I'll try to keep that in mind, but you need to keep in mind that if they're let off, they'll likely keep after you. I can't have them out there as a threat."

"I understand. Do what you have to do."

I sat with her for two hours just providing her comfort. When I left to go to church, she was lying down trying to rest.

The table was full when I got there. Reaper got straight to the point.

"Spawn confirmed it's a burner phone. We know we need to eliminate this threat to Alisse. The question is how. Ink, I'll give you the floor."

"Thanks. Okay, this is a hard one. I want to just take their asses out, but they're still family to Alisse. And I need to make sure whether Amber knew about it or not. Alisse says her aunt would know. The parents tell each other everything. That leaves us with three people we have to neutralize. We could make it appear to be an accident that kills all three."

"What about the boy?" Lash asked.

"I may have an answer for that. I've been digging into those other guys and I think there's one who is more than likely the father than the rest. He comes from a very wealthy family. I found some emails and old deleted texts where Amber tried to get back in his life and used her son to do it. The guy refused to fall for it. He said if the boy was his and she would prove it, then he'd do his duty. She never went through with the test. If we can find the kid's real dad, we might be able to have him take him." Spawn told us.

"Well, she probably didn't want to risk it not being him. If she was with as many as you said, there's at least four that could be. How long ago did that happen?" I asked.

"About a month before she appeared here bugging you."

"That figures. I say we contact the men and get them to take the test. If they don't take it, then we'll have to let him go into the system or to some else in the family. I don't like the idea of foster care. Hopefully, we find his real dad and he takes him."

"What do you think of the idea of getting the evidence to the police and having them arrested? They would go to prison for a few years. By the time they get out, they will have hopefully learned their lesson. Or we could make sure someone helped them to have an accident when they're on the inside," Maniac suggested.

We debated for over an hour. In the end, we decided to get the evidence over to the police, but not until I had all three of them in front of me. I wanted to talk to their asses.

It went smoother than I thought it would. Amber had decided for some reason to actually go through with the paternity test. When she came to the clinic to do it, I got her to come back to the compound with me. She had thought she was wearing me down. I could tell by the smile on her face. She thought she was going to win. I made sure that when I went to the clinic, I left Alisse at home. While I was doing that, Mayhem, Crusher, and Maniac were paying a visit to her parents. They would be bringing them to the compound. They lived not too far outside of Bristol on a big piece of property.

Once I got her here, Cheyenne invited Christopher to her house to play video games. Amber had objected until I told her to let him go. She had no idea Alisse would be there with them. I sat her down in the common room. She looked around. I could tell she wasn't impressed. It might not be the fanciest place, but it was clean, painted and the furniture mostly matched.

She reached over to grasp my hand. I let her. "Austin, I mean Ink, I'm so glad that you came and got us today. I know that we've had our problems and what happened all those years ago, was terrible. I was stupid and didn't realize what I had. It took me a long time to grow up and then I was so afraid to tell you. It wasn't until Christopher started to ask more and more about his dad, did I do it. I know we can be a family and I can make you happy."

"You think you can make me happier than Alisse? What am I to do with her, Amber? She's pregnant with my baby."

She shrugged. "I don't know. I guess pay her child support. I don't want us to raise her kid, but you might need to give her support for it. Who knows, she might not even have it. She's early on, miscarriages happen all the time."

I had to stop my hands from curling into fists.

"Or an accident. If she'd been there when that fire broke out in her apartment, she'd have died," I said, feeling sick to my stomach that I was even saying it and playing with her.

Amber smiled wider. "Yeah, that was too bad. But bad things happen all the time you know. It's a dangerous world. You can't be too careful."

I was astonished at how stupid she was. I was about to say more when the door to the clubhouse opened and in strolled Mayhem, Crusher and Maniac with her parents. They were looking scared. That meant they had to threaten them to get them here. I figured that would happen. Amber jumped to her feet and rushed over to them.

"Mom, Dad what're you doing here?"

"These ruffians came to our house and basically kidnapped us. I told them I'm going to have their asses arrested. What is the meaning of this, Austin?" Leon yelled at me.

I walked over to them. "Why don't we all have a seat and I'll tell you why?"

They reluctantly followed me back to the table I had been sitting at with Amber. I got straight to the point.

"I know Leon that you hired a man by the name of Butch Delany to kill Alisse. He tried with the fire at her apartment and then again when he put a bomb in her car." I saw their stunned faces when I let that drop.

"I-I" Leon stuttered. I held up a hand.

"Don't bother trying to deny it. He confessed it all to us. My brother Spawn has been in your bank account, texts, and emails. He has all the proof he needs to prove you did."

"What are you going to do?" Leon asked. Margaret and Amber were silent and were giving each other scared looks. Neither of them appeared to be surprised at what was done, so I took that as proof they were in on it.

"All of that will be turned over to the local police. They'll arrest you and you'll give them your sworn statements. You will plead guilty when it goes before the judge and then you'll spend time in prison."

"What makes you think we'll swear to anything you just said?" He said arrogantly. He still thought his money would buy his way out of this.

"Because if you don't, before I kill you, I'll be sure you suffer the worst pain you've ever felt for as long as your heart can hold out. That goes for all three of you. Personally, if you weren't Alisse's family, I wouldn't be giving you this choice. I'd just kill your asses. I don't tolerate people threatening my woman."

Amber and her mom started to cry. "What about Christopher?" Amber bawled.

"Like you've ever given a damn about that boy. He's been in boarding school since he was little. He's hardly been around you from what we found out. We'll see if we can find his real father and see if he wants him. If not, he might go to another family member or into foster care. Whatever way it goes, I'll make sure he's taken care of. He's innocent in all this."

Leon kept threatening and when that didn't work he tried bribing me. The ladies cried and pleaded, but in the end they had no choice, especially when Mayhem showed them a couple of his favorite toys. They were almost relieved to have us call the cops. Chief Carlton came out personally to take them off our hands. I knew Reaper had him on standby for this. Like I said, Carlton didn't care what we did as long as it wasn't against anyone innocent.

Before Carlton hauled them off, I had Amber tell him she wanted to leave Christopher in my care. He didn't object. At least I'd know he was safe and cared for while we figured out what to do with him.

At Reaper's house, I found him happily playing a game while the ladies talked in the kitchen. I quietly told them what had happened. Alisse gave me a kiss and thanked me for not killing them. I explained that we'd be Christopher's guardians for a while until we found his dad or placement. She was happy with that.

Later, after we explained his mom had left him with us, I took him and Alisse home. He didn't seem to be surprised his mom left him and he didn't ask where she was. That told me this wasn't unusual for him. I felt sorry for him. He seemed like a good kid. The next few months were going to be crazy, but at least no one was going to be trying to kill the woman I loved.

Alisse: Epilogue- Five Weeks Later

I looked around at the people surrounding me and Ink. We were out on the dance floor slow dancing to our song. It was our first as husband and wife. It had taken a lot to get here, but the day was finally here and it had turned out better than I ever imagined. The decorations were beautiful as well as our cake. The food was delicious. Everyone was having fun and I was finally Mrs. Austin Kavanagh.

I looked over and waved at Christopher. He was grinning from ear-to-ear. With Amber, Margaret and Leon in jail, the guys had worked hard to contact the other men we thought might be his dad and got them to agree to take paternity tests. In the end, the guy she'd gone after before Ink was his dad. Lucky for Christopher, his dad was more than willing to be a part of his life. He had the courts grant him sole custody of his son. Christopher was now living with him and having the time of his life. His dad, Channing, had thanked us. He didn't want anything to do with Amber, but he did his son. He apologized to Ink. He had no idea that when he was sleeping with her, that she was with Ink or anyone else.

My cousin, aunt, and uncle had pleaded guilty and were awaiting their sentencing. The stuff Spawn had sent unanimously to the police and their confessions was enough to get them convicted of arson and attempted murder. They were going to go away for a long time, especially since the judge sentencing them was friendly with the club. It was nice to have friends in high places. Ink had confessed that when they eventually got out of jail, they'd be watched and any attempts to harm me or our family would result in them being killed. They wouldn't get a second chance. I agreed. I was lucky he'd let them off the first time. It wasn't what he wanted.

School was going well. I hadn't gone back to work full time. I found I needed more study time and carrying this baby was a lot of work. The same applied to Cheyenne. Dr. Simpson had promised me that when I got done with my degree, she'd be thrilled to hire me as a RN. Also she told Chey she'd be glad to have her back at any status she wanted after the baby was born. We were going to wait and see.

Ink had been working and doing his best to get the nursery just the way we wanted it. I still had a few weeks to go until we found out what we were having. Reaper and Cheyenne were having a boy. I was hoping for a boy, so that they could be best friends. Reaper liked to tease Ink that we were going to have a girl and his son would grow up to claim her as his old lady one day. Ink told him that couldn't happen until she was seventy, that's how old she had to be before she could date.

I was settling into my life with the Punishers.

They'd become the family I'd always wanted. There wasn't anything I could think of that I wanted that I didn't have.

"What're you thinking, baby?" Ink whispered in my ear.

"I was thinking how good my life is right now and how I have everything I could ever want. It's all thanks to you. I love you so damn much, Austin."

He growled low then gave me a passionate kiss. I heard people hooting and clapping. I ignored them. Once we were done, he smiled down at me.

"Whirlwind, you came out of nowhere and blew me off my feet. I knew as soon as I saw you, that you were the only woman for me. I love you more than words can ever say. Thank you for loving me and giving me a family."

"I think we're both lucky."

"We are. What would you say to us sneaking out of here and starting our honeymoon? These animals can party as long as they want. I need to be inside my wife."

"What're you waiting for? Lead the way."

As he hauled me out of there, I couldn't help but send up a prayer of thanks. I couldn't wait to find out what the next fifty years would bring. Whatever it was, I knew it would be wild, fun, and filled with love and passion.

The End until Maniac's Imp Book 3